BY THE SAME AUTHOR

Strange Files of Fremont Jones

Fire and Fog

DIANNE DAY

doubleday

NEW YORK

LONDON

TORONTO

SYDNEY

AUCKLAND

THE

BOHEMIAN

MURDERS

a fremont

jones

mystery

PUBLISHED BY DOUBLEDAY
a division of Bantam Doubleday Dell
Publishing Group, Inc.
1540 Broadway, New York,
New York 10036

DOUBLEDAY and the portrayal of an
anchor with a dolphin are trademarks of
Doubleday, a division of Bantam
Doubleday Dell Publishing Group, Inc.

BOOK DESIGN BY DANA LEIGH TREGLIA

All of the characters in this book are
fictitious, and any resemblance to actual
persons, living or dead, is purely
coincidental.

Library of Congress Cataloging-in-
Publication Data
Day, Dianne.
The Bohemian murders : a Fremont Jones
mystery / Dianne Day. — 1st ed.
p.   cm.
I. Title.
PS3554.A9595B64   1997
813'.54—dc21   96-40172
CIP

ISBN 0-385-47923-9

First Edition

1   3   5   7   9   10   8   6   4   2

*To all women who
are Keepers of the
Light, in or out
of lighthouses.*

ACKNOWLEDGMENTS

Many people helped with various aspects of the writing of this book. Thanks to Pat Hathaway, Randy Reinstedt and John and Susan Klusmire for helping with research. Special thanks to all the writers who coffee in Carmel, especially Bob Irvine, Bob Campbell, Nancy Baker Jacobs, Adele Langendorf; with extra thanks to Bob Campbell for letting me use twangy boys. Extra appreciation goes to Dorothy Nye, for being such a careful, intelligent reader.

While I have attempted to capture the spirit and flavor of historic Carmel, Pacific Grove and what is now Pebble Beach, no characters in this book are based on people who actually lived there in the early part of this century. There is one exception: The character Hettie Houck was inspired by Emily Fish, who was keeper of the Point Pinos Light from 1893 to 1914.

—D.D.

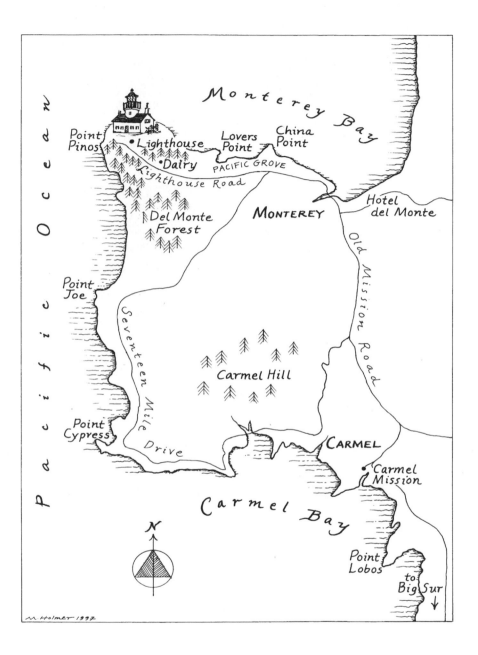

THE

BOHEMIAN

MURDERS

CHAPTER ONE

KEEPER'S LOG
Date: January 9, 1907
Wind: SW, light gusting to moderate
Weather: Cool, some clouds after morning fog
Comments: Moderate swells on bay. Whale migration beginning, one spouter spotted, boat out of Monterey Whaling Station observed in pursuit.

    [signed]Fremont Jones, Deputy
           for Henrietta Houck
           Keeper, Point Pinos Light

I suppose my luck ran out. Or perhaps it was only that I made a mistake, or two, or three. Nothing really disastrous—I have a different, one might say heightened, definition of disaster since last year's Great Earthquake and the fire that followed. Nevertheless my recent mistakes have caused me heartache and embarrassment, and a good deal of inconvenience, not to mention insecurity. Indeed sometimes I look around me in this beautiful yet alien place and wonder what in the world I am doing here.

I do a good bit of looking around because that is part of my job: I make observations and keep a log; I also keep accounts and order supplies and oversee the man who tends the property. I do these things in my capacity as deputy keeper (status: temporary) of the Point Pinos Lighthouse. I tell myself that I am fortunate to have this job for six months, and therefore my luck cannot really have run out—that is what I tell myself.

The lighthouse at Point Pinos is nothing like a certain other lighthouse I visited a couple of years ago, to the north of San Francisco. For one thing, this is in the opposite direction, south, by more than a hundred miles, and for another, it is not the least threatening in appearance or in atmosphere. This lighthouse looks like a Cape Cod cottage with a tower and lantern stuck onto its roof like an afterthought. Point Pinos is the southern headland of Monterey Bay, acres of dunes and scrub rolling down to a rocky, granite coastline, surrounded on three sides by water and on the fourth by thick forest a mile deep. Beyond that forest is the prosperous little town of Pacific Grove; in the other direction, some three miles as the crow flies but farther by road and beyond another forest, is a tiny, rustic village called Carmel-by-the-Sea. If more felicitous surroundings exist anywhere on earth, I have not seen them. Yet I am quite perverse: Often I am discontented and wish I were somewhere else.

I have not given up typewriting; in fact I have a brand-new Royal typewriter, which, like its predecessor, is my most prized possession. However I have had difficulty, due to the aforementioned mistakes, in getting my business started in this new place. I tell myself it will happen, nothing is impossible—that is what I tell myself.

I was telling myself something of the sort around four o'clock in the afternoon of January 9, 1907, as I gazed idly out the watch-room window. The watch room is located at the base of the lantern tower, so it is round and rather small but pleasant enough, particularly considering the panoramic view. Hettie (short for Henrietta) Houck, the real keeper of the light, used the watch room as a sort of office and so I do the same.

I met Hettie last month because I was thrown out of a boarding-house in Pacific Grove on an accusation of immoral conduct, and she happened to be on the sidewalk outside at the time. My so-called immoral conduct was that I had, earlier that evening, entertained a male person in my room with the door closed. This male person was my friend Michael Archer, who now lives in Carmel; the "entertainment" was an argument between us, a very personal sort of argument, which was why I had closed the door. The reason for the argument was that I had made a huge mistake about Michael—or Misha, as he now prefers to be called—but I didn't make it all alone; he misled me. And from that most crucial mistake, all the other mistakes flowed. . . .

"What *is* that?" I asked aloud of no one, and picked up the binoculars. There was something riding the waves just beyond an offshore rock formation that I call the Three Sisters; whether the three rocks have an official name or not I don't know. The object was about the same size as a sea lion, but it was predominantly red and they are always brown. Nor was it a seal. Seals, unlike sea lions, do come in different colors—but none of God's creatures (except humans, who alone are capable of artifice) comes in that particular shade of scarlet.

Try as I might, I could not see the object well enough to tell what it was, even with the aid of the binoculars. I put them back on the desk and went out of the watch room, up the circular stairs that climb inside the tower, and out onto the platform beneath the lantern that houses the third-order Fresnel lens. On the platform there is a powerful spotting telescope, which with some fiddling I managed to focus on the Three Sisters.

"Botheration!" I expostulated; the odd object was gone. Perhaps it had swum away, but I did not think so. I lifted my head and scanned with naked eye, occasionally fighting back strands of long hair lifted by wind gusts, until I found it again. It had drifted, or possibly swum, a few yards north and closer in to the rocky shore. I aimed the telescope and refocused.

Indeed it was not swimming, not moving through the water of its own locomotion, but rather you might say that the ocean was having its way with this thing. Nor was it entirely red—I caught flashes of white and black as well. Whatever it was, the incoming tide brought it relentlessly closer to shore, until it was caught in the crest of a breaking wave, tumbled over and over in flashes of red and black and white, and for a moment I thought—

"Oh, no," I said, pushing my face harder against the telescope as if that alone could clarify my view, and louder I cried: "No!"

But there was no denying it: The object had both arms and legs of a pale, sickly white. And a head with face obscured by a mass of black hair. It was human, probably female, surely drowned.

"Where's Mrs. Houck," the police officer asked in a challenging manner, "and who are you? Why're you driving her rig?"

"My name is Fremont Jones. I'm the deputy lighthouse keeper, serving for Mrs. Houck while she is on a six-month leave of absence. I'm driving her rig because it seemed the best and fastest way to get over here." Ridiculous as it had at first seemed, I had quickly learned from experience how long it took to cross the extensive dunes around the lighthouse on foot. It was far faster to get in the rig and drive around by the road. "It was I who spied the body on watch and gave the alarm."

"Oh." He tipped his cap, which I took for a sort of apology. "Yeah, I guess I did hear about Mrs. Houck being gone. Sorry if I was short with you, Miss Jones, but a body can never be too careful."

"Quite right," I agreed out of politeness, but actually I do not concur with that sentiment at all. There are certainly plenty of people who are altogether too careful and therefore lead rather boring lives. However I do believe that there were more of them in Boston, where I used to live, than in California. This state seems to have been built by risk-takers.

A shout from out beyond the rocks attracted my attention, and that of the policeman. We turned our heads simultaneously toward the sound, and saw that it came from one of the boats of the Pacific Grove Ocean Rescue.

Pacific Grove is a resort community, population about three thousand, nestled along the inner curve of that southern headland which has Point Pinos at its tip. Monterey lies just to the northeast, Carmel to the south. The shoreline of Pacific Grove is spectacular but dangerous for the uninitiated, being made up mostly of jagged pieces of upthrust granite. Hettie Houck, who was nothing if not a stern taskmaster, had trained me thoroughly: Do not walk far out upon the rocks, and even if you think you are at a safe distance, do not turn your back on the ocean—for a rogue wave can rise up and sweep you away in the blink of an eye; and if you are in a boat, stay well out, because the current may trap you and dash your vessel upon the rocks.

Too bad, I thought, that the woman who drowned did not have such a good teacher. She was virtually certain to be a woman because of all the scarlet. Men, unless they are dressed for an academic procession or some sort of religious exhibition, do not wear that much, or that shade, of red.

There are a few places along the shoreline where one may enter and exit the water safely, and my mentor had taught me these as well. Into one such small cove on the north or bay side of Point Pinos, the rescue team brought their boats. But I saw no sign of the drowned woman.

"Where is she?" I muttered under my breath. The policeman didn't hear—he was already picking his way down the slippery rocks to the scant piece of sandy beach below. The tide was on the ebb, so the scent of sea-stuff was strong; and though the day had been balmy for January, there was a bite in the wind coming off the water. I drew my wool shawl closer about my neck, shivering, and suddenly wished I had not come.

Perversely, even as I wished myself elsewhere, I felt bald curiosity nudge me to follow the policeman down to the sand, where I presumed the poor drowned person would be brought ashore. The rescue boats were taking their time, negotiating their way in tandem around underwater rocks whose tips showed above the surface in the trough of each ebbing wave. I lifted the hem of my skirt and regarded my shoes with some dismay—they were soft black leather, fairly new, not meant for clambering about on the rocks of Pacific Grove.

Just as I was about to set forth, good shoes or no, I heard the muffled clomp of horses' hooves on the unpaved road, accompanied by the rattle and clatter of a vehicle that proved to be the coroner's wagon. The wagon was black, of course, ugly as sin, but the matched pair of black horses that pulled it were magnificent. Glad of the distraction, I went over to admire the animals. I'd thought Hettie's bay mare was quite fine, but these black beauties put her in the shade.

"They are so beautiful!" I said to the driver. The horses whuffled and stamped, arching necks that gleamed like onyx.

"Yes, aren't they?" He jumped down with an agility that belied his age. "I take good care of them. Now, where's the body?"

"Are you the coroner?" I asked, unnecessarily as it turned out, for he reached beneath the driver's seat and brought forth the black bag that carried the tools of his trade.

"I am. Dr. Frederick Bright, by name. How-do, Miss." He tipped an imaginary hat. I supposed he habitually went hatless in order to show off his extraordinarily full head of snowy-white hair. He had a white mustache of equally extravagant proportions. With the addition of a beard he might have resembled Santa Claus, except that his body was far too thin. And his eyes were definitely not jolly: They were dark, round, too small for his face, and constantly jumped around in a nervous manner.

I said, "How do you do. I am Fremont Jones, temporarily the lighthouse keeper at Point Pinos. The rescue team hasn't brought the body in yet." I inclined my head toward the water, meanwhile stroking the horse's neck and feeling the tiny quivers of abating exertion beneath his smooth, warm skin. The horse regarded me with an eye of liquid jet, as if he understood that my stroking was as much to calm myself as him. I have heard tell that horses are not intelligent, but that is hard to believe when you look into their eyes.

Dr. Bright made a grunt of acknowledgment and moved off toward the place where I'd been standing before his arrival. He was bandy-legged, I noticed, and walked with an odd little hitch in his gait. His hair was so thick and heavy that the breeze off the bay barely stirred it, whereas my own reddish-brown topknot was blowing down strand by strand. He put his black bag on a rock and waited, jiggling up and down with impatience. I heard him mutter something that sounded like "Come on, come on!"

They did come on, and it was a sight I might wish to forget, but I know I will never be able to as long as I live. A brawny man in hip boots came striding through the surf with the drowned woman in his arms. Her dark hair was hanging down like a dripping curtain and her scarlet dress was sodden. White silk stockings trailed in tatters from her legs; one shoe was missing. The sky behind the man with his tragic burden was streaked with long rose ribbons and the sea was turning purple as the sun went down.

A small crowd of people, alerted by the horn on the firehouse that summons the ocean rescue, had begun to gather but they kept a respectful distance and an equally respectful silence. I stood apart, still stroking the coroner's horse, but I went forward when I heard Dr. Bright say, "Put her down right here. After I've done a brief examination, we'll want the people to come forward, see if somebody can identify her."

Good luck, I thought as nausea rose in my throat, for the one shoe was not all that was missing. So was half her face. I looked away, into the stricken eyes of the man who'd carried her.

"The fishes been at her," he said. Someone in the front row of bystanders heard, repeated, and a murmuring rippled through the crowd.

"How—" My voice broke. I tried again. "How long do you suppose she has been in the water?" There was not much odor; the body was not decomposed, merely . . . eaten. Somehow I found that hard to bear; it made me feel inside as if my spine were a blackboard and someone was scraping his fingers down it.

"Not long," said Dr. Bright, "thirty-six hours at the outside, I'd guess, but I'll know more when I get her back to the laboratory. It's a shame about her face, though. Be that much harder to get an identification."

"The, um, the dress is distinctive," I said. That was my final contribution. I couldn't bear to look anymore at that poor woman. What I had not seen at first was that the bodice of her red dress had been ripped open—by a large fish, or an angry person before she fell into the water, who could tell?—and the fish had eaten away at the one breast thus exposed. They had nibbled at her fingers and at the toes of her shoeless foot. But the dress was indeed distinctive and I guessed it would have been expensive because it looked like velvet. I certainly wasn't going to touch it to find out for sure. I further guessed that her underclothes would be even more informative, for the inch of petticoat that showed beneath the hem of her dress was quite fine. That is, where the sharp teeth of the fish had not pulled the lace into tatters.

Somehow one does not think of fish as having teeth. But obviously some species must—the proof was there on the sandy ground before me. I moved back a few steps, staying close enough to see and hear all that went on. I was certain one of the people who came forward when Dr. Bright beckoned would know her. A woman who wears exquisitely made clothes cannot be a waif or a stray. But one by one each man and woman shook his or her head and moved on.

Last to come was a personage of some repute, by the name of Euphemia Wells. Hettie had pointed her out to me and warned that I should be careful of Euphemia, whose leadership in Pacific Grove goes back to its founding some thirty years ago. Hettie had also told me that the town was founded as a summer religious retreat for one of the larger Protestant denominations, so the religious influence is still strong, which was why my transgression at the boardinghouse had been dealt with so severely.

Euphemia is a large woman, with a bosom like a shelf. She wears outmoded dresses of black bombazine and I have never seen her hatless. Even at seven in the morning, if you should happen to be out for breakfast or having your morning constitutional and you pass Euphemia, she will be wearing one of those dreadful forward-sloping hats. The hat will be black also, and her dress will rustle stiffly (not, God forbid, enticingly) as she moves by. She rustled stiffly now, and her corset creaked as she bent down to get a closer look at the poor drowned woman.

"Humph!" she snorted, backing off. Then she gave me the evil eye, for absolutely no reason I could think of, but she soon enlightened me. "Distinctive dress, my foot. It's disgraceful, that's what kind of dress it is! Only a certain sort of woman wears such a dress, and you won't find that sort of woman in Pacific Grove. If you want to find out who she is, you'd better ask those bohemians on the other side of the hill!" With that, she rustled and creaked away.

By "the other side of the hill" she meant Carmel—where Michael Archer lived, with those bohemians.

A year ago I would have gone ahead to Carmel even though night was falling as the coroner bore the body away. A year ago I would not have let little things like dark, seldom-traveled roads and inexperience in handling a rig get in the way of satisfying my curiosity. A year ago—that is to say, before the earthquake—I had not yet had certain experiences which have since caused me to make some attempt at occasional prudence.

There are only two ways to get to Carmel—that is, assuming one does not go by water: by the Old Mission Road or on Seventeen Mile Drive through Del Monte Forest. The latter is a picturesque, winding route that was built mainly to impress the guests of the Hotel Del Monte in Monterey. Indeed that drive gets its name from the seventeen miles between the hotel and the forest's Carmel gate. The Old Mission Road is more direct, but goes over a hill (the very one aforementioned by Euphemia Wells) so steep that anywhere but in California it would be called a mountain. Furthermore, that hill is supposed to be haunted—and while I do not believe in ghosts, if ever there were an apt place for one it would be the summit of Carmel Hill. There is something about the summit that compels a look over the shoulder to see what might be behind.

"It can wait until tomorrow," I said aloud, giving a shake to the reins. Hettie's bay mare, Bessie, twitched one ear backward but obliged me by picking up her pace. If the drowned woman was from Carmel, or had any connection to Carmel, Michael would know—and he would still know tomorrow morning.

Meanwhile I still had to drive through the Point Pinos woods on my way back to the lighthouse, at twilight, when tree trunks seem to waver in the gathering gloom and creatures that hunt at night come out with their glowing eyes. I am a city person—all my life I have lived either in Boston or San Francisco—and there are times, especially at night, when in the midst of all this glorious nature I feel isolated and alone.

CHAPTER
TWO

KEEPER'S LOG
January 10, 1907
Wind: SW light
Weather: Cool, a.m. fog
Comments:

I noted the wind direction and the early morning fog in the log; I would add to this, on the basis of my observations, as the day went on. I presumed Hettie would approve my frugality with words. I had patterned my style of log-keeping after hers, and she was nothing if not concise. There were no wasted words in her log; I daresay there had been no wasted words, or anything else wasted, in the entire life of Henrietta Houck. I had never heard of a female lighthouse keeper before meeting her. Now I knew there were others, but probably few, male or female, of such exacting standards.

She had been gone since just before Christmas; she'd trained me during the two weeks prior to that. There was definitely a serendipity in our meeting that night on the sidewalk, for although on the surface we seem not at all alike, Hettie and I are sisters under the skin. It did not take either of us long to figure this out, or to see that our respective wants and needs dovetailed exactly: She desired to take a trip (for what purpose she did not say), but the deputy provided by the naval lighthouse service had proved unsatisfactory during his training and so she had dismissed him; I wanted to stay near, but not in, Carmel until I had at least tried for a while to understand what was going on with Michael. Six months at the lighthouse suited me exactly. It not only gave me a place to live, but also a small salary—a great help to me in my reduced circumstances.

Hettie's assistant, now my assistant, is a man named Quincy. He is taciturn, with the sort of tanned and weathered skin that men get from spending their lives on or near the sea. He might be fifty, or he might be a hundred years old; the only thing one can say for sure about Quincy's age is that it is doubtful he'll see forty again. He is thin yet muscular, in a wiry sort of way, and his shoulders have a slight stoop. He usually wears a battered old felt hat with gray locks of longish hair straggling from beneath its brim, and his eyes are such a dark gray they are almost black. He cannot read or write; otherwise Hettie could have turned the lighthouse over to him in her absence. But this lack of literacy is a small deficiency when one considers that he can (and does) do everything else there is to be done about the place.

I do not like to have to rely on people for things, because then what is one to do if those one relies on are not available? However, I do find myself relying on Quincy. He positively adores being asked to do things; his eyes get all shiny with pleasure. They were shining as I explained to him that I needed to go to Carmel, so would he please hook up Bessie to the shay? And would he mind, if it wasn't too much trouble, taking the watch for a couple of hours?

"Righty-o!" Quincy said. It is his favorite expression.

The sun shone through the morning fog with a glowing pearlescence as Bessie and I set out to climb Carmel Hill. Near the summit I hopped down from the shay and walked the steepest part to give the horse a break. The fog was like an army of wraiths, swirling among the dark shapes of tall trees, obscuring the view, creeping along the surface of the road. I hurried, tugging at Bessie's halter, and as soon as the angle of the slope leveled off, jumped back into the carriage.

"Go, Bessie!" I yelled, flapping the reins. The mare took off like a bat out of hell. It was an interesting descent, what with the two-wheeled shay tipping this way and that from our speed. The farther down we went, the more the fog cleared, until the sun broke through just as the road took a southerly bend that would soon lead us to Carmel-by-the-Sea.

Michael has built a cottage for himself on a street called Casanova, which he says means "new house" in Spanish, but I think he is only trying to divert me with that definition. I suspect rather that the name of his street has gone straight to his head, for I gather his behavior in recent months has been similar to that of the Italian Renaissance fellow with the same name—the one who got himself jailed in Venice for his excesses. So I was not unduly surprised when Michael answered my knock on his door in a state of semi-undress. That is to say, he was wearing trousers and a black and gold brocaded vest over nothing else, unless one wanted to count the dark hair that whorled about his chest in the most fascinating manner. Behold, the new Michael!

"Hello, *Misha*," I said.

"Hello, Fremont," he replied sleepily, leaning in the doorway with his black eyelashes at half-mast. His trousers drooped at the waist, exposing his navel.

"I apologize," I said, "if I awakened you." Not that it wasn't high time to be up and about—it was early but not *that* early. I was trying not to stare but my eyeballs had acquired a will of their own. I couldn't keep them on his face to save myself, and now my glance strayed past his shoulder in the direction of what I supposed was his bedroom.

One of his eyebrows quirked upward in a way that was achingly familiar. Ignoring my apology he said, "You're the last person I expected to see. Isn't it a little early for social calls?"

Everything around us was so quiet that I could hear the swish of Bessie's tail, and the chitter of a squirrel in a live oak tree, whose branches curved down to embrace the cottage. I said, "This isn't exactly a social call."

For a moment I thought a shadow of disappointment fluttered in Michael's changeable eyes. They are like the sea, those eyes, changing from blue to green to shades of gray according (I have come to believe) to the man's inner weather. At the moment they were bluish gray and rather cold. He said, "Then there must be some sort of problem."

"N-not really." I fastened my eyes on his face and willed them to remain there this time. I had just discovered that men have nipples, though I couldn't imagine what for; actually I had never thought about it before, which I suppose is what comes of not having any brothers. And only the one sexual experience, which I do not like to think about. Jerking my mind back on track I said, "I know it is rather rude to arrive unannounced—"

"Especially," he interrupted, with that damn eyebrow going up again, "considering that you have led me to believe Carmel is the last place on earth you'd like to be."

"Never mind that; I was upset. I didn't mean— Well, just never mind. My point is that, since there are no telephones in Carmel, or for that matter Pacific Grove, I could hardly help coming unheralded. As it were."

Michael smiled at my awkward explanation. It was a slow, sensual sort of smile that took the chill right out of his eyes. He has a mobile mouth, which is perhaps his best feature, made all the more attractive by an off-center dent in his chin. "Fremont," he said at last, "will you come in?"

"Certainly. That is, if it does not greatly inconvenience you."

He chuckled and moved back, leaving the front door open. As the fog burned off, the day was warming; nearby some ecstatic song-

16

birds had begun to celebrate the sunshine with much trilling. I entered hesitantly, the relative darkness of the unfamiliar room temporarily dimming my vision.

"I'll put on some clothes," Michael said, "if you will excuse me for a moment. There is coffee on the stove. As you may surmise, I have just gotten up. You did not, however, awaken me."

I murmured a word of thanks, then stood straining my ears to hear if any other murmurings, no matter how discreet, came from his bedroom. I have been endowed with unusually acute hearing, which does come in handy sometimes, though lately I would rather have been endowed with something more visible. Large breasts, for example. I had always thought mine were perfectly adequate until meeting the female whose voice I sought to hear from the bedroom.

At any rate I didn't hear anything other than the sound of a wardrobe opening and closing. Thus reassured I crossed the one large room that serves as living room, dining room, and kitchen, dropping my shawl on a rocking chair as I passed. Michael's home is a cottage in the true sense of the word: small, cozy, somehow in harmony with all the surrounding elements. All the houses in Carmel have this unpretentious air about them. Actually if I were in an unkind mood I could say that some are little more than woodland shacks. Shack or cottage or whatever, all have been dignified by names; for some reason I cannot fathom, there are no street numbers in Carmel. Michael's is called Xanadu. After the poem by Mr. Coleridge, the one that goes: "In Xanadu did Kubla Khan/A stately pleasure dome decree . . ."

"Hah!" I exclaimed involuntarily.

"Fremont, did you say something?" Michael called out from the bedroom.

"It's nothing—just that your coffee is rather hot. I almost burned my tongue." I lied, of course; what burned me was the idea of pleasure domes. Especially since the connotation of Xanadu had to be intentional. Michael built and named the cottage himself.

He did not build it with his own hands, though many—perhaps most—of Carmel's small population have literally built their own houses. This in spite of the fact that a group of people with fewer practical skills can scarcely be imagined. They are all artists of one stripe or another, with or without connection to San Francisco's

Bohemian Club, who, like Michael, left the city after the earthquake. As, eventually, did I, although I had allowed him to persuade me— to mislead me—with my own willing cooperation.

"A penny for your thoughts." Michael picked up his coffee cup from the table and carried it over to the stove. He had snuck up on me. When he wants to, he can move like a cat.

"Save your money. I wasn't thinking about anything in particular."

"Then shall we sit and drink our coffee at the table like civilized folk?" He pulled out a chair. "And you can tell me what has brought you to Carmel so early on a winter's day."

"It hardly feels like winter." I smiled and smoothed my dark green corduroy skirt. It was impossible not to enjoy sitting at the table with him. How pleasant the room was, with its glowing wood floors, huge fireplace of golden-hued local stone, and tree-filtered sunlight falling through casement windows. I felt as if I were in an enchanted cottage in a green-gold wood. Around us, all of Carmel seemed suspended in a magical hush. Softly, so as not to break the spell, I asked, "Is it always like this?"

"I don't understand the question." Michael sipped, looking over the rim of his coffee cup. His eyes had caught some of the greenish light, which turned them turquoise. With his pale skin and arched black brows, high cheekbones and black hair grown so long it curled, he looked exotic enough to live in Xanadu.

"It's not important." I shook my head and sat up taller, straightening my spine. "The reason for my being here is, I want you to come with me to look at the body of a woman who was pulled from Monterey Bay yesterday."

"Why?"

"Because, in the first place, no one who was present at the time— which was a goodly portion of the citizens of Pacific Grove—seemed to know who she was. And in the second place, I've been thinking about it and there are some very peculiar things about the way she died."

"She drowned, one would assume. That is not particularly peculiar for a body found in the bay."

He was trying to provoke me, but I pretended patience. "What is peculiar is that she was wearing a dress of red velvet, a rich fabric, excellently cut. Not the sort of dress one buys off the rack at the local department store. Furthermore, I'd be willing to bet my eyeteeth that her underclothes—camisole, petticoats, and so on—were hand-sewn. You know what that means!"

"How should I know anything about women's underclothes? You shock me, Fremont!"

I made a mock frown. "You know, surely, that now that we have sewing machines and methods of mass manufacture, only the most expensive underthings are made by hand."

"Hmm." Michael rubbed his chin. It is a habit of his when thinking, left over from the time (not too long ago) when he used to have a black beard with silver streaks at the sides.

"Don't you see?" I appealed to him, leaning across the table. "A woman of means would not be likely to go walking all by herself along the rocks of Point Pinos wearing such an elegant dress!"

"You didn't say she was found near Point Pinos."

"Well, she was. I saw her myself from the lighthouse at about four o'clock yesterday afternoon, and gave the alarm."

"So you think her drowning—if indeed she did drown—was no accident."

"Yes."

"And you base this assumption on the clothes she was wearing?"

"Together with where she was found. If she had washed up on Del Monte Beach, I wouldn't think it so peculiar."

"Because?"

"Because then she could have been a guest at the Hotel Del Monte, out for an evening stroll, who got careless and turned her back on the water or some such thing. Really, Michael, you're being extraordinarily dense!"

He rubbed at his ear and blinked owlishly. "I suppose I'm a little out of practice, but it scarcely matters. Why come to me, Fremont?"

I sat back, deflated. Yes, why indeed? What had happened to my old friend Michael Archer, a rather bookish older gentleman habitually dressed in a dark suit and white shirt—who used to enjoy playing Dr. Watson to my Sherlock Holmes? He had turned into this new fellow, Misha—what was the last name? Oh yes, Kossoff. I could tell this was Misha by the clothes he wore: pleated fawn trousers, cream-colored cashmere sweater with a gold silk scarf knotted into its open neck, and fringed brown suede vest. This Misha stirred such mixed feelings in me that I wanted to scream.

But I said reasonably, "There was some suggestion that the woman who drowned may have been known in Carmel. I thought, because of your wide circle of acquaintance, that you might care to attempt to identify her."

He tipped his chair back and put one foot up on the table, shod in brown suede that matched his vest. "Let the police handle it, Fremont."

"Somehow I have the impression that they are not likely to try very hard."

"Maybe that's wishful thinking on your part."

It was a deliberately harsh jibe that I did not dignify with a response.

Michael reached out, stretching, and took an orange from a basket on the table. He began, slowly and carefully, to peel it. The fragrance of the fruit made my tongue curl. He said, "There is no point in my going with you. I will not be able to identify the woman."

"How can you know that, when you haven't yet seen her?"

"No one of my acquaintance is missing. She is not from Carmel. We are a very small community here, and as of last night we were all accounted for." He offered half the orange to me, juice dripping from his fingers.

I shook my head, refusing to accept either the fruit or his disinterest, which I believed was an act. To what purpose I had no idea. Act or not, he was letting me down. "I was wrong to come here," I said, rising from the table.

Michael tipped his head back as I passed behind him, and I felt his eyes follow me to the door. But I did not look back. In the doorway I said without turning, "I am sorry for intruding upon your morning. I did not realize how completely Carmel has changed you."

I had set one foot across the threshold when Michael raised his voice ever so slightly. "I had hoped you might have come on business of a more personal nature."

My cheeks burned. I swallowed hard, willing the flush to fade, and as it passed off I glanced back over my shoulder. Now both feet were up on the table, and the green-gold light glinting across the Slavic lineaments of his face turned him into a satyr, or a Pan. I could not think of a reply.

Michael prompted, "A social invitation, for example. I daresay I might feel more welcome in your new home than I did at that rooming house. Of course, if you'd taken the rental cottage I found for you here in Carmel, the rooming house episode would never have happened, nor would we be having these—shall we say—communication problems."

I turned fully to face him. "We've been through this before, Michael."

"Not to my satisfaction." With a thunk he brought both feet to the floor and stood up to face me, half the room's length between us.

"You want to hear it again? Very well: I could not take that cottage because I am first and foremost a businesswoman, and there is not enough business in Carmel for my typewriting service—contrary to what you led me to believe. Apparently it did not occur to you, when you were being so persuasive about my moving here, that your Carmel writer friends cannot afford to pay for having their words typed."

"Some can. You were too hasty," he grumbled.

"My financial resources are limited. I have to be practical, and Pacific Grove is a more practical place to start my sort of business. It is halfway between Carmel and Monterey, so I can attract customers from both places. I've explained all this to you before."

Michael took a few steps forward. "So you have. I did not think then, and I do not think now, that business was the real reason you refused the rental cottage."

My chin came up and my face ignited; this time I did not try to make the flush fade. He was right, that was not the real reason, but I would sooner have died than admit it. In a warning tone I said, "Michael, if you persist in this you will destroy what is left of our friendship."

Eyes glittering, he came forward a few more steps so that we were only some six feet apart. "Why can't you bring yourself to call me Misha, when everyone else here does?"

The answer was too complex. Words stuck in my throat.

He moved within inches. "Why is it so difficult for you to accept the changes I'm making in my life, and in myself? I never dreamed that you, of all people, would react the way you have, or I would not have encouraged you to come to Carmel. Be fair, Fremont. When you left Boston, didn't you do much the same as I have done? You moved to a new place, took on a new lifestyle, and a new name as well. I have done no more than that."

"I suppose, when you put it that way . . . but you must admit, your new lifestyle is rather extreme."

He leaned in to me. I stood my ground, looking up at him, thinking that he must be able to hear the exaggerated thumps of my heart. "No more extreme," he said, "than yours is, for a woman."

"You have me there," I said. I blinked, swallowing hard. I could see cords of tension in his neck, and hear the harsh sound of his rapid breathing. For long moments neither of us moved; we stood locked in a contentious attraction that neither wished to break. But then simultaneously and as if by mutual agreement we both moved back.

I stood just across the threshold, wiping the palms of my hands on my skirt, for they had gone all sweaty. "All right," I said, "a compromise: I will call you Misha if you'll accept the fact that it will take a long time before I can feel comfortable in Carmel."

He did not reply, but stood rubbing his chin with such a strange, faraway look in his eyes that I thought, Ye gods, he is going mad as a hatter!

Suddenly he smiled and reached for my hand, grasping it in a businesslike handshake. Pumping enthusiastically he said, "I accept the compromise, Fremont!"

"I am glad, Misha." I smiled back at him, but in truth such a huge gulf had developed between us during the past month that I felt more distant from my old friend now than at any time in the past. Smiling and wanting to mean it, wanting the problems to go away, wanting above all for *her* to go away, I slowly extracted my hand.

"You'll see, Fremont," he said eagerly, looking boyish although he is twenty years older than I, "things will get better. This is only the beginning. A new beginning."

I replied by rote, "I suppose you are right."

Ever since the earthquake, people keep talking about new beginnings. As for me, I am fairly sick of beginnings—I have begun a few too many of them lately.

Behind me I heard Bessie softly snuffling and browsing in the brush, reminding me that I had a life apart from Michael—*Misha*—and demands upon my time. A living to earn. Duties to fulfill. "I must go now," I said. But as I reached the shay I turned and called out impulsively, "Will you come to dinner at the lighthouse, Misha?"

"Thought you'd never ask," he drawled, with a one-sided grin.

"Sunday evening," I instructed, gathering the reins, "at seven o'clock. And, Misha, in the meantime you might just ask around Carmel about the drowned woman. Maybe someone will know something; you can't tell unless you ask."

Before I drove away I saw his face cloud over, his expression so darkly glowering that I could almost hear the thunder of his mind.

CHAPTER THREE

*M*isha, *Misha, Misha:* I said the new name over and over to myself in time with Bessie's clopping hooves. Perhaps if I repeated it often enough I might get used to it . . . but I didn't think so. The truth was that I hated the name, because it meant to me at best a lack of consideration and at worst a betrayal of my most tender feelings.

"Why," I had begged of him that night behind the closed door of my boardinghouse room, "why didn't you tell me before I came down here that you have turned yourself into this totally different person, this Misha Kossoff?"

And he had answered, "Because I was afraid that if I did, you wouldn't come. Michael Archer was an experiment that didn't work, Fremont. Mikhail Arkady Kossoff is who I really am."

How could I tell him the truth after that? How could I tell him I had fallen in love with Michael Archer, an experiment that didn't work? How could I tell him I'd believed he loved me too? Why else would I have uprooted myself from San Francisco, a place so dear to me in spite of the dirt and noise and sky-high prices of post-earthquake reconstruction, except to be near the man I loved?

I could not possibly tell him these things.

I could—I did—believe his real name was Mikhail Arkady Kossoff. Early on in our friendship he had told me he was an American of Russian descent, and had taken his American name, Michael Archer, from his first two names in Russian: Mikhail Arkady. I could even believe that something he had been doing while he was going by the name Michael Archer had not worked out, because even though he would not admit it in so many words, I knew that, by whatever name he was called, the man was a spy. Or had been a spy, since he said he was "retired." Those things were not the point. The point was that I did not, could not, would never believe Michael was really Misha. If I did, I would have just packed up my bags and gone home.

Except, of course, that right then I did not have a home.

"Oh, *shit!*" I yelled at the top of my lungs—it is a word I learned from Father, who would always change it to "shoot" if he knew I was within earshot. Not a word I would ever utter except in moments of direst frustration. At that very moment an automobile tootled its horn and chugged past my horse and carriage. I sincerely hoped the driver had not heard what I'd said.

I gave the reins a flick, for Bessie was plodding even though the hill is much less steep on its Carmel side. The mare did not speed up much and I let her be, because my thoughts were also plodding. I am forever trying to be fair, and I do feel an affection for the Carmelites, as Carmel's residents call themselves. Any resemblance to the religious order of the same name is in the spelling only. These Carmelites are a colorful, eccentric bunch, so unconventional that they quite leave me in the shade. I went back in my mind to that December day, my first in Carmel. . . .

I had arrived on the Monterey Peninsula via an elegant, fast train called the *Del Monte Express*. I was in a celebratory mood, due to the satisfactory outcome (I knew the sod was guilty, and the jury agreed) of the trial of one Mickey Morelock. I was the principal witness against Mickey, and in order to appear at the trial I had stayed in San Francisco for three months beyond the time I'd told Michael I would move to Carmel.

I knew he had found a cottage for me to rent. But I am stubborn, and some people—my father, for instance—would say excessively independent, so I had reserved for myself one of the less expensive rooms at the Hotel Del Monte, for three days, just in case.

In the middle of the afternoon on the first of those three days, Michael called for me in his Maxwell auto. We were going to have a picnic in Carmel. Everything was beautiful—the weather, the scenery, the company—and I was positively giddy with joy. I wore a smart new suit with one of those tightly fitted, long-sleeved, waist-length jackets that were the latest style. Perhaps the material, an olive silk gabardine, was a bit fine for a picnic but that did not deter me. Especially when Michael said, "You are looking exceptionally well today, Fremont. And well worth waiting for these past three months."

I thanked him, feeling as if I glowed from the inside out. He was looking exceptionally well himself, in clothes far more casual than I was accustomed to seeing him wear: a shirt of some loosely woven wool in an interesting teal shade, worn over a black sweater and black trousers, and a black fedora that slouched enticingly over one eye.

Michael kept up a running commentary as he drove, telling me interesting little scraps of history, such as how Carmel got its name: from the Río Carmelo, the Carmel River, which was in turn named for some Carmelite monks in the party of an early Spanish explorer. I had scarcely noticed any time pass when we bucketed into Carmel on Ocean Avenue, an unpaved street with the texture of a washboard. Michael identified the largest building on the right, the Pine Inn, then shortly he veered left and said, "This is Monte Verde Avenue, where Oscar Peterson and his wife, Mimi, live. My cottage is on Casanova, one block farther down." He pointed out, on our left, the

Petersons' cottage and its attendant cabins, all but swallowed up in the surrounding greenery.

"Where is the ocean?" I asked, as to my surprise he nosed the Maxwell into a bush of marguerites and stopped the motor. "I thought we were going to picnic on this beach of pure white sand that you've told me so much about."

"We are," he replied, "but everyone is gathering here at Peterson's first. We'll all go down to the beach together. We do this most every night, to watch the sunset. It's beautiful. A peak experience."

I smiled at his enthusiasm but felt bitterly disappointed: I'd thought that Michael and I would be picnicking alone. In my fantasies, our first time together on the white sands of Carmel would be the occasion of his telling me, at last, that he loved me. He would thank me for giving up San Francisco in order to be near him. And I would say something like "Oh, it's nothing, because I love you too."

Oscar Peterson's place reminded me of a summer camp I used to go to when I was a child: It smelled all woodsy and appeared barely fit for human habitation. A scrawled sign had been tacked on a tree trunk near the graveled turnaround that served for a drive: PETERSON'S PLACE. Not a very novel name considering, if I remembered correctly from the various stories of Carmel Michael had told me, that Oscar was a poet.

"Here's Oscar now," Michael said, taking my elbow. I drew in a deep breath, raised my chin, and assumed a smile.

The man who approached us was tall and thin and pale, with sparse graying hair that hung limply to his shoulders. He wore round glasses with silver frames and thick lenses that magnified his gray eyes. His clothes looked as if they might once have belonged to somebody else, or alternatively, as if he might once have *been* somebody else: shirt and trousers both so much too big that they hung in folds, gathered in at the waist by a knotted red scarf for a belt. His trousers were chopped off just below the knee, exposing a pair of fish-belly-white shins, and he wore sandals on his long-toed bony feet. In sum, his appearance was rather off-putting, or so I thought until Michael completed his introduction.

"Fremont, I am charmed," Oscar said, with a smile so radiant it instantly eclipsed all his oddity.

"Likewise, Oscar," I said, meaning it.

"We're all back here amongst the trees." He waved vaguely and started off. Michael and I followed, and soon I was knee-deep, so to speak, in Carmelites.

One fellow, an artist with an Arabic-sounding name I didn't quite catch, wore flowing robes of black and white, complete with a burnoose. His companion was a woman who looked older than he—if one could judge his age by his face, since every other part of him was covered. She also looked less exotic, wearing a fashionable auto-travel costume of duster and veiled hat, in a delicate but dull shade of pink called ashes-of-roses. Her name was Irma Fox and her face resembled one, with her small mouth and sharp nose and beady eyes all squinched together in the center of it.

Just beyond Irma three fellows sat in a row on a redwood bench. They were all in their shirtsleeves, with collars removed and varicolored vests hanging open. They introduced themselves as Tom, Dick, and Harry and I wondered if they were joshing me. I was just about to ask, when *she* appeared. All bedecked in flowers, she floated up out of nowhere to hang on Michael's arm.

"*Dahr*-ling," she said in a voice dripping honey, "you *must* introduce me to my *rival*."

Before that, I hadn't even known I had a rival. Another josher, like Tom, Dick and Harry—that was what I thought at first.

Michael chuckled and said smoothly, "Artemisia Vaughn, may I present Caroline Fremont Jones, who prefers to be called Fremont."

"How-do-you-do," I said by rote.

She said, "Charmed. I prefer to be called Artemisia, though there are some cretins around here who insist on calling me Art. One doesn't want to be *called* Art, one *creates* art."

"Artemisia is an artist," Michael said, smiling down at her, "in more than one medium. She paints and writes, and does amateur theatrics."

I said, "How impressive." It was hard not to stare at this artistic paragon. She looked as if she might be somewhere between Michael and myself in age—that is to say, in her thirties. Her face was arresting but not beautiful, dominated by a long nose with a bit of a hook at the tip. Large, dark brown eyes were her best feature, balancing a wide mouth. She had braided into her long brown hair some of the daisies that bloom so profusely here, and she wore a Grecian-style gown that showed off a pair of pointed and obviously unbound breasts.

"I paint nocturnes," said Artemisia, "and I write stories out of my dreams. I am only interested, you see, in things of the night."

"Then one would presume," I said brightly, "that is why you are named for Artemis, goddess of the moon."

"Of course!" She laughed, sounding a good deal like a shower of golden coins, and laid her head with the greatest of ease against Michael's shoulder.

"And of the hunt," I added.

"How clever your friend is, Misha," she purred. "But of course you told me she was, didn't you?"

"Fremont is indeed clever. Too much so, sometimes."

"You are too kind, both of you," I said; I was thinking, What was that she called him? A pet name? This was becoming a tad unbearable.

"Don't be silly!" She tweaked Michael's nose. The easy way she touched him quite astonished me. He smiled down at her, not minding her familiarity in the least.

"One can never be too clever," she asserted. "Isn't that right, Fremont?" Lifting her head from Michael's shoulder she winked at me and, without waiting for a reply, twirled off, the folds of her Grecian gown rippling around her.

That was my first encounter with Artemisia Vaughn, the Other Woman. It left me so stunned that I met the rest of the Carmelites in a kind of daze. In order to remember people, I had to pair their names with their clothing. This was easier than it might have been, because this picnic was the nearest thing to a costume party I'd seen since Halloween.

Brunhilde, a sturdy blonde of Germanic appearance, was Mimi Peterson. Although she did not wear a horned helmet, she had hair as yellow as corn, knotted carelessly on top of her head and spilling down her cheeks and nape in a most attractive way.

There was La Señorita—an extravagantly flirtatious, extremely thin brunette in ruffles whose name I promptly forgot; the Medium

Brown Man, named Arthur Something—a quiet, brown-suited fellow who was medium everything: height, weight, age, length of nose, size of ears, etc. etc. etc.; and Diogenes—an older man, white-haired and round-bellied, in a shapeless drab robe, carrying a lantern—a professor by the name of Stork or Storch. Finally there was Phoebe, who looked like one of those little gray-brown birds but also like a softly rounded Jane Eyre, in a chocolate dress with a white collar, center-parted light brown hair, and hazel eyes. Her last name, which equally suited her, was Broom.

My reverie was suddenly and rudely interrupted with a snort and a jolt—Hettie's bay mare had achieved the crest of Carmel Hill and was attacking the downslope with rather too much enthusiasm. "Easy, Bessie, easy!" I yelled, pulling back on the reins to slow her down. Since the fog had cleared I was able to see the magnificent blue curve of Monterey Bay over the tops of the trees as we began our descent. But in my mind I remained in another place, by the edge of another bay: Carmel Bay, on that first and fateful December day.

All the colorful Carmelites, plus me, had finished eating a potluck picnic supper on the sand—which was as white as Michael had said it was. The sun was a fiery red ball sinking toward the Pacific when Artemisia came running over to the blanket where Michael and I sat, and grabbed us both by the hand.

"You must come, both of you!" she exclaimed. "I am constructing a living tableau to the dying day!"

Michael allowed her to pull him to his feet but I resisted, saying, "No, thank you. I much prefer to be part of the audience."

She pouted and Michael's mouth curved in a sensual hint of a smile. "Are you sure, Fremont? Artemisia's tableaux are quite the thing."

Not quite my thing, I thought, but I forced yet another smile and waved them on. Then I watched with a strange combination of envy and sadness as Artemisia assembled her little group of men and women and laid her hands on them, moving arms and legs and tilting heads into various poses, as if they were living statues. The setting sun stained their bodies red-gold.

"She's good at that," a voice behind me said quietly.

I looked around, startled because I'd thought myself more or less alone; the nearest picnic blanket was perhaps ten feet away, and both its inhabitants were in the tableau. "Phoebe," I said, recognizing her. "I agree; Artemisia seems endlessly talented."

Phoebe sat down next to me, tucking her feet beneath her skirts. She wore brown high-button shoes, an odd choice considering the sand. She said, "You didn't take my meaning. I meant she is good at manipulating people."

"Ah," I said, in the way that Michael does when he either does not know what to say, or does not wish to give anything away. I waited, but Phoebe did not elaborate.

In silence we watched a scene so lovely it made me ache. The declining sun gilded the wave crests, while elsewhere the sea was dark as wine; a family of seagulls wheeled on the wind and dipped into a streak of sunset that dyed them pink as flamingoes. Except for that single shaft of sun, the air was thick with purple twilight.

Artemisia, not quite satisfied with her arrangement, placed her hand on Michael's inner thigh and rotated his leg outward. A sliver of ice slit my heart. She stroked his throat, forcing his head back; she took her own long white scarf and draped it around his neck so that the tails of it streamed in the wind. His arms were flung back as she had placed them, after the manner of the Winged Victory of Samothrace. The others held positions slightly less dramatic—Artemisia had made Michael the hero of this scene.

At last she was satisfied and stepped back. The living statues held their poses while the sun, grown gigantic in its declension, released a final scarlet flash that turned them all to blood-red gods.

And Phoebe said, "I didn't realize Misha was so handsome."

"Misha?" I whispered, so as not to spoil the dramatic moment.

"Misha. Your friend."

At that moment Diogenes lumbered to his feet and began to sing, or rather to chant, a wordless melody in a minor key that was quite affecting—even to me with my divided mind. Artemisia clapped her hands once, and the tableau shifted smoothly to another pose. A collective sigh rose from all the observers, myself included. The living tableau to the dying day was both beautiful and eerie; it gave me goose bumps.

Phoebe's voice broke the spell. "I wonder if Misha would pose for me in the nude," she mused.

I recalled that she was a sculptor, and was grateful the last rays of sunset would camouflage my cheeks, for they flamed at the thought of Michael posing in the nude. But I did not make any objection; a few hours in their company had taught me that these unusual people were true bohemians, artists and intellectuals, the most *avant* of the avant-garde—even if a few of them did seem to me slightly insane. So I only asked, "Why do you call him Misha, Phoebe?"

"Because," she replied, "it's the Russian nickname for Michael, and he's Russian. You didn't know?"

"I thought he was an American."

"Well, maybe he's both. All I know is, when he first came looking around Carmel, not long after the earthquake, he was Michael Archer. Then when he bought the land, the title was drawn up for Mikhail Arkady Kossoff, which he said was his legal name, the one he was born with. He was born in Fort Ross—which used to belong to the Russians before California became a state." Phoebe shrugged. "We didn't think much of it—all artists know lots of people who have changed their names. Anyhow, it was Artemisia who first called him Misha. He liked it, and it stuck, and now as far as I know, Michael Archer is no more."

"How very interesting," I said. I stared across the sand where the tableau was breaking up and the living statues were embracing one another, saying their good nights amid arpeggios of laughter. The central figure in this sharing of affection was Artemisia, the white of her Grecian gown glowing as if it fed on the little remaining light, and even as I tried to swallow my jealousy, Michael—whom she had first called Misha—leaned over her, removing her scarf from about his neck and wrapping it around hers.

I had looked away then, because I'd been afraid he would kiss her, and I hadn't wanted to see. Phoebe had continued to talk but I hadn't heard a word she said; my ears were roaring and my mouth had gone drier than the sand on which I sat. At that exact moment it had all come together for me: I would be miserable living in a cottage in Carmel, where I would have to deal with this sort of thing every day; there would be no I-love-you's for Michael and me on the white sand or anywhere else; I had come within inches of making a complete fool of myself. In other words, I'd made a great mistake.

I hadn't cried then; somehow I'd gotten through that night and the rest of the days and nights that followed. I don't cry easily. But now, with the wind in my face as Hettie's mare flew downhill toward Monterey, I felt tears drying on my cheeks.

An earthquake is a great learning experience. I suppose the same is true of any disaster that shakes you up and turns your life upside down; when you start putting yourself back together again, you find that nothing looks quite the same as it did before. And if you have lost a great deal, as most of us did in the quake and fire, you will quickly learn what means the most to you by the ferocity with which you long to have it back.

Love and friendship aside (for at the moment I am understandably confused on that score), what I missed most after the earthquake, with a longing that was almost physical, was the daily routine of going to my office and having a job to do that earned me a living wage. I learned that any work, paid or not, is better than none; and that forming one's own routine and sticking to it can be the equivalent of a port in a storm. Therefore I lost no time, once I'd decided to stay in Pacific Grove, finding an office and setting up my daily routine. Though it did have to be modified when I agreed to become temporary keeper of the light.

Hettie was to be gone for six months, so at least until July my schedule would be as follows: In the mornings I generally would be at the lighthouse, doing all the paperwork associated with the keeper's job—the log; the ordering and monitoring of supplies; recording the hours worked by Quincy and his occasional helpers; accounting for the ingress and egress of monies; and so on. In the afternoons I would go to my office in town, from noon until about three-thirty. Though I would of course have liked to stay at the office longer, I did not feel I could ask Quincy to take the hourly watch past four o'clock. And since I was a whiz at the lighthouse paperwork, I could spend the occasional morning away without much harm done.

It was just after eleven-thirty when I returned from Carmel and checked in with Quincy, who told me about the logging schooner that had entered the bay from the north during the last hour. I thanked him and went up to the watch room, where I added the schooner to the "Comments" section of the log. Everything observed on the bay—traffic in or out, sightings of marine animals, any unusual event—had to be recorded there. Such as the drowned woman, I thought on my way back downstairs.

Much good I'd been able to do her, I reflected while making myself a sandwich of bread and cheese for lunch. I wondered if anyone had reported her missing. And if not, how the police would proceed to make an identification. Perhaps they would have a photograph taken of the good side of her face, publish it in the newspaper. That's what I would have done. . . .

Not being as fond as Hettie apparently was of milk straight from her spotted cows, I helped myself to some of Quincy's coffee. He is a coffee fiend, it is his one indulgence, and he keeps a pot of coffee on the stove in the lighthouse kitchen all day. This stove is a black iron thing that positively eats wood and looks as if it has been there since the lighthouse opened half a century ago; I couldn't cook on it to save myself. But then, I am not much of a cook in any circumstance. *Why oh why did I ask Misha to dinner?*

"I just won't think about it," I said briskly; "what's done is done." And in short order I finished my sandwich and set out walking to my office, just over a mile's distance, in downtown Pacific Grove.

FREMONT JONES TYPEWRITING SERVICES: My sign, a portable one that has graced several different working arrangements since the earthquake, now hangs in a window on Grand Avenue, between Lighthouse Avenue and the main street, which is appropriately called Central. I smiled when I saw it and my heart gave a little leap of gladness. How good to be in business again, even if only for a few hours a day!

The office is quite different from my first one, which was on Sacramento Street in San Francisco and burned right after the earthquake. This one is smaller but somehow has more personality. The building itself is brick, rather narrow, two-and-a-half stories tall. My office is located on the ground floor; what is over my head, I am not sure, as I have not yet seen the occupant nor heard anyone moving about. My door opens onto the sidewalk; right next to it is a window so wide it takes up almost all the rest of the storefront.

Inside, the ceiling is high, providing a sense of spaciousness that offsets the sparse square footage.

I furnished this office quite economically with used household furniture from a shop in Monterey. Furniture designed for offices proved to be entirely too pricey. So my "desk" is an old library table, and my typewriter stand is an end table cut down to the right height. File folders reside beneath the desk in a wooden milk crate I begged from the dairy on Point Pinos because it happened to be the right size. Supplies are stashed on the shelves of an old bookcase, the kind with glass doors that drop down to keep out the dust; much of the glass has been cracked and mended with adhesive tape. Two undistinguished straight chairs have cheerful yellow cushions tied onto their hard seats. The pièce de résistance is my new Royal typewriter, which has a moving carriage and a little bell that dings when you have reached the end of the line and must perform the carriage return.

Filled with pride of possession I uncovered the typewriter, then went to the window and flipped over a card that says OPEN on one side and CLOSED on the other. Since the day had turned so fine, I left the door open. A breeze wafted by, bearing scents of salt and kelp. The streets were quiet; Pacific Grove is nearly always quiet. But compared with the lighthouse on Point Pinos, the little town was abuzz with activity. Traffic sounds were like music to my oft-isolated ears.

I waved at the man who tends the photography shop across the street. He ignored me, as usual. I presume he is one of those people who believe a woman has no place in business—the world is full of them. I pay such folks no mind. With a smile for extra measure I turned my back on him and proceeded to the typewriter.

Business was far from brisk, but most days a few customers trickled in. I had two letters to type from yesterday afternoon, so I got right to it. I was completely absorbed in the second one, trying to decipher the author's endlessly inventive and sometimes amusing misspellings, when I sensed another presence. I looked up.

A man stood in the doorway, a distinguished older gentleman who was yet by no means *old*. His hair was so silvery it glistened in the sun. His skin, contrastingly, was tanned, suggesting that he must spend a good deal of time outdoors. He wore a black-and-gray-pinstripe vested suit, a white shirt with a starched collar, and a black tie. In one long-fingered hand he held a black top hat by the brim.

I smiled and said, "Good afternoon."

His face was all the more handsome for its lines of experience. But he did not return my smile. He said, "So it's true, then, what I heard."

CHAPTER FOUR

KEEPER'S LOG
January 10, 1907
(Additional comment) Coast Guard vessel up from Point Sur reports gale-force winds moving up coast from S.

"*I* beg your pardon?" I said.

"Braxton Furnival, at your service," he said with something between a nod and a bow of his silvery head. "May I come in?"

"If you have business, Mr. Furnival, by all means." I stood up behind my typewriter. I was wishing that I had placed the library

37

table/desk out in the room instead of against the wall, so that I might shelter behind it. On the other hand, I hate the fact that I have become so suspicious of people—even if his initial remark was odd enough to merit it.

He advanced, turning the brim of his hat in his hands. "At the moment I'm merely curious, but I may have business after we have talked. You are, I take it, Fremont Jones?"

He kept eye contact; his gaze did not roam up and down my body. I counted that a good sign and relaxed a bit. "I am indeed. Will you take a seat, Mr. Furnival?"

He was so large and long-limbed that he quite dwarfed the yellow-cushioned chair. Seemingly at his ease, he crossed one ankle on top of the other knee. His socks were black with silver clocks. Now came the smile. "I heard Hettie's replacement over to the lighthouse was a woman with a kind of odd name, and that this woman keeps a business afternoons in town. So I came to see for myself."

"I'm replacing Mrs. Houck on a temporary basis only. Typewriting is my main business, which I will pursue full time after she returns to the lighthouse in July. Provided, of course, that there is sufficient need for my services here."

"I see. Are you any good?"

There was a certain roguishness to the question, and a roughness in general about Mr. Braxton Furnival, in spite of his excellent clothes. I rather liked him—but then, I have always liked older men. So I did not take offense but answered with a touch of roguishness myself, "Yes, I am. Quite good."

He laughed and slapped his knee. "A female with spirit, and good-looking too! By thunder, I'll take you on."

"If by that you mean you have something for me to type, I'll be glad to look it over. Do you have the material with you?"

"Nope. I've got me a secretary, but he don't do typewriting."

"What sort of business are you in, Mr. Furnival?"

"Land, my dear. Land. I'm the man on the spot for the Cypress Coast Company." This announcement pleased him; he grinned, put both feet on the floor, and tipped his chair back, lacing his fingers across a broad but tight belly.

"On the spot?" I inquired.

"Del Monte Forest. I live out there, keep an eye on things, participate in development plans, that kind of stuff."

"So presumably you might have reports to type, and correspondence?"

"Yep. Where you from, m'dear?"

The question was personal but I was determined to keep this conversation on a professional basis, so I replied, "My previous business was in San Francisco. I can, however, provide you with local references since I have been at work in this location for several weeks. I'm sure you'll find the quality of my typewriting satisfactory."

He shot me a knowing look and nodded his head a few times. I interpreted this to mean that he had received my subtle message. "I'm sure I will," he said as he reached out and plucked his hat from the end of the desk where he'd placed it. He put the hat on his head, adjusted the brim to his satisfaction, and stood up with his right hand extended.

I rose and joined in a brisk handshake. He was a head and more taller than I, although I am tall for a woman.

"Fremont Jones. Fremont's a famous name in these parts. Do you mind my asking—"

"Not at all," I broke in, although in truth I could not help being tired of it. "John Charles Frémont was a distant relation. Fremont was my mother's maiden name."

"Oh. That explains it, then."

He lingered and I waited, though my feet were feeling a bit fidgety beneath my skirt. I did have work to get on with.

"Lots of folks around here didn't have much use for him, you know. Frémont, I mean. Hope that's not causing you no trouble."

"Not at all, Mr. Furnival. I quite understand. John Charles Frémont seems to have been a person whom other people either liked very much or disliked with equal intensity. No one felt neutral about him. It was the same in Mother's family. He was something of a black sheep, and his wife, Jessie, was not mentioned at all. However I have always admired them both and wish I could have known them." I gestured toward my typewriter. "Now, if you'll excuse me . . ."

"I see. You got work to do. Well, one of these days soon I'll be back with some work for you, Miss Fremont Jones." A few long-legged strides took him to the door, but there he turned back. "Or is it Mrs. Jones? You wouldn't be a widow by any chance, and you so young?"

Naturally he assumed I would not have a living husband and be working. I knew it was unreasonable to be irritated—anyone would have assumed the same; nevertheless my throat felt tight as I said, "I am unmarried and self-supporting, Mr. Furnival. Good day."

On the way back to the lighthouse I stopped at the tobacconist's shop, where one may also buy newspapers and magazines, and obtained a copy of the afternoon paper, which is called *The Wave.* Once I had smiled and nodded my way through the most populous part of town—that is to say, up to Pacific Street—I unfolded the paper and scanned headlines as I walked. I turned page after page, every so often hefting the strap of my bag up higher on my shoulder.

So assiduously did I search through the paper that I was unaware of entering the wood until relative darkness among the trees made the newsprint difficult to decipher.

"Oh, botheration!" I swore, pages rattling as I folded *The Wave* without attention to neatness. Various woodland creatures, startled by my noisiness, ceased their chattering and scampering. The wood became unnaturally quiet. A chill slithered down my spine, feeling like a premonition, in spite of the fact that I am not the least bit superstitious.

"Why?" I didn't realize I had spoken aloud until I heard the word resound through the silent wood. Even my footsteps on the sandy dirt trail made scarcely a sound. Why, I reiterated silently, was there nothing at all in the newspaper about the Poor Drowned Woman?

I was beginning to think of her in capitals, as if that were her proper name. Surely there should at least have been a simple report that the body of a woman had been brought from the bay by the men of the ocean rescue. The ocean rescuers are local heroes; therefore one would assume their actions to be newsworthy.

I quickened my steps, with the consequence that grit from the sandy road worked its way between my shoes and stockings. The price of living near the beach! No matter; the sooner I got to the lighthouse, the sooner I could give *The Wave* a thorough perusal. Some sort of article had to be there. I told myself as I hurried along that the lack of a photograph was a good sign. Probably someone had already identified the unfortunate woman.

I came out of the wood to discover that there was more than one source of the gloom that had stopped my reading. The day was clouding over, and not with simple fog. A massive dark gray cloudbank rose up from the south, spreading so fast that its progress could be seen with the naked eye.

Quincy, laconic as always, was herding the Holsteins into the barn. "Dispatch come from the Coast Guard," he called out as soon as he saw me. "Stuck it on the door."

"Thanks, Quincy," I called in return. Lifting my skirts I ran up the walk. My heart was pounding, not so much from the climb plus that final burst of speed as from sheer excitement. We had not had a storm since Hettie left, but if that ominous sky did not portend a storm I could not imagine what would!

The dispatch, which would have been delivered by a Coast Guardsman on bicycle from the Monterey station, said that their cutter returning from Point Sur (approximately twenty nautical miles south) had reported gale-force winds headed up the coast. I dumped newspaper and bag at the foot of the stairs and charged up to the watch room with its panoramic view. The ragged, rocky projections of Point Pinos were directly ahead of me, a northwesterly direction; to my right or eastward the vast curve of Monterey Bay dipped farther than my eyes could follow; and to the left or south lay the shallow curve of Spanish Bay and the jutting outline of Point Joe. The scene was breathtakingly bizarre. To the left was darkness, to the right was light, with Point Pinos the line of demarcation . . . but not for long. In this battle of dark versus light, the dark was winning. One could watch its progress either in the sky or on the water, where waves responded to the creeping darkness overhead by turning black in their troughs, and spurting forth whitecaps. A flock of seagulls, trying to fly southward, encountered a wall of wind that brought them to a standstill in midair, wings flapping frantically to no avail.

I confess a sort of sneaky fascination with wild weather. As a child, I thought a storm on the cape was better than any trip to the amusement park—including a ride on the Ferris wheel, which in my childhood was everybody's idea of the ultimate thrill. But this approaching storm would have to thrill me later. For now, I had work to do. I took the procedures book from the shelf and read through the storm protocol, then proceeded to follow it.

The main thing was not to let the light go out. The same earthquake that rocked San Francisco in April of last year had jangled the Fresnel lens and sent the lamp's flame soaring, but the only real damage had been to the tower structure. A crack opened up in the round wall, which had since been rebuilt with reinforced concrete. I checked the oil tank, which continuously supplies the lamp by means of a pump, and the water tank in case there should be a fire. Both were full.

Quincy had already closed the exterior shutters on the keeper's quarters, and he had secured the horse and Hettie's Holstein cows in the barn. I saw him out at the edge of our little oasis of grass, walking slowly around the storage building and making it secure. I caught his eye and waved, and he waved back as he started across the grass toward his lean-to beside the barn.

The wind was tearing me to pieces—it was most exhilarating! I went back into the lighthouse, put on the kettle, and tidied my hair while waiting for the water to boil, then fixed myself a cup of tea, which I took up to the watch room. There by the light of a kerosene lantern I read every word of *The Wave* and watched the storm come on. Long after total darkness fell and I could no longer quite watch, I listened. The wind howled around the tower and pushed against its walls like a frenzied thing. The sea crashed so violently on the rocks that I was glad this lighthouse had acres of dunes around it. The foghorn regularly emitted its doleful sound even though it was not precisely foggy. And the ships stayed away. Not a single little light bobbed on the bay.

In the midnight watch I climbed into the lantern itself. Shielding my eyes, I looked out into the wild night. It was a hypnotic experience to follow the broad white beam, which seems to turn, an impression produced by a metal drum that revolves around the constant, stationary light. Hypnotic to catch glimpse after glimpse of foaming waves, strands of sand borne on the wind like ghostly, gossamer scarves, scraps of uprooted scrub scudding over the dunes like fantastic crabbed creatures. And in the midst of it all I thought again about the Poor Drowned Woman, for I had found not a mention, not a single word about her in the newspaper. She might as well not have existed, for all anyone seemed to care.

"At least we found your body before this storm," I said aloud, and then I made her a promise: "Even if we never know who you are, I will see to it that you get a decent burial."

KEEPER'S LOG
January 16, 1907
Wind: W moderate
Weather: Mild and humid, high overcast
Comments: Tender off-loaded supplies in a.m.

The storm had done no damage to speak of, and three days later I survived cooking dinner for Misha—not to mention consuming it—with no damage to myself or to him. In fact the evening was quite like old times, until I mentioned my concerns about the Poor Drowned Woman. He refused to discuss her beyond reiterating that she could not have been from Carmel because none of Carmel's residents was missing. The fact that I wanted to pursue the matter, and he did not, only pointed out how far apart we'd grown. He left soon thereafter. My great personal victory was that I neither burned the beef nor cried myself to sleep that Sunday night.

When an entire week had passed with no news whatsoever of the Poor Drowned Woman, I left my morning's ledger and asked Quincy to come in and have a cup of coffee with me. Which I suppose was presumptuous as it was his coffee to begin with, but anyway he came.

To my great surprise, he took off his hat at table. I had never before seen him without it. Ducking his head, he scraped long gray locks behind his ears. I busied myself with putting a few cookies on a plate, to give him time to compose himself.

When I sensed he was ready I put the plate on the table and sat down myself. "Quincy," I began, "I need some advice."

He looked a bit wary. "I dunno, Miss Fremont—"

"Really, Quincy, if I call you Quincy, and I do all the time, you must call me simply Fremont. When you say 'Miss' like that, it makes me feel like somebody's maiden aunt!"

He grinned and picked up his coffee mug without responding.

I picked up mine, too, and said, "I hope you don't mind the mugs. I know Hettie always used china cups, but I prefer a mug myself."

Quincy grinned wider and said, "You're a caution, Miss Fremont, and no mistake."

I sighed and rolled my eyes in an exaggerated manner.

Quincy said, "Sorry, I forgot. Just Fremont. This is good coffee, Fremont."

"It should be. You made it yourself." We both laughed, and I got back on subject. "Seriously, Quincy. You've lived here in the Grove for a long time, haven't you?"

"Yep," he nodded and slurped a bit.

"Do you have any friends on the police force?"

He reared back in his chair, looking at me as if I'd suddenly grown two heads. "Police?"

It was perfectly clear he didn't consider the police as potential friends, so I tried another tack. "How about the coroner, Dr. Bright? Do you know him?"

"Nope."

As I have previously observed, our Quincy is a laconic fellow. I tried again. "Have you any idea where Dr. Bright would have taken the body of that woman we found off Point Pinos a week ago? As far as I have been able to ascertain, there is no morgue either here or in Monterey. Would they take her as far away as Salinas?" Salinas, thirty miles away on the other side of the Santa Lucia Mountains, is the county seat.

Quincy scratched his head, his gentle eyes going all soft with thought. Eventually he said, "Don't think so. Think the coroner took her over to Community Hospital—that's what usually happens to people that drown in the bay. He hasta do that whatchama-callit—"

"Autopsy?"

"Right. Before their people can come take 'em away for burying."

"That's just it, Quincy. I don't think anybody could take that poor woman away, because nobody knew who she was. And there hasn't been one single thing in the newspaper about that body being found. Don't you think that's odd?"

He looked at me solemnly and slowly shook his head. Without a word.

"Well?" I sounded impatient. Not being the laconic type myself, after a while it wears thin. "Come on, Quincy. You know something more, I can tell. Talk to me!"

"Dunno as I should," he mumbled down into his coffee mug.

I got up and poured more coffee for him. No sugar or cream—he drank it black. As do I.

I sat down again and leaned toward him. "Please?"

It took him a while to make up his mind, and while he was doing it he looked everywhere but at me. The clock ticked. The wind, which blows variably but constantly out here on the point, whispered at tiny cracks along the window frames. Finally Quincy graced me with his dark eyes.

"I heard tell," he said, "that she weren't no better than she should be. So it ain't fitting that a lady like yourself should be concerned about her. Mrs. Hettie would say as how the thing to do is leave well enough alone."

"From whom did you hear this?" I had tried myself to get people in town to talk about the subject, with no success.

He shrugged his thin shoulders. "Folks at church. You know how they talk."

I didn't; I am probably the only halfway respectable female in Pacific Grove who does not go to church on Sundays. Hettie had advised me to pick a church and start going, if not for religion then for the social contacts, but this was one piece of her advice I hadn't heeded. I would feel like a hypocrite, and hypocrisy is something I cannot bear in others, much less in myself. I persisted. "Did the folks at church happen to mention the woman's name?"

Quincy tugged at his earlobe and said to my left shoulder, "Them kinda women don't use their real names. But anyways, nobody said nothing 'bout a name."

Under cover of the table, I impatiently tapped my foot. "By any chance do you happen to go to the same church as Euphemia Wells?"

45

He seemed startled and reared back again. If Quincy were a turtle, most likely he'd have retracted his head into his shell. "No s'ree bob!" he declared with his Adam's apple quivering.

I surmised that Quincy was just as awed by Euphemia as everyone else was reputed to be. Since he said nothing further, I decided it was time to take pity on his obvious discomfort. "I only asked because Euphemia was there when the ocean rescuers brought the woman in, and at the time she implied something similar, while also admitting that she did not specifically know her. I fear that Euphemia Wells and others like her may be impugning a dead woman's reputation without one shred of proof."

"Say what?"

"Telling tales, Quincy, spreading rumors about a poor dead person who cannot defend herself."

He shook his head. Sadly, I thought. "They say as how Miss Euphemia has some very definite ideas. And what she says goes in the Grove. That's just the way it be."

I stood up decisively. "You've been very helpful and I do appreciate it. I shall have to go into town an hour earlier than usual today. Can you take the eleven o'clock watch?"

"Sure can. I'm always here, Miss—er—Fremont, always glad to help out. Mrs. Houck, she had her social engagements and her committees and such. You have your other work. I reckon as that's important."

I thanked him and got ready to leave. I wasn't going to work, at least not right away, but Quincy didn't have to know that.

Dr. Frederick Bright was not only the coroner, he was also the pathologist at Community Hospital. I discovered this salient information by the expedient means of looking him up in the telephone directory at the public library. I decided against calling ahead for an appointment, and hopped on the first streetcar going down Lighthouse into Monterey.

One transfer and some small confusion later, I strode confidently into the hospital pathology suite as if I knew exactly where I was going and had every right in the world to be there—which was

46

hardly the case. I'd chosen to wear my good suit of olive silk gabardine and had put my hair up, which I don't usually bother doing but it does make me look older. Therefore, one would hope, more authoritative. This pathology suite was a rather depressing place: no windows, rather dark, and at the moment it felt empty as a tomb. Also it smelled, an odd, acrid odor I could not quite place.

Through a partially open door on my left I saw long tables topped by laboratory equipment, beakers and vials and such, and high stools on which the laboratorists—or whatever they are called—might sit. At the moment there was no one in the room. Two doors on my right were closed. I drew near the first and listened, hard, for the sound of voices behind it, but I heard nothing. Likewise at the second door. I went to the end of the hallway down the center of this suite of rooms, where a double door bore two words, one on each side: AUTOPSY THEATER. How macabre!

I hoped I would not have to attend any performances in this theater. For one thing, the unpleasant odor (which I mentally tagged "eau de post mortem" to keep up my spirits) was stronger inside the doors. I let them close behind me and looked around, even though the large room was as empty as the rest of the suite seemed. Who knew when I would have an opportunity to examine such a place again?

As a theater they would go bust, for there were no seats. So I supposed it was just a quaint medical custom to call the place where autopsies are done a "theater." No seats, but a lot of shelves with a lot of large glass bottles containing things I did not want to look at too closely. In the center of the room, a metal table with holes in it like a colander; under the table, a drain in the floor. Near the table a two-tiered cart, also of metal, with some objects upon it resembling instruments of torture. Against the opposite wall, a pair of large sinks. Hoses. Buckets. Mops. Aprons. Scales.

I shivered, not so much because the place was rather distasteful but because I was physically cold. "The dead probably prefer it chilly," I mumbled, briskly rubbing my arms. So where were they, the dead?

With a *whomp!* the double doors exploded inward and I jumped at least a foot. I also emitted an involuntary yelp and lost no time scrambling out of the way. I had wondered where the dead were, and now here was one of them rolling right through the doors! Shrouded beneath a sheet was the unmistakable profile of the human form.

"Who're you?" growled the male nurse or attendant or whatever he was. He looked like a pugilist in pajamas, one who has lost a few too many fights. And he challenged: "What're you doing in here?"

"Waiting for Dr. Bright," I said with more confidence than I felt.

"Come to watch the autopsy?" he asked over his shoulder as he maneuvered the gurney alongside the metal table.

"Perhaps," I said noncommittally.

"You don't look like a doctor," the huge fellow remarked, folding his arms in a belligerent stance.

I raised my chin. "Women are entering the medical profession now. Haven't you heard?" Without giving him a chance to reply I went right on: "If you would be so good as to direct me to Dr. Bright's office, I would be most grateful."

Perhaps to test my mettle, he whisked the sheet off the dead body before deigning to frame a reply. The body was male, either fat or bloated, with jaundiced skin. I didn't even blink but my stomach climbed several inches up my backbone.

"Doc Bright's office is the first door on the right. His name's not on it. He likes to pretend like he's not here, but he's in there. Just knock."

"Thank you," I said, and left without looking back. A moment later I was tapping on that first door, behind which I'd heard no sound earlier. Still hearing nothing, I tapped again. Harder.

Aha! At last, the sound of uneven footsteps—I recalled the hitch in Bright's stride. The door jerked open and we stood nose to nose.

"Well, well, well!" he said, those jittery eyeballs rolling. "What have we here? Do I remember you? I think I do. Yes, I do! You're the young lady took over for Hettie Houck at the lighthouse."

"Yes." I smiled and extended my hand. "I'm Fremont Jones. I would be grateful for a few minutes of your time. I understand you have an autopsy to do. I won't keep you long."

"There's lots of good things about having dead folks for your patients," he said, pumping my hand and doing his best to twinkle. "For one thing, they don't talk back. For another, they don't mix up their medicines. And for another, they don't get all hot and bothered if you keep 'em waiting! Heh, heh, heh!"

"I never thought of it that way," I admitted, following him into one of the strangest offices I had ever seen in my life. There were bones and specimens in various forms—floating in liquid, desiccated like dried flowers, pressed under glass—everywhere one looked. And books, piles and piles of them. And papers, scattered willy-nilly. But it smelled of pipe tobacco, which was a big improvement over that other smell.

"Come to visit an old man in his lair, Miss Jones? What's on your mind?"

I took the only chair unoccupied by books. "I am sure you must have done an autopsy on the woman I sighted from the lighthouse."

"The Jane Doe. Yeah, um-hm. That was an interesting one." He picked up a paper knife and scratched the back of his head with it. "She didn't drown."

"Didn't drown?" Somehow that did not surprise me.

"No water in the lungs. Death probably caused by a blow to the head. Skull was fractured on the side where the flesh was eaten away. Other bruises too."

"Other bruises," I said flatly, as I have discovered that repeating a person's words back without inflection often keeps them talking.

"Head and neck. Twisted left ankle."

"Left ankle." If I remembered correctly, that would have been the foot missing the shoe.

"You any relation to Hettie?" he asked abruptly, surprising me.

"Not at all. Why do you ask?"

"Because Hettie's as nosy as you are. Or vice versa." He grinned.

I felt my lips curve, but my mind was working too rapidly for much grinning. I sensed that Dr. Bright was about to clam up. "Hettie and I do seem to have certain character traits in common, but we are only recent friends. I am curious to know if the woman has been identified."

He shrugged, playing with the paper knife, turning it end to end. "I have no idea. That part's up to the police. Missing persons, you know. In my report I told them the death could either have been an accident or homicide. I lean toward accident. She's out walking by herself on the rocks—not a good idea, by the way—"

"I know."

"Anyhow, she twists her ankle, falls, you get that first leg bruise. Tries to get up, a big wave takes her, cracks her head open. Other bruises would be from battering on the rocks."

"I see," I said, rising. "Thank you for telling me."

"Thank Hettie. She got me accustomed to satisfying her curiosity. But you keep what I told you to yourself, just the same as she would. And come see me again sometime. Always glad to have a pretty woman in the place."

"You're most kind, Dr. Bright." I smiled, winningly, I hoped. "There is just one more thing. Where is the morgue? It does not appear to be here in the pathology suite."

"Morgue? What do you want to know that for?" He frowned, and I feared I'd gone too far. But I had to know.

There was nothing for it but to lie. "I met someone recently who may be able to identify her, but he is one of those people who feels an inordinate amount of caution about the police. So I thought I might serve as a go-between. I feel some responsibility to help, you see, since I was the one who first sighted the body."

"Oh." He rubbed the tip of his nose, then seemed to make up his mind. "We don't have much of a facility for holding on to unclaimed bodies in Monterey County. I stashed Jane Doe at Mapson's Mortuary. They'll let you in if you say I sent you. If your friend can identify our Jane Doe, now mind, he'll have to talk to the police."

I thanked Frederick Bright again, profusely, and left the hospital—none too soon for I saw by the clock in the main lobby that it was nearly noon. I would be late to my office, but I thought it scarcely mattered as I have so few clients anyway. My mind was positively seething with questions. Did Jane Doe (I could no longer call her the Poor Drowned Woman, since she hadn't drowned) die as a result of her own carelessness? Or did some unknown person hit her on the head hard enough to kill her, and throw her into the sea? Who was she? Why weren't the police doing anything? Or if they were, why was there nothing in the newspaper? And most important of all, how could I find the answers to any of these questions?

Thus occupied in my mind, I hopped off the streetcar at the corner of Lighthouse and Grand and did not even see the person waiting on the sidewalk outside my office until I was practically upon her.

"I must say, it's *about* time!"

That voice made my toes curl. The waiting woman was Artemisia Vaughn.

CHAPTER
FIVE

She was dressed all in shades of purple, from head to foot. Where she got such clothes I could not imagine, but I did have to admit (to myself—never to her, or God forbid to Misha!) that they looked good on her. She seemed to be swathed in layers of veils. Like me, Artemisia does not wear a corset. Unlike me, she is so generously endowed that one cannot help noticing she does not wear one.

"I apologize for being late," I said, as sincerely as possible while unlocking the door, "but I had some business in Monterey and it took longer than I'd thought it would." I gritted my teeth and uttered the expected: "How nice to see you again, Artemisia."

She flowed gracefully through the door. "Likewise, Fremont. Misha assures me you are absolutely *the* perfect person to whom I should entrust my manuscript, which I have brought with me. Oh, what a *darling* office! I adore these yellow chairs."

It was the cushions, not the chairs, that were yellow; but to say so would be nitpicking. Grudgingly I noticed that the lavender and purple of her dress presented quite a pretty picture against the yellow cushion, like a patch of spring crocus.

No sooner had she sat than she bounced up again. Very sprightly for a woman of thirty-some-odd. Her hair was down in the way I myself prefer, and intertwined with narrow purple ribbons. "Is this the typewriting machine? It's very handsome, isn't it? You know, Fremont, what you need is a few pictures on these walls. I always think a blank wall looks so *naked,* don't you?"

"My budget does not extend to paintings," I said dryly.

Artemisia whirled around, and I saw that her ensemble was not made of veils after all. There was actually a dress under there of solid fabric in a medium-purple shade, and over it several top layers, each of a different cut and different shade, in a thin material such as georgette. "Oh, I'll get some together for you. We'll all contribute one or two. Myself, Tom, Dick, and Harry, Khalid—"

I said without thinking, "Khalid is the Burnoose Boy?"

She laughed: the gold-shower-of-coins effect. "Exactly!"

Her laugh was so infectious that I laughed, too. Then I recovered myself. "I couldn't possibly allow you to do that. You see, I can't afford insurance either, and original artwork—"

She interrupted me, laughing again. "You are living in some other world, Fremont. *Insurance?* Do you think any of us could possibly care about something so *mundane?* Of course I do sell my paintings, and so does Khalid but only to Irma's friends, and Tom, Dick, and Harry can't *give* theirs away but I'll sort through them and find some that aren't too bad."

"Artemisia, are Tom, Dick, and Harry their real names?"

"I doubt it." She plopped down again and all her layers subsided with a little *poof.* "Just between us girls, I call them the Twangy Boys."

"Twangy Boys? Oh, I see. At least, I think I do." In spite of myself, I giggled. "All three of them? Together?"

Artemisia giggled, too. If her laugh was like a shower of golden coins, her giggle was like pixie dust. "They are a ménage à trois of a different kind!"

We both whooped. I hadn't laughed so hard in months. For the moment I didn't care that I was laughing with the enemy. "Y-you must understand," I gasped, "it is not their—uh—preferences I'm laughing at, but your powers of description."

"Oh, quite," she replied, which for no reason at all set us both off again.

"Well, to business," Artemisia said, wiping her eyes—carefully, for she wore something to blacken her lashes. Instantly she was sober as a judge, reaching down beside her chair where she had placed a large, flat leather bag. "Here is my latest creation. You must guard it with your *life*, Fremont. It's the best thing I've ever done. With words, that is."

Her handwriting was a careless scrawl, but legible. The title of her book was *The Merchant of Dreams*. I flipped to the last page, which was numbered one hundred and fifty.

"It's a novella," she explained. "It's going to be a terrific sensation. You'll see why when you type it. My publisher will be so pleased to get a manuscript that is typewritten. Did you know they are beginning to prefer it? I predict the day will come when they no longer accept manuscripts done by hand."

"That can only be good for me! I charge ten cents a page, Artemisia. And since I am only typing part-time, it's difficult for me to say exactly how long it will take."

"Well, no matter. As long as it doesn't take forever. I'll stay in touch." She folded her hands on top of her bag and cocked her head to one side, considering. "Why haven't you been back to Carmel? Did we in some way offend you? I, at any rate, thought we would be seeing you on a regular basis. Actually I assumed you were going to rent the cottage Misha arranged for you. But he told me you'd changed your mind."

I felt my face begin to flush, so before answering I pretended to have dropped something under the desk and bent down to retrieve it. When I straightened up again the flush was conquered. "Sorry," I said, "where were we? Oh yes, the cottage. After getting the lay of the land, so to speak, on the Monterey Peninsula, I decided that my typewriting service would do better in this location. And then I met Mrs. Henrietta Houck, the keeper of the light at Point Pinos, and she asked me to take over for six months so that she could have time off for personal reasons. Between the two, I haven't much time to go visiting."

Artemisia looked at me for what seemed an excruciatingly long time, her large, dark eyes gleaming and teeming with thoughts I would have given almost anything to read. Finally she said, "You are a serious, hardworking woman, I see."

I sat tall. "I have my moments of levity, but I've chosen to earn my own way—if that is what you mean."

Her eyes narrowed. "You think Misha has become a playboy."

It was a statement, not a question. I did not respond.

She waited.

I waited. Until I began to feel like an elementary schoolchild in a staring contest, and then my devilish sense of humor rose to the occasion. "As long as he hasn't become twangy," I said.

KEEPER'S LOG
January 18, 1907
Wind: NW, moderate to gusting
Weather: Cold; heavy clouds, rain, and drizzle
Comments: Two passenger steamships from N in but not out (laying over for better weather?)

Try as I might, I could not get away from my office the next day to go to Mapson's Mortuary. Not that I'd look a gift horse in the mouth, but there is a certain perversity in the way one can sit for days, bored to bits with nothing much to do, and then the work comes all in a clump.

So it was that virtually on the heels of Artemisia's novella another Carmelite arrived with an even lengthier manuscript in need of typing. This was none other than the Medium Brown Man, whose actual name proved to be Arthur Heyer. His book was a collection of local legends, under the title GHOSTLY TALES OF THE CENTRAL COAST, and while Arthur was still prattling on about how he had collected his legends, Braxton Furnival loomed larger than life through the door, quite eclipsing the Medium Man (who was not brown but plaid that day).

So Arthur, who was being more entertaining than one would have thought him capable of, scuttled away and Braxton held forth for long after his charm had worn thin. He did, however, leave one letter to be typed over and over again—seventy-three times, to be exact—for a long list of names and addresses. Potential investors, he called the addressees. Doing the same thing so many times was bound to be tedious, but I did not greatly care as it was also lucrative, especially since I decided to charge him three cents apiece for typing the envelopes. I judged Braxton could afford it, and I must have been right because he didn't bat an eye. Add to all this a certain amount of walk-in traffic off the street, and I was suddenly busier than I had been in a very long time.

Thus it was that on the eighteenth of January, which was a Thursday, I drove the rig into town at noon instead of walking. My plan was to take the typewriter (which I could lift, but not easily) back to the lighthouse and do some typing that night, to compensate for the fact that I intended to post a sign saying the office would be closed that afternoon. I was going to Mapson's Mortuary come hell or high water.

High water seemed the more likely: It was raining, and Bessie the bay mare was none too pleased to be left standing in the street. She twitched her ears back and snorted while I wrestled the typewriter—covered, of course—into the bottom of the shay. I had also put the top up on the carriage, but with the wind blowing off the bay it did not do a tremendous lot of good. Nevertheless I was fairly dry, in an unfashionable but serviceable rain slicker I had found some months ago in the donations box at the tent city in Golden Gate Park. I believe my slicker—which is black and shaped rather like a tent itself—is a garment intended for males, which is why it is so comfortable and roomy. Were it made for a woman it would probably be restrictively narrow through the shoulders, tight in the neck, with tiny buttons clear up to the ears. The clothing we women have to put up with is one of my pet peeves. Someday I will do something about it—if I can only figure out what.

I was about to climb into the carriage when through the steady rain I saw someone coming along the sidewalk from Lighthouse

Avenue. A short woman in a yellow canvas duster. It was Phoebe Broom, looking a lot less like Jane Eyre and more like a canary.

"Oh dear," I muttered, then hoped she hadn't heard me. I gave Bessie's neck a pat and whispered a word of patience in her twitching ear, then pasted a smile on my face and met Phoebe as she came alongside the office door. "Phoebe, isn't it? What brings you out in the rain?"

"I like rain." She smiled up at me in her unassuming way. "Though it does interfere with my sculpting. The roof of my studio leaks. So I caught a ride over the hill with Oscar—he's gone on into Monterey. I've brought something I thought you might like to have. If we could go inside? Or are you on your way out rather than in?"

"I am going out—" I indicated the sign in my window that said CLOSED "—but I can delay for a few moments. Come on in."

I unlocked the door and we dripped across the floor. Phoebe went straight to the desk, wiped her portfolio off with a handkerchief, and opened it out. "Come and look," she beckoned to me, "you can choose the one you like best."

Uh-oh, I thought, remembering part of our last conversation, but I went ahead and looked. And soon felt teary—the drawings were of Misha, my Michael, and they were that good. "You drew these, Phoebe?" I asked. "I thought you were a sculptor."

"The drawings are the first step. You have to draw before you can sculpt. At least, that's how I was taught." She grinned and poked me gently in the ribs with her elbow, a mischievous light in her eyes. "I'll bet you thought you were about to see some drawings of Misha in the nude. Didn't you?"

I nodded, smiling. "Something like that."

"Well, I want you to know I tried, but he went all priggish on me and wouldn't take off his clothes. So I'm having to do Misha's head on Khalid's body."

"How did you know Khalid's body would be worth doing, considering those voluminous robes he wears?"

"I know Irma Fox. She can afford anything, so why would she keep a man who's less than well put together?"

"Good heavens!"

"What did you think? That Khalid was Irma's adopted son? Surely you aren't that naive, Fremont."

"No," I admitted, "and why shouldn't she, considering that it's done the other way around all the time. It's just—I don't know—I suppose it's just that I'm not accustomed to talking openly about these things."

Phoebe shrugged, and looked down at her drawings as if dismissing the topic. "That's because the world is full of hypocrites, except for those of us who choose to live in Carmel. Now, which one of these do you want, Fremont? Or do you want one at all?"

"Of course I do! They're wonderful." She had captured him so exactly that I could see the familiar expressions of my Michael within the curling hair and gypsyish neck scarf of Misha. The drawings were ink on heavy paper, done with a sure hand and great skill, not a tentative line among them. And as I went through them one by one, I had an idea that had nothing whatever to do with either Michael or Misha. A wonderful idea!

"This one," I said, taking out a three-quarters profile that was so perfect it almost broke my heart. I might have lost him, but now I would always have this to remember him by. "Thank you so much, Phoebe."

"You're welcome. There's a framer on Calle Principal in Monterey who's pretty good. I've never learned to frame."

"For the moment, at least until it stops raining, I'll leave the drawing here in the office. Tell me, Phoebe: Are you free for the next couple of hours? And can you keep a secret?"

I have observed that conspiracy produces a certain amount of camaraderie. I do believe, however, that Phoebe and I would have become friends even without conspiring. She was plainspoken and straightforward, both qualities that I appreciate in a person, male or female. Though I have made some disastrous mistakes where choosing friends is concerned, I did not believe that Phoebe would turn out to be one of them.

"Don't worry," she said when I inquired about materials, "I have my sketchbook and pencils with me. I never go anywhere without them. And I shall play my part to perfection, I assure you!"

Mapson's Mortuary is in a boggy part of Monterey near Lake El Estero, where a cemetery is also located. Bessie did not quite enter

into the spirit of our adventure; she couldn't have been more recalcitrant if she were a mule, and I could hardly blame her for not wanting to sink her fetlocks in the mud. A double row of eucalyptus trees
with scabrous bark leaned mournfully over a peeling adobe building
with a moon gate—a cultural mixture that one sees occasionally in
California.

"Ugh!" Phoebe said.

"My sentiments exactly. But look, there is a sort of shed at the
side. At least we can get the horse and carriage out of the rain."

We secured Bessie and entered the mortuary through a side door.
Inside it was dark and dank, but at least there was no unpleasant
smell.

"I suppose there's nobody lying in waiting, or whatever you call
it," Phoebe whispered. "The place seems deserted."

My eyes had grown used to the gloom. I picked a door and said,
"This way." Of course I didn't have the slightest idea where I was
going, but I have found that in such a situation it is not a bad idea to
act as if one knows.

We had entered into an enclosed side porch with a tile floor. The
door I chose was at the far end of this porch, leading to what I
surmised would be the back of the building. The door was locked, so
I knocked. While waiting for it to open, I glanced down at Phoebe,
who was so excited she almost shot sparks. "Calm down," I whispered, "and try to look doleful or morbid or something."

The door opened outward, so I had to step back; I trod on
Phoebe and she yelped. "My friend is rather nervous," I explained to
one of the tallest, thinnest men I had ever seen, not to mention one
of the most silent. He wore an apron and a stern expression, which
led me to speculate that we must have interrupted something unspeakable.

As he was obviously not going to say anything, I continued: "I
hope you can help us, as we are on a difficult errand. My friend is
looking for her cousin, a woman who seems to have disappeared on
a trip to this area about a week ago."

"Just over a week, actually," Phoebe chimed in, demonstrating
an excellent memory of the facts I'd told her in the carriage on the
way over.

"My name is Fremont Jones. Dr. Frederick Bright told me that you have the body of an unidentified woman here, and—oh dear, this is really very difficult—"

Head bowed, my co-conspirator had begun to cry, not at all silently (and probably not with tears, but I didn't intend that anyone should look closely enough to find that out). I put my arm around Phoebe, whose small stature helped her to look all the more bereft and helpless. She shook most convincingly.

"So if you would just allow us to take a look at this Jane Doe," I pleaded, "we'd be most grateful."

Phoebe sobbed.

"I'm the only one here, and I got no authority. You can come in, but you'll have to wait for Mr. Mapson."

At least he could speak! I was beginning to think the man had started out a normal size but somehow had been stretched like an Indian-rubber band, and in the process had lost the use of his vocal cords.

Mr. Long and Tall led us through a dark corridor, turning on gas wall sconces along the way that did little more than cast strange shadows. The rain, falling harder now, rattled on the tile roof of the adobe. Our footsteps echoed on the floor, which was also tile. There was a musty smell about the place, and I brooded over what might be behind all the closed doors.

"You can wait in here," he said. It was a parlor with a gas chandelier hanging from an already low ceiling. He lit two of its six globes, which immediately began to do their work of casting fantastic shadows. And then he faded away.

"I wonder how long we'll have to wait," Phoebe fretted.

"Not long. In about five minutes I'm going to go and bribe him."

"Fremont!"

"It will be much better that way, because if he takes money to break the rules, he's not very likely to tell anyone we were here. Don't worry. I'll tell him you're just too distressed to wait. It was your crying jag that kept him from closing the door in our faces, I'm sure of it. Keep up the good work!"

Long and Tall's name was Tom and he took the bribe with alacrity. We went back to the parlor for Phoebe, who began sniveling as soon as she heard our footsteps; then Tom showed us through one of the closed doors that led to yet another corridor. "The cold room," he said, pushing open the door at the end.

"This is where we keep 'em, but we can't keep that one you came to see much longer. After a while the ice isn't enough, if you know what I mean. She's about to go over. It's this one right here. I'll wait outside."

He left, and I put my right hand over my nose and mouth while with my left hand I drew down the cloth that covered the body. That face! And the stench! Oh my God.

Phoebe was made of stouter stuff than anyone has a right to hope for. "Go on, Fremont, keep him occupied. I can do it. I can extrapolate the other side of the face from the bone structure. It won't be an exact likeness because the two sides of the face aren't exactly alike—did you know that?"

It was a rhetorical question; her hands were busy sketching already. I said, "If you're sure you'll be all right . . ."

"Of course I will!"

I squeezed Phoebe's shoulder in mute thanks and slipped through the door.

"I wanted her to have a minute alone with the body," I said to Tom in a hoarse whisper. "She isn't sure. With the face half gone like that—you understand."

"Sure," he said. He was smoking a cigarette; the smell of the burning tobacco masked the faint odor that seemed to make its way through the door, or perhaps it was the memory of that odor that still lingered in my nostrils.

I thought of what he'd said about them not being able to keep Jane Doe much longer; after seeing the condition she was in, I could understand that. But I also remembered my promise to see her decently buried.

I cleared my throat. "Ah, Tom? My friend is not exactly affluent. Assuming that this is her lost cousin, have you any idea how much the least expensive sort of funeral would be?"

"I don't do that part," he said, blowing smoke over my head.

"We'll have to see Mr. Mapson, I suppose," I said resignedly. Whatever it was, I wasn't likely to be able to afford it.

"I don't do it," a slow and rather unpleasant smile spread across his face, "but I know how much everything costs. I'm an apprentice, see. Some day I'll take over this whole business. Your cheapest funeral, wood box and all, will cost you about a hundred-fifty."

"I see. Thank you." That was three months of Hettie's salary, half of what I was earning taking her place. I concluded drearily that making promises to the dead is not such a good idea.

A commotion at the door caused Tom to look around and down, and me to hasten to open it. Phoebe collapsed against me in a coughing fit, but she'd had the presence of mind to stash her sketchbook and pencils inside her duster. Her eyes were streaming—for real, this time.

She shook her head. "It's not my cousin. That poor, pathetic creature isn't any relation of mine!"

Tom looked skeptical.

I said quickly, "You took plenty of time to make sure. That's all anybody could ask." I bundled her back up the corridor and said to Long Tall Tom over my shoulder, "Thank you so much. You can see that she couldn't have stood the strain of waiting any longer."

He followed us to the outside door, and every hurried step of the way I felt his eyes boring into my back. He was avaricious, but also smarter than I'd at first taken him to be. I could only hope the bribe would keep him quiet.

As for Phoebe, the experience had positively electrified her. "Fremont," she exploded the moment we reached the carriage, "as soon as I'd done the whole face I was sure! I know that woman!"

CHAPTER SIX

"That's very interesting," I said, "particularly since Misha has told me more than once that she cannot be from Carmel. I asked him right at the beginning to try to identify her and he refused, saying it would be a waste of time."

"I didn't mean I know her from Carmel," Phoebe said. "Just that I've seen her somewhere. I'm sure of it. I have a good memory for faces—most artists do."

"And how is your memory for names?" I asked, clucking up my hoof-dragging horse. Though the rain had diminished to a drizzle, Bessie still did not want to go back out in it.

Phoebe's plain but lively face puckered in a frown. "I don't think I've ever actually met her, I mean as in being introduced. . . . I'm pretty sure I haven't . . . if only I could remember *where* I saw her. . . ."

I said, "Oh, dear." But I hadn't really thought it could turn out to be that easy—and I was glad Misha hadn't lied to me.

Once Bessie got the idea that we were headed home, I was able to take one hand from the reins. I stretched my fingers toward the still-pondering Phoebe: "May I see the drawing?"

"Hm? Oh, certainly. Just don't let it get too wet." Phoebe flipped open her sketchbook and handed it to me.

I took a quick look, for a steady wind drove the drizzle right beneath the carriage canopy, and every now and then an errant gust would fling fine drops, stinging, in our faces. The lines of the drawing were no less sure for the necessary haste of its execution. "She was pretty," I observed. I stared at it, hard, as if to engrave it on my brain, then returned the book to Phoebe.

"Bright blue, the shade called 'royal,' " Phoebe mused. "I seem to connect that color with her, so that's what she must have been wearing when I saw her."

"The dress she had on when they pulled her from the water was red. So perhaps we may conclude that whoever she was, she liked strong colors and wore them with impunity." Suddenly I snapped my fingers. "Oh, damnation!"

"What, Fremont?"

"I meant to ask if we could look at her clothing, but I forgot!" We clattered over a bridge that spans an inlet, and the street did a jog toward the large, shabby whaling station overlooking Monterey's inner harbor. Misha's sailboat—a sloop called the *Katya*—is anchored there. A busy wharf lies off to the right, and just at the left looms Presidio Hill. There is an old building on that hill which is popularly called Fremont's Fort, after my illustrious relation. On my first day in this area I went there, simply to stand where he might have stood.

"Why would we want to see her clothes? Ugh!" Phoebe said.

"Never mind," I said, "it doesn't matter now. We already know three important things, Phoebe: She was not from Carmel, or you would have known her; she was not from Pacific Grove, for several reasons I won't go into; and that leaves Monterey. My own pet theory, that she was a guest at the Hotel Del Monte, no longer holds water because you've seen her somewhere. Unless that was where you saw her?"

She wrinkled her small, upturned nose. "The Del Monte is hardly a place I frequent. But you are forgetting the whole of Del Monte Forest, Fremont, along the Seventeen Mile Drive. There are some houses—estates, really—in there. We Carmelites often go exploring and picnicking in those woods, especially around Point Cypress."

"Oh? Do you know Braxton Furnival by any chance? He lives over there, and is a new client of mine."

"Hah!" Phoebe said. "Yes, I know him, but I'm hardly his type. . . . Oh, my goodness! Fremont, you're a genius!" She practically leapt out of the carriage.

Startled, I tightened my grip on the reins. Bessie does not like this stretch of road, which skirts the burned-out remains of a China-town; she tends to act as if she might bolt along here. I said, "I beg your pardon?"

"Braxton Furnival had a huge party at his place about six months ago, and he invited all of us. Have you ever seen his house? It's simply amazing."

"No, I haven't. By us, you mean everyone in Carmel?"

"Yes. He's friends with Oscar Peterson's family. They're promi-nent in the East Bay, you know, around Oakland, though they have practically disowned Oscar. I'd guess Braxton didn't know that. I don't know if he really meant to invite everyone or just Oscar and Mimi, but you've seen how the Petersons are—the evening of Braxton's party they just said to whoever was around, 'Come on, let's go!' and we went. Most everyone, except now that I think of it, Misha wasn't there; I think he was up in San Francisco."

"And . . . ?" I encouraged, when for all her former animation Phoebe fell silent.

"I'm thinking. I want to be sure." She was quiet again. I glanced at her and then past her at the wide water of the bay. So gray and dreary today. The hills far across on the other side were only dimly visible through a veil of blue-gray mist. The seals that often play along the rocks in this area had gone into hiding, along with every-one and everything else. Not even a gull flew overhead. At least for the moment, we were alone.

I was itching with impatience by the time Phoebe said, "I can't be *absolutely* sure, but I think that's where I saw your Jane Doe. At Braxton Furnival's party! There were at least a hundred people there, all milling around and making noise and drinking too much, especially the men. I'm sure I never got a proper introduction, but I remember that face, the long black hair, the blue dress . . . Yes! Oh, Fremont, come on. Let's go right now to Braxton's house!"

Thus, in a high fever of excitement, Phoebe and I undertook a wild goose chase. I began to suspect she had been among those who'd had too much to drink at that party, because she couldn't remember the way to Braxton's house. She directed me down half a dozen or more side tracks through densely wooded stretches of forest, and more than once it was only the roaring of the sea that warned me when the track was about to dead-end. We would come out on the edge of a cliff somewhere, all rocks and scraggly cypresses flat-topped from the wind, and below, the crashing waves; and while this was all beautiful in a wild sort of way, it wasn't getting us anywhere.

Finally I had no choice but to take Phoebe home to Carmel. She had missed her ride back with Oscar, and I had to return to the lighthouse to relieve Quincy from watch duty. I admit if I had been driving the Maxwell instead of a fatigued horse, most likely I'd have kept on going, regardless of the inconvenience to Quincy. Of course if more people in the area had telephones (particularly myself and Braxton Furnival), it would have made a world of difference. As it was, I supposed I should either have to write to him or wait until he next appeared at my office.

Waiting is not my long suit; therefore I proposed to Phoebe that she make several copies of her sketch overnight, which I would pick up from her the following morning. She agreed, and it was well after four o'clock when I finally got back "home" to Point Pinos.

• • •

The lighthouse has your basic two-by-two cottage design: two rooms down and two up, plus the round watch room just above the roofline, in the base of the tower. I decided it would make eminent sense to type in the watch room, thus saving myself the bother of going up and down the spiral stairs every hour. Quincy volunteered to carry the heavy typewriter up for me. Fortunately the machine had suffered no damage from its jouncing afternoon under the seat in the shay.

Typing with the dark of night always in my face was not easy; I required a while to settle down. But once I started on Artemisia's novella I was simply *gone*. The story had me in thrall, as I am certain she intended her readers to be.

The Merchant of Dreams told the story of a young woman who is suddenly widowed and left penniless. Without skills, much education, or experience, and desperate to support herself without turning to prostitution, she answers an advertisement in the newspaper that reads: "I will buy your dreams."

Artemisia's heroine is named Heloise. It was some measure of Artemisia's skill as a writer (aided by the story's setting, which was Boston) that in no time the voice of Heloise began to sound in my head as if it were my own:

> I thought, what harm can it do for me to go and talk to this buyer of dreams? The address was quite a respectable one, on Commonwealth Avenue, with a business name as well: The Morpheus Foundation. I had heard that the famous Viennese psychoanalyst, Dr. Freud, had done some researches on dreams and I supposed this was something of the sort.
>
> I could not have been more wrong, but of course I had no way of knowing it then. So all unaware on a fateful Friday I put on my only good dress (the others having been sold to purchase firewood) and rode to Commonwealth Avenue on the trolley.
>
> The servant who opened the door had a visage so angelic that for a moment I did not know if I were face to face with a man or a woman: a cloud of golden hair, curiously elongated blue eyes more darkly lashed and browed than the hair color would suggest, a

straight nose with delicate nostrils. Altogether, it was a face worthy of Botticelli; and when at last my eye traveled downward, I found that this incredible creature wore trousers. Therefore, I concluded, he was a man.

"I have come in answer to the advertisement," I said. "I should like to speak to the person who offered to buy dreams."

"Come in," the angelic being said, dropping back into darkness, and I stepped over the threshold.

For a few moments I was blinded by the abrupt change in the level of light. I felt around and over me a sort of huge quiet, the hush of a house sufficiently grand that it knows it will go on long after those who built it are lying in their graves. There was a sweetish odor in the air: not quite perfume, perhaps incense. As sight returned I looked down a long hall and saw the figure of the beautiful gate-keeper dissolve in the distance, become one with the shadows in the far reaches of the corridor. He had not told me to wait and so I thought of following, but my feet were curiously reluctant to do so. I remained rooted to an oriental runner near the front door.

The walls, I observed, were panels of a dark and gleaming wood; the coffered ceiling was made of the same wood, as were the stairs. Mahogany, or the darkest walnut, and very fine. Directly overhead a small, unlit chandelier shed transparent crystal droplets, like frozen tears shimmering suspended in time.

Indeed, in all this dark luxury and enveloping quiet, I myself felt a sudden sense of dislocation, of alienness, as if I had stepped into another dimension where time as one knows it had ceased to exist. And though I chided myself for this fancy, still I strained my ears for the ticking of a clock—only to encounter circles upon circles of silence.

Suddenly I, Fremont Jones, jerked my head up and pricked my ears. What was that? Had I heard something? Or had Artemisia's story fired my all-too-active imagination?

I left the typewriter and went to the window, which the lamplight had turned into a dark mirror. I cupped my hands around my eyes, put my face to the cool glass, and looked out. It was black as pitch out there: no moon, no stars, no nothing. Nothing but a regularly recurring bright band of light streaming from the great Fresnel lens. And the wind: a steady and insistent visitor, ever pressing up against doors and windows, moaning to come in.

I expelled a short, exasperated sigh. Surely there was nothing untoward going on, but I had to be certain. Pulling the shawl up to the tips of my ears and taking up the binoculars, I climbed the twisting stairs and went out onto the circular platform. The wind rushed to grab me and, in the rudest (not to mention chilliest!) manner, tried to get beneath my skirts. Slowly I walked once around the tower. The lighthouse beam is meant to be seen, not to see by; indeed, the contrast between bright and dark is more dizzying than illuminating. It occurred to me that a clever person might actually hide in the border of the beam—if he or she could keep up with its movement, which was doubtful.

Having made the complete circuit, I stood in one spot and raised the binoculars to my eyes. I knew from experience that on a relatively clear night it was possible out there to see by starlight alone; with so little as a quarter moon, one can see of a Point Pinos midnight as much as at noon on a dark and stormy day. But on a night like this . . .

I searched the ground for lambent glimmers of light, as from a handheld lantern or a candle. I tried to hear beneath the wind, and above the waves breaking nearby. I listened so keenly that I discerned the rustle of cattle in the barn, a distant barking of sea lions, and the snarl of some feral cat. Yet of any intruder I saw not a sign, and heard not a sound.

"So," I muttered as I went back in and down to the watch room, "it was my imagination after all." At least I had performed a most thorough watch—some twenty minutes before it was due.

Reassured, I returned to *The Merchant of Dreams* precisely where I had left off, with Heloise waiting amid circles of silence:

I shifted my weight restlessly from one foot to the other; closed my eyes and held in my mind the face of a clock, with a sweep-second hand ticking away time in an orderly fashion. When I had passed a few seconds in this fashion, the angelic fellow's voice called out: "Dr. Morpheus will see you now, if you care to proceed along the hall."

I opened my eyes and, after a brief bit of disorientation, saw that a door had opened far down the hallway. From that open door a square of golden light proceeded. The same light bathed the Botticelli head and turned its fair hair into a halo. I felt dazzled and most strange, burning with desire to see what lay beyond that golden door while deep inside me something whispered: "Turn away and run!"

But alas! I did not run. I did not fear the strange situation as much as I feared the things I knew poverty could drive me to do. I would sooner kill myself than live as a fallen woman. So I uprooted my reluctant feet and step after step went down that long, long hall.

Once again the change in light made it difficult to see; the tall, standing figure of Dr. Morpheus wavered for a moment in my vision and then, as my eyes adjusted, took shape: an intensely handsome man of exotic mien, as if from another place and clime. Long black hair that swept his shoulders, totally out of fashion; broad cheeks and a high brow; pale eyes but with dark rings around the iris like a Persian cat.

"My name is Jonah Morpheus," he said. His accent was British but that did not tell me where he was from; the British empire reaches all over the world.

"Heloise Goodenough," I said. My voice came out clear as a bell. "I have come in response to your advertisement about dreams."

Jonah Morpheus invited me to take a seat; he dismissed the man who looked so much like an angel, calling him Thad; he himself sat behind an imposing desk upon which stood a fantastical lamp fashioned all of colored glass, even its shade. This lamp threw jeweled light across his face as he made a steeple of his fingers and set his chin atop it. "Tell me about your dreams," he said.

I smiled, albeit rather stiffly. "I am here to strike a bargain. Your advertisement made no mention of the particulars. I should like to know these before I talk about my dreams."

"A wise woman," said Dr. Morpheus, and he smiled. At that moment a cat leapt upon the desk—huge, black, long-haired. The cat went first to Morpheus, rubbed its chin on his hands, and purled a greeting deep in its throat; then with its plume of tail held high, padded daintily across the surface of the desk and sat at the edge, regarding me soberly through eyes that were exactly like its master's.

This is some kind of a strange test, I thought, but how he had arranged it I could not imagine. I decided to ignore the cat. I said, "Well, sir?"

Again, that smile. Slow and sensual, it played over his face and drifted through the air to touch me like a caress. His voice was both rich and rough. "I am collecting dreams for a project whose purpose must remain secret until all collection is complete. And as the advert said, I will pay."

He seemed to think that was enough explanation, but it was not—at least, not for me. I asked, "Presumably at some point this project would be for publication?"

"Presumably."

"In other words, if I tell you—*sell* you—my dreams, they'll be out there someday for all the world to see?"

The smile grew broader. I fancied that the cat smiled, too. Jonah Morpheus said, "Your protection will be complete anonymity. No one will know which dreams are yours."

"I . . . I see." I moistened my lips with my tongue, for my mouth had gone dry. "How much?"

"For each night's dreams, ten dollars."

Ten dollars! Why, in a month I would have three hundred! It was a fortune! So much that I immediately grew suspicious. "Why so generous a sum?" I asked.

He leaned forward across the desk. The cat turned its elegant but flat-faced head to watch him. "Because," he said, "it is not easy to buy dreams. Or to sell them, for that matter. There are conditions, and a contract, which is binding."

"Ah. Tell me."

"First, the duration of the contract is three months. For that time you must either live here at the Morpheus Foundation—room and board provided, of course—or you must agree to come here first thing each morning; in either case, you are not to speak to anyone until you have told me your dreams from the night before."

I nodded my understanding.

"Second, you must tell me everything you dream, in its entirety, no matter if the subject matter is nonsensical to you, or repulsive, or embarrassing. If you attempt to hold anything back, I will know, I assure you. I am highly skilled in this area." His strange eyes bored into me hypnotically, and I could well believe him. The cat turned its head back and stared at me, too, making an eerily doubled effect.

"And what," I asked, "if there is a night when I do not dream?" I did have such nights, frequently.

He laughed, a rough rumble. "That is extremely unlikely. One interesting finding I have made already: the more a person tells his— or her—dreams to another, the more vivid the dreams become, and the more frequent." He leaned back again and steepled his fingers, a pedantic posture. "Did you know, Miss Goodenough, that there are some cultures which are based on the sharing of dreams?"

I shook my head.

The cat jumped down from the desk with a light thud and to my great surprise, sprang into my lap. "Good heavens!" I said.

Jonah Morpheus smiled approvingly as his cat turned around three times in my lap, kneaded my skirt a bit with its paws, then curled itself into a warm, purring lump. "The cat's name is Shadow," he said.

"Is Shadow a boy or a girl?" I stroked the pretty creature's silky head.

"Neither," he said enigmatically.

I did not inquire further.

"So what is it to be? Do the conditions pose a difficulty for you?"

The cat purred, Morpheus smiled, and I tried to think. But all I could think was that in three months of selling my dreams I would have earned almost a thousand dollars. Perhaps 'earn' was not the right word. It seemed so easy. . . .

"I will do it. Draw up the contract," I said.

"Ask him," said Quincy early the next morning. He pointed to a male figure across the dunes, bent almost double as he walked along the rocky shoreline. "That's Junior, so-called on account of his name's Joe and he claims to be the son of the one what they named Point Joe after. Anyway, Junior's kind of a hermit; he's lived in the Del Monte Forest all his born days. He smells a mite rank, but he wouldn't hurt a fly, Miss Fremont."

"All right, I'll catch up to him and ask, but I swear, Quincy, if you don't quit calling me Miss I'm going to fire you!"

Quincy seemed shocked, but soon the twinkle was back in his eyes. He was getting to know me. Good!

"Hitch up the shay while I'm gone, will you?" I grinned, and set off over the dunes.

When I caught up I soon saw why Joe, Junior was so bent over. The poor man was ancient and almost blind, his eyes clouded with milky cataracts. "Eh?" he said, rearing back and almost losing his balance. I grabbed at his ragged arm for fear that he would fall off the rocks into the sea.

I said loudly, though I did not know if he were also slightly deaf,

"I'm Fremont Jones. I live in the lighthouse, and Quincy, who works there, said you might be able to tell me where in Del Monte Forest a certain person lives."

"Might," he conceded, stepping from the rocks onto the sand and laying down his burden, a large burlap sack full of who-knew-what. Junior was, apparently, a scavenger. He put his head over on one side in a canny manner. "Depends who the certain person is."

And what the reward might be, I thought, reaching into my pocket. I pulled out a quarter; not much, but all I had with me. "Braxton Furnival," I said, holding up the money. Overnight the weather had cleared, and the morning sun struck silver from the coin.

"That be a siller dollar?" Junior asked.

I moved upwind before answering. "No, it's just a quarter, but if you tell me where he lives and follow me up to the lighthouse, I can get another seventy-five cents."

Junior shrugged. "Ain't hardly worth a dollar no-ways." He reached out his hand palm up and I deposited the quarter in it, relieved that he did not want more. My relative poverty both embarrassed and scared me at times; in truth I did not have a whole dollar to spare.

Junior said, "You goes in the forest by the Pacific Grove gate. First two times the road forks, you take the left fork each time. Pretty soon you comes on up a rise and there she be. Can't miss 'er. Biggest darn house you ever seen round these parts, and ugly as sin. Har!" He laughed raucously, which made his poor eyes stream. He wiped at them as he continued: "Lives all by hisself in that big place—leastways, that's how he tells it. Har!" He wiped his eyes again and squinted. "You going up there by yer lonesome?"

I nodded. "Yes."

Junior shouldered his pack. "Then you best be careful."

CHAPTER SEVEN

KEEPER'S LOG
January 19, 1907
Wind: W light
Weather: Cool; clear and sunny
Comments: Steamships out to S in early a.m.; also whales going S, local boats in pursuit

*B*raxton Furnival, or his architect, had read too many novels about European royalty and/or made one too many trips to the Black Forest. His house was in the Grand Germanic Hunting Lodge style. If it were mine (a staggering thought) I should name it "Grosse-Dark," I thought as I came up a track overhung by the low-sweeping branches of old cypress trees. Although the forest between Pacific Grove and Carmel certainly had space for such a monstrous dwelling, in every other way it seemed out of place. In fact, it was quite jarring to come upon anything so large and dark and bulky all of a sudden, even if one were seeking it out.

"Well, really!" I commented to Bessie, as with a touch of the reins I guided her through a stone gateway, one side adorned with a wooden shield-shaped heraldic crest, which I presumed Braxton had invented. The crest featured a boxing bear on one side, three pinecones on the other, the name FURNIVAL arched across the top, and on a sort of waving banner at the bottom the words VITA ET PLENITUDO. "Life and wealth," if my memory of high school Latin served. Such ego the man had! And, it seemed, the wherewithal to support it. Certainly no baron of the German kaiser's court ever had a grander woodland hunting lodge; but who would want to live in a place like that all the time?

Not I! It was all great gables and rough shingles and huge beams intentionally left unfinished so they still resembled trunks of whole trees—and all of it, down to the last splinter, an oppressive dark brown. One got the idea that Fafnir could not be far off, and Siegfried (who I personally think must have been thick between the ears) would come bounding along at any moment. It was all so excessively masculine and virile that for a moment I stood in the entry portico feeling overwhelmed.

The knocker on the massive front door was iron—what else?—and raising it required both hands. I squared my shoulders, took a deep breath, lifted, and discovered that the knocker made quite a satisfying racket when it came crashing down. Once, twice, three times I repeated this process before concluding that Braxton Furnival was not at home.

"O-o-oh . . . botheration!" I said, biting my lip because I wanted to say something much stronger.

Now what? I found it hard to believe that anyone would live in such a huge house without at least one servant to help take care of it. So in spite of what old Joe, Junior had said, I walked clear around it and every now and then called out, "Hello? Anybody home?"

In the back I had a surprise—a broad patch of cleared land, planted with grass to make a sloping lawn, rolled down a considerable distance toward the sea. Ocean and sky seemed to be having a contest out there, to determine which could be the purest, deepest blue. Neither won; the result was a perfect tie. Deer grazed on the grass, but they bounded gracefully away, white tails flashing, as soon as they got my scent.

"He probably hunts them," I grumbled, wishing I could tell the shy, pretty animals to come back because I would do them no harm. Deer came to the lighthouse grounds, too, whole families, each with their antlered buck, to eat the scrub grass among the dunes. Actually I had found that they will eat almost anything, including some things you'd prefer they didn't, such as Hettie's daisies.

I turned around and looked at the house from this side. Impatient as I was to be getting on with things, I was also curious, so I went across a flagstone terrace and looked in through a gigantic bow window. As one might have expected, it was dark and gloomy inside. I gazed at a large, open room that, with the addition of a long table and chairs, would have made an impressive banqueting hall. Its most notable feature was a stone fireplace large enough (predictably) for a person to stand inside. I wrinkled my nose in distaste.

As I left the window I chided myself for intolerance. Bostonians of some affluence have a kind of reverse snobbery that I seem to have been born with. I know it is just as bigoted to scorn the ostentatious rich as it is to shun the poor, yet still I do the one while I would never do the other. I cannot help being uncomfortable with people who make a show of wealth.

"How ridiculous," I said to myself. "It is no concern of mine how Braxton spends his money." Yet my opinion of him had gone down a notch since seeing his idea of a grand house, and I was sorry, for he was undeniably an attractive man.

Equally undeniable, he was not there; and as I had no knowledge of his daily habits, there was no way I could track him down. Would there be no end to all these delays?

Patience, I thought as I stamped my foot. Of all the virtues I do not have, patience seems the most impossible to acquire. I do, however, try it from time to time. So instead of flouncing off in a huff, I decided to take my leave in a calculated manner. I strolled deliberately across the terrace and looked out over the rolling expanse of lawn, making an effort to picture the party where Phoebe said she had seen Jane Doe.

The deer had ventured out once more to graze. One by one, my imagination replaced them with party guests, until one deer—small, no antlers—raised her head and gazed directly at me. A doe! In my mind she became Jane Doe, with dark liquid eyes and an arched neck. Beautiful. Vulnerable. Her scarlet dress was the wrong shade of red, not the same red as the hunter's vest, no protection from a human predator. Had he been among the crowd I envisioned: the Carmelites in their odd-assorted garb, the friends of Braxton Furnival in their dark suits and proper yet fashionable dresses?

"Were you both at the party, Jane?" I asked, my voice all on its own dropping to just above a whisper. And for a chilling moment I thought I heard a whispered answer: *Yes!* Then I shook myself all over, like a dog, and got on with things.

Bless Phoebe's lively heart and talented hands. She had stayed up late the night before making ten copies of her Jane Doe sketch. Five she'd kept to show around Carmel, and five I had with me. I took one and wrote a note across the bottom:

Dear Mr. Furnival,
Do you know this woman? I am trying to find out who she is, for reasons I will gladly explain if you will contact me either during my office hours on Grand Street or otherwise at the Point Pinos Lighthouse. At your earliest convenience, if you please.

Sincerely yours,
Fremont Jones

I folded the paper and placed it under the knocker on the front door.

"Come, Bessie," I said as I got back into the shay and took up the reins. "We must think where and how to use these other sketches of Jane Doe."

I need not have worried—within half an hour the sketches of Jane Doe were no longer within my possession, nor was I in any state to do much about it.

I thought at first that I was hallucinating, or that I had come across an unusually vivid example of one of Arthur Heyer's ghost tales. A title flashed before my eyes: "The Bleeding Bandito." But this bandito wasn't bleeding so far as I could see; he was riding like fury out of thick pine trees in that section of the Point Pinos woods that always makes me nervous. I reined Bessie in; she pranced and tossed her head, harness jangling. The thrum of the other horse's hooves was like thunder in the earth. And though the man was masked I froze there like a fool thinking perhaps he would pass on by.

Need I say he did not? Whoever he was, he was an excellent horseman. I had time to observe the masterful way he whirled his horse to a stop from a full gallop, seeming to hang in midair beside the carriage—just before he hit me. There was pain, and a great roaring and a red flash inside my head, and then darkness.

"My, my, my, tch-tch-tch!"

I opened my eyes to Quincy's doleful visage, considerably too close to mine. I blinked, and all the cymbals of Siam went off at the same time inside my head. I think I groaned; I know I closed my eyes again.

"Miss Fremont—"

"*Fremont!*" I barked automatically. My head reverberated like a gong.

Quincy cleared his throat and tried again. (Incidentally, he never called me Miss again after that!) "Fremont, you just lie there nice and easy, don't try to get up nor nothing. I'm gonna get you a doctor."

"No," I said. I winced and squinted at him, then put my hand up to feel my poor head. There was no blood, only a lump that probably felt much bigger than it was. "Don't do that." I put my feet down to the floor and sat up gingerly. Quincy had laid me on the couch.

"How did I get here?" I asked. "I was in the woods when some man just came out of the blue—or the green, to be precise—and attacked me."

"Bessie came home with 'er reins draggin'. There you was, all slumped over to one side of the carriage. Gave me such a fright,

Fremont! That's a big bump you got on the noggin. Best let the doctor have a look, that's what I think." He nodded emphatically.

"I appreciate your opinion, but I worked for the Red Cross after the earthquake last year and I know about concussions. Hold up one finger, Quincy, and watch my eyes. See if I can track your finger as you move it from side to side."

He did as I asked but it was no use; even I could tell that my eyes did not focus properly. With a sigh I gave up and gave in, collapsing back on the couch. "There are demons hammering inside my head. I suppose you had better fetch Hettie's physician, though I already know what he will say."

"You betcha!"

"Quincy?" He was already loping toward the door but I called him back. "The leather bag that I carry with me everywhere—was it in the carriage? And a manila folder with some papers?"

"Nope. I'll look again, but far as I recall there weren't nothing but you. Reckon as you got robbed. You want I should fetch the police, too?"

"Police!" I grimaced, which caused only more pain. "No, I can't deal with the police, not the way I feel at the moment. The doctor will be quite sufficient. Thank you very much."

"Righty-o."

I slept. The next thing I knew the doctor awoke me, poking at my head and peering into my eyeballs. He pronounced a mild concussion and told Quincy I must be awakened every few hours for the next twenty-four, which was about what I expected. I slept and woke and slept again, and when I next awoke, Michael was there.

"Michael?" I asked, on the off-chance I was dreaming.

"Yes, Fremont. How do you feel?"

"Where is Quincy?" I got my elbows underneath me and lifted up my head.

"I sent him off to get himself some supper. Which is what I propose for you, if you feel you can keep it down. Hold your head still and let me look at your eyes."

I really felt much better. The headache had subsided to a bearable dullness, but I decided not to tell him just yet. I liked too much the way he held my head in his hands, and the nearness of his face.

"Hmm," Michael said. "I believe you will live, with your brain intact."

"Is it my imagination, or do you sound slightly disappointed?"

"Your sense of humor is also intact, I see." Michael smiled. His eyes roamed my face, and for a breathless moment I thought he was going to kiss me. But he didn't. He smoothed my hair instead, and in the process his fingers grazed the place where I'd been hit.

I jumped and yelped: "Yowch!"

"That's where you were struck? Hold still, Fremont. Let's see how bad it is."

"The doctor has already done quite enough poking about, thank you very much!"

"The skin is not broken, but you do have a sizeable lump."

"So I have already surmised." I brushed his hands away and sat all the way up, swung my legs around, and put my feet to the floor. Someone—Quincy? Michael?—had removed my shoes and covered me with an afghan. "How long have you been here?" I asked. "And what brought you here to begin with? News of my misadventure cannot have reached Carmel already."

"I stopped by your office, so I came along here."

I groaned. "I should have sent Quincy with a note to post, but I never thought of it. I hope I haven't lost much business."

"I should think that's the least of your worries at the moment."

I did not want to know what he meant by that, so I inquired as brightly as I could manage, "Did you bring something for me to type?"

He smiled. "No. I was passing through Pacific Grove and only wanted the pleasure of your company for a few minutes. Instead, I have been watching you for hours."

"Well, that is very kind of you, if more than a little embarrassing to me. I shall be all right now. There is no further need for you to stay."

"I disagree. Since I've sat with you so long, the least you can do is offer to let me share your supper. Especially as I've already cooked it."

I raised my eyebrows, a tiny movement that did not hurt . . . much. "You can cook?"

"Passably. I made a vegetable soup with the broth that was already simmering in the well at the back of your stove."

I folded the afghan on my lap, put it aside, and stood up. My head swam; I blinked and steadied myself. "How very enterprising. As long as you do not expect scintillating conversation, you may stay."

I excused myself and visited the facilities, where I looked into the mirror and wished I hadn't. The whole upper-right side of my face seemed slightly swollen, and there was discoloration along the cheekbone and into my hair. I bent closer and turned my head: The egg-shaped knot bulged just above and a little behind my right ear. My hair, which is long and straight, reddish brown in color, and ordinarily pulled back in a tidy fashion, had escaped its ribbon and resembled a rat's nest. Brushing proved out of the question, as even the slightest tug at my scalp brought stinging tears to my eyes. I decided to let it go, let the whole heavy mess hang down my back. What did it matter? Why should I care in the least what Michael thought? My blouse, which has a high collar that buttons on the side, was undone at the neck as the doctor had left it. I left it, too. Only Michael—why bother?

"It is remarkable," I said on entering the kitchen, "how one can be hit on the head yet subsequently hurt all over."

"That's trauma," Michael said from the stove, his back to me.

"A fine Germanic word, to be sure." I lowered myself into a chair at the kitchen table. I was glad to see that Michael had set our places here, glad to be eating in this warm, friendly room rather than in Hettie's dining room, which was elegant, formal, and cold.

"An injury to one part of the body insults the whole of the body," he said, placing a glass of clear liquid in front of me. "Mineral water from the mountains north of here. I've a case of it in the Maxwell. It's very good, and who knows? The minerals might help your insulted body to repair itself."

I thanked him and watched in achy dullness as he served a simple meal of soup and bread with butter and cheese. We did not talk, which was just as well, for I cannot seem to be civil to Michael these days without making an effort, and any sort of effort was for the moment beyond me.

He finished before me and pulled out his pipe. "Do you mind?" he asked, waving the pipe under my nose. Its bowl was aromatic even when empty.

"Not in the least. My father smokes a pipe. I am well trained."

"Hah!" Michael threw his head back and laughed. "That's a lie if I ever heard one!"

I tried to glare at him but even that required too much effort. So I shrugged. "Suit yourself."

He performed the pipe ritual. I observed that he was rather better at it than Father, who always accumulates a pile of matches before producing much smoke. Michael's pile consisted of only two. "Aah!" he sighed, loosening the scarf at his neck. It was silk, black with bluish-purple paisley. His shirt was cream, also quite likely silk, beneath a V-neck sweater of fine black wool. The Beau Brummell of Carmel-by-the-Sea.

I was still slowly spooning up soup. It was tasty, quite revivifying. I felt his eyes on me but perversely declined to meet them.

"Your man—"

"Quincy," I interrupted, without looking up. "He is Hettie's employee, not my man. Pray, proceed."

"*Quincy,*" Michael said with special emphasis, "tells me that you were robbed."

I shrugged again, still not looking up. "The robber got that leather bag I carry for a purse. There was nothing of much value in it. What is more of a bother is that he apparently took a file folder with some sketches."

"The sketches are valuable?"

"Not really. They were only copies; I can get more." Now I let him draw my eyes. The smell of the pipe tobacco was getting to me, in spite of the aches in my head and body; not the aroma itself but a sort of emotional aura it evoked—of home and warmth, closeness, love.

Michael's brow was creased with concern. His eyes were very blue tonight. "You didn't notify the police that you'd been attacked and robbed."

I put down my spoon, reached for the mineral water, and drank before trusting myself to speak again. "I don't see much point to it, since nothing of real value was taken. Nor do I wish to call attention to myself."

The frown deepened. He leaned forward and dark, curling hair fell down over his brow. A few silver threads glimmered among the black. "I know," he said, "that you had some bad experiences with the police—"

"That is putting it mildly!" I interrupted, but he went right on talking. "—in San Francisco when your housemate was killed, but this is Pacific Grove. And you've been physically injured, which concerns me far more than the loss of your purse and a few sketches. Let me take you to the police station, Fremont. The Maxwell is outside."

"No, thank you. As the adage says, 'Once burned, twice shy.'" That can apply to a lot of things, I thought.

"Um-hm," said Michael. He leaned back in his chair and puffed contemplatively at his pipe; I broke off a piece of sourdough bread and buttered it. I could hear Hettie's mantel clock ticking in the living room, and the rhythmic roar of the sea, muffled by sand dunes and windowpanes. Suddenly I began to feel hot, not ill but feverish all the same. I glanced swiftly at Michael, but I saw a stranger, I saw Misha: a face transformed by naked desire.

"Fremont," he said in an oddly deep voice, "you are beautiful."

Dear God but I was hot! I laughed on a high, false note and said, "Misha, you are quite insane." I couldn't bear the intensity any longer, so I got up and went to the stove, where I checked the coffeepot. It was empty.

"Don't call me that." He came up behind me and stood too close.

"Why not? I thought that was what you wanted everyone, including me, to call you." I jabbed my elbow back as I picked up the coffee percolator, forcing him to move. I carried it to the sink; he followed.

"Everyone except you. From you it requires an effort. On your sweet tongue, Misha rings false." His lips were near my ear and his breath was like fire.

Suddenly I was furious, and so energized by my fury that I no longer felt aches or pain—or caution. I forgot about making coffee and whirled around, my voice low, deadly: "How dare you talk about my sweet tongue! You have not the slightest idea whether my tongue is sweet or not, but the same cannot be said about *hers,* can it? *She* who gave you the name, who first called you Misha, how sweet is *her* tongue?"

He went all pale; his still-naked eyes flared forth pain. And then a veil descended within those eyes and he became the old Michael, in spite of new curls and clothes: an enigma, with depths impossible to fathom. He stepped back stiffly and in a tight voice said, "My mother was the first to call me Misha."

I was still angry. As if I had tasted blood and been crazed by it, I ranted on, my voice now steadily rising: "But *she* does not remind you of your mother, does she? Or perhaps you committed incest in your youth? Were you a little Oedipus, Misha?"

"Beware, Fremont! My mother is dead, she lies in the ground beside my father. What you are suggesting is obscene."

I lifted my chin. "And the things you are doing over there in Carmel are not obscene?"

I saw with deep satisfaction that Michael could not keep up his facade. The enigma cracked, the veil dissolved, his eyes blazed. But what came next was unexpected. In the space of a heartbeat he had me trapped against the sink, pinned by the weight of his body, and he was swallowing me whole.

The heat of him dissolved all my bones. I could no more have pushed him away than I could . . . could . . . I couldn't think of anything.

His mouth left mine. He held my face in both his hands, and I felt his strength. "Say it," he hissed on the *S*'s, "say my name!"

I trembled. He could crush my head like an egg. "W-w-which one?"

"Who am I to you, Fremont?" He had agony in his eyes.
"Michael!"

He kissed me again, now tenderly. I clung to him and cried without knowing why. He wrapped his arms around me and murmured soothing sounds, nonsense, then finally words. Words I wanted to hear: "Fremont, listen to me. I am not in love with Artemisia. It isn't what you think."

"It's not?"

"No. It's not." He released me, came to stand beside me at the sink, and took up the percolator himself. Which was just as well—in my still-boneless state I certainly could not make coffee.

"Then what is it?" I asked.

"I, ah—" He glanced over his shoulder at the open kitchen door, then out the window over the sink. The white beam of the Light swept by. "I can't talk about it. Not yet, and certainly not here. Where do you keep the coffee?"

I got it from the cupboard and gave it to him. My ability to think was returning, along with the dull ache in my head and various other parts. "More spy stuff," I said bitterly, "is that it, Michael?"

Looking truly miserable, he carried the percolator over to the stove and placed it on a burner. "I can't talk about it." He bent over, opened up the stove's firebox, and tossed in a couple of pieces of wood. "But the 'spy stuff' is not what you think, either."

"Dear God in heaven!" I exclaimed, even though I am hardly sure there is one. "Now you're driving *me* insane!"

Bent over, poking up the fire, Michael muttered something. His face glowed as if licked by the flames of hell.

I said, "I beg your pardon?"

He flung the stove door shut with a clang, straightened up, and nailed me with a gaze as hard as iron. "What I said was: Better insane than dead!"

CHAPTER EIGHT

"You had better explain what you mean by that." My legs would not support me any longer. I fumbled for the nearest chair, grabbed it, and sat down rather too hard. "I confess this—this—" I made a stirring-around gesture. "All of this is a bit beyond me!"

Michael said, "I cannot."

He withdrew into himself, becoming a sort of hyper-alert automaton. He watched me, he watched the about-to-perk coffee; me, the coffee; and so on. His face had gone utterly expressionless.

I waited.

Finally he spoke again. "I apologize for losing control of myself with you, Fremont. What I did was, under present circumstances, inexcusable. I hope you will forgive me."

"It was nothing," I said—which was of course an utter lie.

Michael winced.

"I suppose I might have rather enjoyed it," I continued, observing him from the corner of my eye, "if I were more my usual self this evening. That is, of course, provided you told the truth about your feelings for Artemisia."

He rubbed the top of his head: back to front, then front to back. An old habit that had caused less disastrous results in previous times, when his hair was clipped short. The motion meant he was anxious.

"You forgive me then?" he asked.

I hardened my heart, though he had made the most endearing mess of himself. "I did not say that. There is more at issue between us than a few moments' indiscretion."

The coffee began to perk and fill the room with its tantalizing fragrance.

"I told you: I am not in love with Artemisia," Michael said.

I waited; the coffee perked; the silence grew. He waited, too.

Michael Archer—Misha Kossoff: By either name, he is one of the few people who can outwait me when I am determined. After a while it became apparent that he would not say more tonight. He would not lose control of himself again. He would not explain why these things were not what I thought they were, and the bubble of energy that had been holding me up had collapsed a good many minutes ago.

I sighed and put my head in my hands, elbows resting on the table. Michael, the self-appointed coffee monitor, got up and rooted around the kitchen. With my eyes closed I listened to the sounds of drawers and cupboards opening and closing; I did not offer to help him find anything. He had done perfectly well on the soup without me—why spoil his record?

Yet it was still a pleasant surprise to open my eyes when he said, "Here, Fremont," and to see before me the coffee mug that I prefer, rather than a cup and saucer, which most women would have wanted. Solicitously he continued, "You are not concerned that a cup of coffee will keep you awake?"

"Surely you jest," I said wearily, picking up the mug.

When most of the tangy brew had coursed warmly down my gullet, I asked one question I could not make myself let go of: "Does Artemisia know how you truly feel?"

He looked deep into my eyes and solemnly replied, "Yes, she does. But she thinks she can change my mind."

"Ah," I said. And then I left him sitting there and went to bed.

KEEPER'S LOG
January 20, 1907
Wind: N, strong and gusting
Weather: Heavy clouds, no rain a.m.
Comments: Whitecaps all across the bay; swells to eight feet; no boats in or out

The face that peered into mine off and on during the night belonged neither to Michael nor to Quincy, but to Mimi Peterson. "Misha was concerned that the doctor's orders be followed while still observing the proprieties," she said in explanation the first time she woke me. "We do know what they are—the proprieties, I mean—even if we generally ignore them. Therefore I have come to monitor you. Now be still, Fremont. I understand that I'm supposed to see if your eyes go all wobbly."

My eyes did not go all wobbly, not during the night and not when I got up shortly after six o'clock. The same could not be said for the Petersons' automobile, which wobbled a good deal as Mimi drove away at six-thirty. Their car reminded me of Oscar—spindly struts but a certain charm—whereas Mimi was more of a steam locomotive. Perhaps it's really true that opposites attract. So where did that leave me and Michael? Actually we are rather alike, Michael and I.

I sighed as I went back into the lighthouse after seeing Mimi off, wondering how this would all come out in the end. At least he had absolved me of calling him Misha. I supposed that was something.

After breakfast I felt a little fragile, and my head was sore but otherwise I was fine. It took quite some time, though, to convince Quincy that this was so. I was glad when he said, "Then mebbe I'll take me a walk into town for a coupla hours, iff'n it's all right with you."

"Of course it's all right," I agreed, but I was curious, for Quincy is not generally much of a one for taking walks. I climbed to the platform around the base of the lantern and watched him disappear into the woods. It was good to be alone again—I'd had entirely too much close company for the past day and night. So why, as soon as I lost sight of him, did I feel apprehensive?

Cold wind tore at my dress. I raised my shawl up over my head, walked halfway around the platform, and looked out upon a gray and deeply disgruntled sea. Neptune was definitely in a difficult mood this morning. I raised the binoculars to my eyes and scanned the choppy waves, praying that I would not find anything out of order. Still with the same prayer, I turned my attention to the shoreline. Slightly nasty weather aside, all was well. I went down to the watch room and so noted in the log.

The typewriter sat on the watch room table, its handsome black-and-silver presence reminding me that I had a lot of work to do. Today was a Saturday, and in the normal course of events I would be going to my office on Grand from twelve to three-thirty. But the thought of carrying that heavy machine down the stairs, putting it into the shay, and so on nearly undid me. Actually I did not feel like getting in the shay myself, though a part of me wanted to dash over to Carmel and see Phoebe, then check by Braxton Furnival's house again . . . while another part (the part that speaks in my head with the voice of my mother) said *You do not always have to go dashing about. If you wait quietly, they will likely come to you.*

"Perhaps by noon I'll feel stronger," I said to myself, canceling the Voice as I trailed a finger across the typewriter keys. Really, I wanted to work, to keep my mind off everything else—I just did not want to transport the machine. *Or,* said the Voice, *to drive the rig through the woods where it happened!* The Voice has an inconvenient way of telling me the truth when I least want to hear it.

Then I realized: The log was done, the accounts were up-to-date, the animals could look after themselves, and Quincy would have let me know if any supplies needed ordering. There was not a reason in the world, at least none that I could think of, why I should not just sit right down and type.

I did ten of Braxton's letters in an hour, and twenty-five envelopes in another thirty minutes. By then I was bored out of my mind—so bored that I started thinking about things I didn't want to think about. Such as: Who was the masked man who struck me? Was he really a robber? Did he just want my purse, or had he really been after the sketches and taken the leather bag merely as an afterthought? Did he know me? Did I know him?

"Never mind," I mumbled, stacking Braxton's letters neatly, the envelopes on top and a paperweight on top of all. "Phoebe has more sketches." And as soon as I felt physically stronger, or got back my nerve or whatever, I would go get them—if she hadn't already come to me by then. I supposed I might as well admit, to myself at least, that I didn't actually believe I was merely robbed.

I went out and did the ten o'clock watch a few minutes early. Everything looked exactly as it had before, except for a straggly line of black cormorants gleefully flapping along, their flight aided by a strong tailwind. I wasn't really seeing cormorants, and my mind was not on the weather. I was seeing eyes that flashed through the holes in a mask, a plain black mask such as both adults and children wear on Halloween. He'd had a bandana folded into a triangle over his nose, mouth, and chin. And he'd worn a Western-style wide-brimmed hat.

A month ago I would have said the only thing I could be certain of was that the masked person was male. Now, after exposure to the Carmelites and their penchant for colorful modes of dress, I could not even be sure of that. The force with which I'd been hit also suggested a man. But I thought of Mimi Peterson's strong arms and legs; of Phoebe, who worked in stone (no, scratch her—her arms might be strong but this person had been much bigger than Phoebe); Artemisia? "Surely a man," I said aloud, as if that settled it. But of course it didn't.

That blow might have snapped your neck! the Voice said. And I said, "Hush up!" but I was rubbing the back of my neck unconsciously as I went back inside.

I returned to the watch room and sat down again at the typewriter. Should I work on Artemisia's novella or Arthur Heyer's ghost stories? I decided on the latter, due to their lack of any Artemisia connection. The title of Arthur's manuscript was *Ghostly*

Tales of the Central Coast. I prepared two title pages, inserting the word *California* on the second, as one can only suppose that many regions must have coasts that are central to them. Perhaps Arthur would be grateful for my suggestion; on the other hand, taking into account the way my luck had been running, perhaps not.

Then I typed Arthur's long preface, in which he thanked half the population of Carmel and Monterey and every hermit in Big Sur (or so it seemed), and described his method of collecting "oral histories" in boring, pedantic terms. I had always thought titillation was the point of ghost stories, but to Arthur these tales were cultural artifacts. One could only hope the tales themselves would be less dry than the preface.

The first story, "The Little Lost Child," got off to a less-than-promising start with a catalog of the communities and regions in which variants of this same tale appear. Then it listed the variations, thereby giving away part of the story and ruining the suspense. I made a note to suggest that he might place these bona fides, or whatever he wanted to call them, after the stories rather than before. And then I began to type "The Little Lost Child."

A dashing *Californio* was riding his handsome horse over Carmel Hill one foggy summer night. He had been courting his *señorita*, who lived with her parents on a *rancho* in the Carmel Valley; it was late and he was tired and eager to get back to his house in Monterey.

Just as he approached the summit, he thought he heard something. What was that? He slowed his horse and listened carefully. It was the sound of . . . the sound of . . . someone sobbing!

The *Californio* walked his horse at a snail's pace while his sharp eyes darted from one side of the road to the other, looking for the one who cried. It was a still night with no wind; the jingling of his spurs sounded clear and bright as bells. The sobbing had stopped. Perhaps he had imagined it?

But no; there it was again! With the heavy gray mist shrouding everything, the *Californio*—for the sake of convenience, shall we call him Juan?—Juan could barely see beyond his horse's pricked ears. A sudden chill came over him, and an inexplicable desire to spur the steed to a gallop, to come down from Carmel Hill as fast as man and mount might fly.

"For shame!" He upbraided himself; then he called out more loudly: "*Hola!* Where are you?"

Ahead in the middle of the road a patch of fog swirled and cleared; the crying stopped midsob, and a child in a white nightgown was standing there.

"*Pobrecito!*" said Juan, sliding down from the saddle and approaching the child, a beautiful infant of about a year old, with golden hair and big dark eyes, a button nose and rosebud mouth, and a tiny chin that trembled. "Do not cry anymore," said Juan. "We will find your mama and papa."

The child smiled and raised its chubby arms in a plea to be picked up, which Juan did, smiling and marveling. Just such a beautiful child would be his one day soon, when he and his *señorita* were married. Tucking the infant against his chest, with a graceful bound and a jingle of spurs Juan leapt back into the saddle.

The horse, which was a strong animal with a brave heart, whinnied and reared. "What is wrong with you?" Juan scolded, struggling to get the animal under control with one hand, while with the other he held tightly the little lost child. The child whimpered. "See what you have done?" Juan went on to the horse. "You have upset the *pobrecito,* a poor little thing that has lost its parents."

When the horse settled down Juan urged her forward at a slow pace, expecting at any moment for the fog to thin and reveal an overturned wagon, or perhaps a woman pinned beneath her fallen steed—for how else could this child come to be along the road?

"Can you tell me your name, *pobrecito*?" Juan cajoled. The child obligingly began to babble, but nothing it said made sense. Indeed, the sounds it made were like some strange foreign tongue, all full of gnashing and hissing. And yet the child was happy, for it laughed and waved its chubby starfish hands in the air. There was no overturned wagon, no fallen horse, nor any breaks in the brush along the side of the road where a wagon might have gone over.

A most peculiar feeling had come over the *Californio.* Although, like his horse, he was very brave and afraid of hardly anything, the chill he felt would not go away, and a sick sort of emptiness was creeping up his spine. Where had this child come from? It was really most peculiar.

The little lost child babbled on in its strange language, waving its hands about, quite content in Juan's arms. But Juan was not content, he was in dismay. He looked down at the babe, and for a moment was reassured by the baby-grin and the angelic cloud of golden hair. "Truly you are a beautiful child," Juan said. "I suppose until we find your mama and papa, I must take you home with me."

The grinning child opened its rosebud lips, smiling wider . . . and wider . . . and wider. And the dashing *Californio's* eyes grew wider, too, for the child's mouth was full of teeth, crammed with teeth, row upon row of sharp, pointed, animal teeth.

"*Madre de dios!*" exclaimed Juan, crossing himself. "You are not human! What are you?"

The front doorbell jangled. "Oh, for heaven's sake!" I exclaimed, thoroughly caught up in the story. I yelled out, "Just a minute!" although there was very little chance that I'd be heard down two flights of stairs and through thick stone walls. I did not type, but quickly read the last few sentences of "The Little Lost Child":

A growl came out of the infant's throat, dark and low and threatening. "My name is Legion," the baby said. And a very frightened but still dashing *Californio* leaned down out of the saddle, deposited the child by the side of the road, galloped off, and left it there. A warning: If ever you are crossing Carmel Hill and you hear a child crying, stop your ears but not your journey. Ride on by!

"Well," I said, hastening down the stairs, smoothing my skirt along the way, "that was quite a story!" My head, which still felt a little strange, warned me to go more slowly, and I called out again, "I'm coming!"

I glanced at myself in the dining room mirror as I hurried past— the bruise along my cheekbone looked ghastly but there was not much I could do about it. I do not wear powder, and I doubt anyway that mere powder would have done much to disguise such a seriously awful shade of purplish red. Whoever was at the door would just have to take me as I was.

I had already jerked the door open when the thought occurred to me that I should have been cautious, opened it only an inch or so and peered out. Next time I would remember; this time all was well. The caller was none other than Braxton Furnival.

"Good morning," he said, losing his polite smile as his eyes flickered over my bruised face. But Braxton was smooth; he recovered immediately, hiding his expression by tucking his head into a suave little bow that did not go at all with his big body. He was as well dressed as usual, though in a style less formal than I had heretofore seen him wear: a leather jacket in a sort of butterscotch color, a yellow ascot tie at the neck, soft wool trousers, boots. No hat.

"I found your communication," he continued, "took you at your word, and came on to the lighthouse."

"I am so glad you did," I said, smiling, and stepping back. "Will you come in, Mr. Furnival?"

"Braxton." He winked. "Don't mind if I do."

We sat in the parlor, and I wished for the first time in ages that I had someone to bring in coffee or tea. Hettie's parlor is quite formal, due to the fact that before she was widowed and became a lighthouse keeper she had lived in a rather fine house. She had brought that lifestyle and some of its furnishings with her: colored glass lamps dripping crystal pendants, brocaded upholstery, lacy antimacassars, Oriental rugs, a silver tea service, and more. Braxton Furnival seemed quite at home in these surroundings. So much so that I wondered if he had been there before.

I asked, "Are you acquainted with Mrs. Henrietta Houck, the lighthouse keeper, by any chance?"

He smiled. His face was so cleanly shaven that it shone as if polished. "No, I am not. I thought you were the lighthouse keeper. In addition to your typewriting service, of course."

"I am, but only temporarily. Mrs. Houck will return in six months."

"Oh, yes. So you said; I remember now. But after her return you'll be staying on in Pacific Grove?"

"That depends on a number of things," I said vaguely, then changed the subject. "I've done some of your letters and envelopes. I have them here rather than at the office. If you want to take them with you . . . ?" I deliberately skirted the subject most on my mind, which was the sketch of Jane Doe that I'd left under his knocker.

He introduced it himself, pulling the folded paper from an inside pocket. With a snap he unfurled it. "Nope. I came about this—you left it on my front door. I'm not sure when, because I do my coming and going from the side door. Anyhow, I found it this morning and thought I'd best come right along."

"It was only yesterday. Do you know her?" I asked, with an effort to appear casual, whereas actually my heart had begun to beat too rapidly.

Braxton turned the sketch over and studied it; he was farsighted and held it at arm's length, frowning slightly. "I might. Then again, I might not. Is it a good likeness?"

"I am not sure. The woman is dead." I closely observed his reaction, which was minute, only a twitching of the tiny muscles about the eyes. "She was pulled from the bay about ten days ago, with only half her face. The fish had eaten the rest. That sketch is a postmortem extrapolation."

He grimaced, and for a moment there was censure in his expression—which did not surprise me in the least. I had been deliberately rather grisly. "You're the artist? You drew this?" he asked.

"No. I caused it to be drawn by a friend."

"On whose authority?" He sounded suddenly sharp.

"On my own authority."

Oddly enough, this bold reply seemed to satisfy him. The set of his shoulders relaxed and he smiled, showing even teeth that seemed very white against his tanned skin. "May I assume that you are not working with the police?"

I inclined my head, which cost me; pain flashed behind my eyes while I replied in the affirmative.

"Then on whose behalf," he persisted, "are you making an attempt to identify this woman? She cannot mean anything to you, or you would know her identity yourself. Are you an agent, Miss Jones?"

"No," I said. But what an interesting idea! "How do you mean, an agent?"

Braxton's eyes narrowed. "You're an unusual sort of woman, Fremont. The sort, I think, they would choose."

My head throbbed dangerously. Stress, I supposed, must make it do that. "They? I'm sorry, Braxton, but I haven't the slightest idea what you're talking about."

"Pinkerton's," he said.

"The detective agency? I've heard of Pinkerton's, of course. Do they employ females?" I was genuinely interested. For the moment I forgot poor Jane Doe.

"Yep." Braxton stretched his long legs out, crossing his booted feet at the ankles.

"I suppose," I mused, "they must have an office in San Francisco, or perhaps Oakland, since one hears they do a good deal of work for the railroads. I confess it never occurred to me they would have women detectives, but I do think it is a splendid idea." I gave Braxton a brilliant smile.

He waved the sketch at me. "Far as this woman goes—d'you think I could take a look at what's left of her? Without the police knowing?"

In spite of the fact that I have little use for the police myself, I get rather suspicious when someone else tries to avoid them. Perverse of me, I know, but there it is. I decided that an attitude of complicity might elicit some information, so I said, "I quite sympathize. I am not overfond of the police either."

"Oh?" His eyes flashed interest. They were gray, and flashed silver, like his excellent hair.

"The police in San Francisco are sometimes not entirely honest," I explained. "Last year a corrupt policeman did his best to have me accused of a crime. He did not succeed, fortunately."

"And were you innocent or guilty?"

"Innocent, of course!"

"Of course." His eyes roamed my face, lingering on my bruised cheek. But he did not mention it; to do so would have been rude in the extreme. His voice dropped and took on a suggestive tone. "Well, how about it? Shall we go take a look at this dead woman, see if I know her once I've seen her in as much flesh as she's got left? That's what you want, isn't it?"

"Indeed," I said, rising slowly because my aching head was telling me to move with care. "I will just get my shawl."

Braxton's automobile was one of the new touring models, a natty Oldsmobile, dark green with brass trim. It quite put plain old black Max in the shade. All the jouncing, however, was not good for my head. I was most relieved when Braxton, following my directions, pulled up alongside Mapson's Mortuary.

"I know the man," Braxton said, assisting me from the passenger seat. For once such assistance was not just female foolishness—I needed it. "Know him through the business community," he added. "I'll handle this."

I acquiesced willingly, even walking a few steps behind. I stood back, too, when the door was opened by a different person this time. Not Long and Tall Tom, but an altogether rounder, older man whose immediate recognition of my silver-haired companion suggested it was Mapson himself. They greeted each other heartily and after the usual ritual of handshaking and meaningless comments, Braxton said, "I've come to take a look at that Jane Doe you're holding. Heard about her through the lady here, Miss Fremont Jones. She's lighthouse keeper out to Point Pinos and discovered the body in the first place."

I peered around Braxton's shoulder, but Mapson hardly glanced at me. Instead he pulled a well-practiced, mournful face and held out his hands, palms up. "Wish I could help you but I can't. The Jane Doe's gone, and that idiot assistant of mine lost the paperwork. I don't even know who she got released to."

CHAPTER

NINE

KEEPER'S LOG
January 22, 1907
Wind: NW, moderate, some gusting
Weather: Cool; heavy cloud cover; choppy seas with whitecaps
Comments: Fishing boats in and out; freight steamer down from S. F.
grounded S of Santa Cruz at Capitola, no injuries reported.

*I*n spite of the bad weather I set out for Carmel on Monday at the earliest possible time. I was beginning to think that if I waited for it to clear I'd be waiting until spring. The previous day the weather was the worst I'd yet seen here: The wind flung rain and surf-spawned mist at the lighthouse with such force that often it was impossible to see through the glass, either in the watch room or from the lantern, and it howled around the tower like some demented ghost in one of Arthur Heyer's stories.

When the rain stopped and the wind died in the early morning hours, around 3:00 A.M., the change was so abrupt that the very silence woke me. Naturally enough, I expected that the day would dawn to those glorious blue skies one sees after storms, so clear and clean they seem scrubbed. But no; when I went up to the watch room at six o'clock and looked out, I was seriously disappointed. Not that I cannot enjoy Nature in all her guises, especially on Point Pinos, where every one of those guises has its own particular beauty—but it would have been so much more pleasant to do what I had to do in better weather.

"At least it is not raining," I observed to myself and to Bessie, who put one of her ears back. Apparently the comment did not rate the attention of two ears. The horse was in fine fettle after being confined to quarters, so to speak, for two days straight. I was in similar fettle after being likewise confined, albeit by a half day less than the horse.

On Saturday, Braxton had returned me from Mapson's to the lighthouse considerably worse for the experience. I did my best to keep my physical and emotional distress from him—physical in the form of a renewed headache so intense that persistent nausea accompanied it; emotional because the loss or disappearance or abduction of Jane Doe's body filled me with such a variety of emotions that I doubt I could have named them all even had I been entirely well. Not for a minute did I believe the story Mapson had foisted on us: that some of Jane Doe's relatives had arrived and taken her away for burial. Braxton, however, brightened right up and said, "That takes care of that, then!" And I thought: Hah!

Subsequently Braxton had taken me home. Whereupon Quincy, who seldom says much of anything unless prodded, took one look at me and gave me the dickens for going out. He insisted that I—in his words—"stay put for a while!" So I did; he spent the rest of Saturday afternoon and much of the evening in the watch room rather than coming and going—I think to be sure I didn't cheat.

Sunday I was a good girl, even if I did not go to church: I honored the Sabbath (not to mention my head injury) with a day of rest. I watched the storm and read all of Arthur's ghostly tales; the two went quite well together. I did not consider the reading of the tales as work, even though it is perfectly true that I can type faster and with fewer mistakes when I do not actually read while I am typing. Lack of absorbing reading material was the only fault I could find with Hettie's well-ordered house, and one that could easily be remedied. A single idle day reminded me that I should obtain a card for the public library.

Just before supper last night, Quincy came into the kitchen with one hand behind his back. "You look a deal better, Fremont," he said.

I turned from the stove, where I was stirring a cream sauce to which I intended to add some leftover chicken and peas, and said, "Thank you. I feel much better this evening than I have since it happened."

Quincy ducked his head, cleared his throat, shuffled a bit, and then looked straight at me. "I found this," he said, bringing the hidden hand from behind his back and thrusting it at me.

I dropped the spoon. "My leather bag!" I cried, grabbing it up. Quickly I looked inside. A useless activity—the bag is so capacious that looking into it is a good deal like peering into a cave. So I dumped the whole thing out onto the kitchen table.

"Found it in the woods," Quincy said, scratching his ear and watching me prod through the collection, "not too far from where you said you was attacked."

"Thank you!" I said fervently. My nose warned me that the cream sauce could not be left alone for long; I went back to the stove and removed it from the burner, then returned to pick up and snap open the little purple cloth pouch in which I keep coins and a few rolled-up bills. Looking into it, I thought: How very odd!

I laughed, sounding false to my own ears, but maybe Quincy could be fooled. "I guess the bandit picked the wrong person to rob," I said with a shrug, "and when he saw what a paltry haul he'd gotten, he just threw it away." I shook the purple pouch; it jingled obligingly. "The bandit took the currency but couldn't be bothered with a few coins. And of course all this other stuff," I made a sweeping gesture across the table, "is worthless to anyone except me."

In fact there were several dollar bills still rolled up in the change pouch. Nothing whatever had been stolen from my bag; it had been flung to earth with all its contents intact.

"I reckon," Quincy said.

I thanked him again, profusely, as I scraped things off the table into the bag: a small comb and brush; a couple of hair clips; a black grosgrain ribbon that had come unwound (black ribbons are what I most often use to tie back my hair); a box of honey pastilles with the picture of an extremely self-satisfied cat on it; tiny scissors in a green velvet case—they are supposed to be for embroidery but I use them on my nails—a few hairpins; some pencils; a couple of disreputable-looking handkerchiefs; a small notebook, the stub of a ticket from the last moving picture show I went to in San Francisco; etc. These items disappeared under Quincy's fascinated gaze, and then he excused himself.

I tried to salvage the cream sauce, with some success, while my thoughts and fears boiled out of control. Only the sketches of Jane Doe were missing. For those sketches I had been viciously attacked; but the last laugh, so to speak, was on the bandito—he didn't know about Phoebe, and Phoebe had more.

So now on Monday morning I took the turn from the Old Mission Road onto Carmel's Ocean Avenue with the rig tipping on one wheel and Bessie at the gallop. Due to the inclement weather no one was about, and I did not have to slow down much until crossing San Carlos Street. I turned to the right on Lincoln, just before the Pine Inn. Phoebe's cottage, Hibiscus House, was one down from the corner of Fifth and Lincoln; having been there once before, the day I'd brought her home, I located it again with no trouble.

But Phoebe was not at home. I knocked and knocked. I called and called. Bessie whuffled softly, upset, I supposed, by my nervous urgency. Animals, I have heard, are able to sense the moods of humans.

Holding one hand on top of my still-sore head (as if that could do any good!) I ran around the cottage, peering in all the windows. It was only two rooms, empty of people but crammed full of other things. Behind the house I found a long sort of shed, roofed over but otherwise open to the elements: her sculpture studio. The works caught my attention and slowed me down, the better to look at them. There were several heads in clay, including one of Michael (Misha, Phoebe would say) just begun but already recognizable. One of Oscar Peterson in a melancholy mood. Also in clay, a small but full-length statue of a man I did not know—thank goodness, for he was entirely nude and embarrassingly well endowed! The largest and most impressive piece was a wood carving of a bird-woman: a woman turning into a bird, or vice versa. The expression on her face was fierce—I loved it. And the texture of her feathers invited my touch, I stroked the wood and fancied that it actually felt like feathers.

I walked back to the cottage slowly, pondering the prodigious talent in one small woman's hands. On the outside, Phoebe Broom was as plain as the sound of her name, but on the inside she was as beautiful and as fierce as that bird-woman. And brave: I remembered how without flinching she had stayed alone with a decomposing body, her talented fingers producing a sketch in record time.

"I must have those sketches!" I said aloud, approaching the back door. Trying the knob, I found it unlocked. I pushed it open, stood on the threshold, and called out, "Phoebe? It's Fremont. Are you home?"

Of course there was no answer—I hadn't thought there would be. In no time at all I had persuaded myself that since this was Carmel, not Boston or even San Francisco, no one would mind if I went into an unlocked cottage when its owner was not at home. Certainly Phoebe wouldn't care if I looked around for the sketches. When I had found them I would leave her a note, if she still hadn't returned. I proceeded inside and began my search.

The main room was cluttered and gloomy. Phoebe was apparently an inveterate sketcher. Drawings of all sizes and shapes, on all kinds of paper from the thickest and most expensive to the veriest scrap, littered almost every surface. Checking over them all in the gloom strained my eyes; my head got the tender feeling that precedes an actual ache, and I decided I'd best have some light.

A simple kerosene lantern with a clear glass chimney sat on a big round table that, by the look of things, served both for eating and work space. I went over to light this lamp, and at its base found a piece of paper that at first I took for another sketch. In fact there was a sketch on one side of the paper. But on the other side there was a note: *Dear Everybody—I've gone away. Don't know when I'll be back. Love to all, Phoebe.*

My hand, holding the note, began to tremble. I read it again, and then a third time. A prickly feeling started at the base of my skull and traveled down my spine. I have had this feeling before—it is a sign of danger. An intuition, if you will. Or even a premonition.

I bit my lip, took a deep breath, got hold of myself, and put the note back down exactly where I'd found it. Then I again set about looking for the sketches of Jane Doe, and this time I conducted a search that was as methodical as it was thorough. It took a long time; I examined the bedroom as well. When I finished I was certain: The sketches were not there. Like Jane Doe's body, like Phoebe herself, they had vanished.

When Quincy was giving me the dickens, he'd said something I had since tried to put out of my mind: "A blow like that to the side of the head, specially from somebody comin' atcha full tilt on horseback, could snap yer head right off yer neck, like a flower off its stalk!" Now, as I drove away from Phoebe's cottage, those words came back to haunt me.

Clucking and flapping the reins, I took the rig into Del Monte Forest by the Carmel gate. Bessie tossed her head and pranced, testing her will against mine. She was unfamiliar with this road, it had begun to rain, and she wanted to go home. "We are going back to the lighthouse," I called out over the noise of hooves and wheels, "but by another route!" The horse was not impressed, but my will prevailed and she settled into her smooth, trotting gait.

The rain was a fine mist, picked up by a burgeoning wind and sharpened into infinitesimal needles that fell like pinpricks upon the skin. The pine forest smelled primeval: rich, earthy, fertile, green. The road twisted near the shoreline cliffs, past Pescadero Point, Point George, Point Cypress, then plunged inland over tree-covered sand hills, but never far from the roaring surf. With Quincy's words going around and around in my head—"snap yer head right off yer neck, like a flower off its stalk . . . flower off its stalk . . . off its stalk"—I suddenly felt dizzy, and a sinkhole opened in the pit of my stomach.

I blinked rapidly and gulped at the cold, wet air. Wrong thing to do; it became harder to breathe than before. Bessie's iron-shod hooves rang on wood as the shay clattered over a bridge spanning a steep-sided gulley. I was panicking. The tall trees, dark green and threatening, were closing in on me. Trapping me in a forest full of danger, full of shadows, the same sort of shadows that not so long ago had flung a masked bandit in my face. *Snap yer head right off yer neck, like a flower off its stalk!*

Had he really tried to kill me? Was I alive simply because he'd misjudged the strength behind his blow? Or had he pulled back mercifully at the last minute? Was he really a he? Or a she? And had this same person, this bandit-who-was-not-a-bandit, made Phoebe disappear?

I took a deep breath and let it out slowly, a technique for controlling fear and tension that Michael had taught me in our more comradely days. I would not—absolutely would not—give in to my fears.

"Gee-ha!" I yelled, as much to encourage myself as to make the horse go faster. I had a good reason for taking the long way home: Braxton Furnival. I had to see him, because he possessed the only remaining copy of Phoebe's Jane Doe sketch.

I burned with wanting to know who Jane Doe was. She had been an important person, that much was sure—important enough to keep the newspapers quiet, maybe even to squelch a police investigation, though in all fairness I supposed the police could have been investigating all along. When the newspapers do not make their reports, who is to know? Maybe the police had found the next of kin, as Mr. Mapson suggested, and the kinfolk had come and picked up the body. Maybe good old Tom really had lost the paperwork after releasing Jane Doe to them.

I snorted. "Not very likely!"

There is an interesting clarity that comes over me when I am fired by a certain sort of anger. In this clear state of mind I can do things I might not otherwise be able to accomplish. Thus I found Braxton's horrid house with no difficulty whatever, even though I approached it from the opposite direction. What is more—and I count this pure, sheer luck—he was at home. He answered the door rather sooner than I might have wished, for I was enjoying a satisfying pounding of the knocker.

"Fremont! Thunderation, you're all drenched. Come in, come in!" he boomed heartily.

"Thank you," I said, drawing my shawl more closely around me, "but actually I am merely damp, and in somewhat of a hurry. I will get to the point. I should appreciate it if you would return to me that sketch I left on your door the other day."

"Why? What for?" Braxton put his hands in his pockets and rocked back on his heels, staring down at me.

I hadn't anticipated such a question, and so I stumbled on my answer. "Why, because I, I . . . Oh!" I raised the back of my hand to my forehead, closed my eyes, and deliberately swayed a bit on my feet—the only delaying tactic I could think of. "You know, Braxton, I believe I will come in just for a minute. I suddenly feel a little strange."

He was extremely solicitous, and I found that I rather enjoyed being fussed over by a tall and handsome older man. Never mind his atrocious taste in houses. He hovered over me, guiding me through an enormous great hall, the sort of place where one imagines people in horned helmets regularly consuming whole roast boars with their bare hands and teeth; thence to a smaller room with a welcome fire in a fireplace of near-normal size.

"Sit yourself down by the fire," Braxton said. "You'll have to excuse me for a minute while I go get us some refreshment. I'm on my own today—servants' day off."

I demurred, but only halfheartedly, and so of course he went off. There is no stopping a man like Braxton Furnival once he has made his mind up about something—I know the type from the years after Mother's death, when I acted as hostess for my father. The fire felt good; I held out my cold hands to warm them, while I used the time alone to think of a reason why I might want Jane Doe's picture. Other than the real reason, which I had no intentions of telling anyone.

Aha! I had it!

I could hear Braxton's footsteps long before he came through the door, because the great hall was uncarpeted. So was this room. Perhaps the bare floors were intentional, a pretension of the royal-rustic style. He placed a tray on his desk. This small room was his study—or at least I presumed it would be eventually, when he finished furnishing it. At the moment most of the bookshelves that lined the walls were empty.

"Brandy," he said, holding the decanter up to the light. He gazed at me, then at the crystal container, turning it to catch the light. "Did you know, Fremont, that your hair is about the color of brandy?"

"Chestnut, that is what people usually say. As for myself, I call it reddish-brown. I do not want any brandy, thank you all the same. I will have just a little of that soda water, however."

"A woman without vanity," he said in a musing tone, as if he were talking to himself. "Amazing!"

I ignored the remark, as it is not quite true of me, but it would be awkward to admit it. "You asked earlier why I wanted the picture of Jane Doe: because it was drawn by a friend of mine. She's very skilled, and since I cannot afford to buy any of her work, I thought I would keep the sketch. She is bound to be famous one day, so I expect it will increase in value." The last concept was one I was sure he would understand.

"Damn!" Braxton swore. He came over to me, handed me a glass of soda water, no ice, then sat in a chair that was a twin to mine. "Beg pardon, Fremont. My tongue gets away from me sometimes, I guess because I don't get much chance to be around the fair sex. I'm a lifelong bachelor, you see."

"I see." I could not help smiling. I wondered how old he was exactly—in his fifties, surely?—and how many hearts he had broken.

He leaned forward smiling, rolling a glass of glowing brandy between his palms. "Where was I? You being here, it's downright distracting."

"My sketch," I prompted.

"Oh, yes." Braxton hung his silvery head and addressed the floor. "I can't give it back to you, I'm sorry. I had no idea it was valuable." He looked up at me, contrition in his eyes. "I thought, since she was gone, we were done with it. I wadded that piece of paper up and burned it last night, in this very fireplace."

My disappointment must have showed in my face—it was so extreme that I could not mask it. I swallowed hard and said, "What a pity."

"Fremont, how can I make it up to you?"

I took a long sip of soda water. Braxton leaned over and placed his big, warm hand over my free hand, which lay in my lap. Lowering the glass, I tipped my head, looked into his eyes, and lied. "It is not important enough for you to be concerned about. Just a whim I had, nothing more."

He squeezed my hand and dropped his voice to a near-growl: "Then tell me who's responsible for that bruise on your cheek, and I swear to Almighty God I'll have him beaten within an inch of his life!"

"Oh, dear, I am in trouble! I did this to myself, you see." I smiled, shook off his hand, and brushed mine against my cheek in illustration. "I have an unfortunate tendency to be clumsy, and there are all manner of metal protuberances around the lighthouse. I slipped and hit my head, that is all. So you do not have to beat anyone, but thank you for offering."

He sat back in his chair, took some brandy in his mouth, and rolled it on his tongue. Watching him I could almost taste the pungent liquor myself; when he swallowed I felt a burning in my throat. His eyes bored into me with an intensity that made me wish I could read minds.

Slowly Braxton shook his head back and forth, his eyes never leaving mine. "Sorry, Fremont, but I don't quite buy it. I just can't get the idea out of my head that you're not what you seem. But I like you, so I'll tell you what I'm going to do. . . ."

I raised my eyebrows in silent inquiry. I felt as if I were skating on the edge of a precipice—one false move, one tiny push, and I might fall off.

"I'm going to tell you who I thought your Jane Doe was."

CHAPTER

TEN

"*N*ow mind you," Braxton continued, "I'm not certain. That's why I wanted to have a look at the body. I sure would like to know why it's so important to you. Not that I really give a hoot in hell, I'm just curious."

"Who did you think she might be, Braxton?"

The fire glinted red off his silver hair. A wolfish look stretched over his features. "If I tell you, will you satisfy my curiosity?"

"I will try."

"Fair enough. Okay. I think maybe Jane Doe was Sabrina Howard, an actress. Aspiring actress, I should say, wanted to break into the moving pictures."

"I can't imagine why. Surely motion pictures are merely a novelty and will soon go the way of most fads." I did not really believe this; in fact, quite the reverse. I simply wanted to keep him talking and perhaps throw him off-guard. "I should think an actress would prefer the stage."

Braxton chuckled. "Some pretty women have caught on to the fact that for the moving pictures you don't have to have a lot of training, the way you do for the stage. Sabrina's talented, though. I guess I should say she *was,* if that was her in your sketch. Did some vaudeville up to San Francisco, singing and dancing, that sort of thing. Wanted to get enough money put by to take her to New York, where most of the moving picture business is."

Warming up to his topic he leaned forward, elbows on knees, the brandy forgotten in one hand. "I put her on to a good thing, her and a few others. Introduced her to this fella named Boggs who wants to make pictures down south of here, little place near Los Angeles called Hollywood. He's looking for backing, hasn't got it yet; I tried to put him together with some people but it didn't pan out. That's what I do—one of the things, anyway—put people with money together with people who want to use it."

"And Sabrina Howard was a part of this, um, equation?"

"Huh?" Braxton's thoughts had apparently meandered off on a tangent of their own. He called himself back on track. "Oh, no. Not exactly. She was, you might say, more of an ornament. You see, actresses like Sabrina, sometimes when I have a big party down here and entertain prospective clients and all that, I hire them for an evening or a weekend or whatever. Nothing out of line, you understand," the wolfish look was back, "they just mix with the guests, look pretty, and act pleasant. It's easy work, they like the money, maybe sometimes they make an important contact for their careers or maybe they don't. Either way, I like to have them around."

"I see. And when did you last have Sabrina Howard around?"

"It's been a while. About six months ago, I guess." Braxton tossed back the rest of his brandy.

Six months . . . the party Phoebe had attended at Braxton's had been around six months ago.

"And you haven't seen her since?" I asked.

"Nope." He got up and poured another finger of brandy in his glass. I wondered at this, as it could not yet be past noon, and I was the one who had been chilled, not he. From behind me Braxton added, "Last time I had a party, as far as I recall, she said she was busy and couldn't come. That's the last I talked to her."

"You must have an address, then, or a telephone number!"

The fire popped suddenly, and I jumped, putting a hand to my throat. Then the flames made a hissing sound as they licked at a damp place in the wood. A tendril of fragrant smoke escaped the fireplace and curled through the air.

"If she's dead," Braxton said, returning to his chair and draping one leg over the armrest in a pose that made me think of Michael being Misha, "what does it matter if I have an address or not?"

"Because if Sabrina Howard *isn't* dead, and can be reached at the address you have for her, then the dead woman is not she and must be someone else!"

"So what? What's all this to you anyway, Fremont? You promised to tell me."

I could not sit still; I wanted to strangle him if that was what it took to get Sabrina Howard's address. I jumped up and, for something to do, strode over to the desk, where he'd put the brandy decanter, and set down my glass there. Time for more dissembling. I forced a wistful tone into my voice. "You will think me foolish."

Of course he reassured me that he would not.

"Well then," I said with a reluctance that was not in the least feigned, for I was about to embroider upon a core of truth: "I made a silly promise that I just can't get out of my head and I feel bound by it. When she was pulled from the bay and nobody knew who she was, I promised the dead woman I would make it my business to see she got a good Christian burial. I wake up in the night thinking about her, about my promise to her." I shuddered; it started as an act but then I found my shoulders quivering in earnest. "She haunts me!"

"Poor Fremont." Braxton left his chair and his brandy to put his arms around me.

With one last shudder I murmured into his yellow ascot, "The address?"

"I reached her through the place she most often worked, the Rialto Theater. I never knew where she lived; in fact, I don't know if Sabrina Howard is her real name or a stage name. Let it go, Fremont. You have no obligation to a dead woman you never met."

"I'm sure you are right." I pulled back but his arms tightened so that I could only move my head. I was trapped all too near those interesting lines in his tanned face. "Perhaps I could let it go, if only she would stop haunting my dreams."

"I'll help you. I can make you forget." His face came down to mine and his lips opened, emitting the sweet-sharp smell of brandy.

And I, minx that I am, turned my head and twisted out of his grasp.

KEEPER'S LOG
January 31, 1907
Wind: SW light
Weather: Clear, mild, sunny, bay waters calm
Comments: Two passenger steamers in, one from San Francisco and one from Vancouver; counted five whales well off Point Pinos headed S.

Business was not booming for my typewriting service. I sat in my office at two o'clock on a Wednesday afternoon at the tail end of January and wondered what had happened to my life.

"My life is broken," I muttered, stacking papers so vigorously that I bent the bottom edge of one and now would be obliged to do it over, "and I shall just have to figure out how to fix it!"

Michael was staying away, out of embarrassment or regret or sheer contrariness; Phoebe had not returned to Carmel; I had written to a friend in San Francisco about Sabrina Howard over a week ago, and as yet had had no reply; and Braxton Furnival was becoming a positive pest. He was a pest I could not exterminate, however, because aside from Arthur Heyer's and Artemisia Vaughn's long manuscripts, his typing business was all I had.

It was time to write out a check for my February rent on the office. Without new business, the office would not pay for itself, much less turn me a profit. Instead of putting pen to checkbook I sat staring out the window, pondering my plight. To tell the truth I was unhappy, which is quite unlike me; and indecision was making me unbearably restless. I am one of those people who would rather do something than nothing—even if that something is the wrong thing, as in my own case it frequently turns out to be.

I thought of circulating a new flyer advertising my business. Thought of dropping my rate to seven cents a page. Thought of taking out an advertisement in the newspapers in both Monterey and Pacific Grove. None of these felt like the right thing to do, they felt like throwing away money—of which I had precious little.

"Think, Fremont," I exhorted myself, "analyze!"

It seemed to me that people around here were too set in their ways, or perhaps they were merely satisfied with the status quo—at any rate, many had tried my typewriting once and then failed to return. This could not be due to the quality of my work, for I turn out a neat presentation even if I do say so myself, and I guarantee my work to be 100 percent accurate or I will do it over free of charge. Therefore the problem had to be either that they did not like *me,* which was a bit bothersome to consider, or they just did not see the point of paying to have something typewritten when they could do it themselves by hand.

Oh dear, I thought, beginning to face the inevitable; then I put a sign on the door, BACK IN HALF AN HOUR, and walked the few blocks down to Lovers Point. I walked past the public bathhouse and the Japanese tea house, out to the rocks, along the way disconsolately trailing my skirts in the sandy dust. The rocks themselves, large chunks of upthrust granite worn by wind and sea into a semblance of smoothness, were relatively easy to climb. Lovers Point is the tallest, most rock-bound promontory on the south side of Monterey Bay; nevertheless it is quite tame compared with some rocky places I have walked along the bay in San Francisco—Land's End, for example.

Tame or wild, foggy or clear, I find that simply being by wide water will eventually put me at peace and clarify my mind. I do not know why this is, unless it is that great forces of nature make my own problems seem small. I thought of the whales I'd seen from the lighthouse on the ten o'clock watch, creatures so huge and magnificent and mysterious, yet so hunted by man that now there are few where once they were many . . . and the memory of the whales too helped me find perspective.

When I returned to my office on Grand Avenue half an hour later, I sat down at the typewriter knowing what I should do. I wrote two letters, which I would post on my way back to the lighthouse at four o'clock. The first was to the owner of the building, giving the requisite thirty days' notice. The second was to my friend Meiling Li, who is a special student at Stanford:

Dear Meiling,

I realize that I have not written since Christmas, which is very bad of me. Things have been more than a little odd, and I am having some trouble adjusting, which is why I have not yet invited you to come visit. There is another reason as well: There was a huge fire here in Pacific Grove last year, in which a Chinatown that predated the town itself was burned completely to the ground. No one will openly discuss this fire; it is still only mentioned in hushed tones. I gather that arson was suspected, but on whose part no one seems to have been able to ascertain. Suffice it to say the Chinese would hardly set fire to their own community! And while no one here is overtly hostile to persons of your race, still I think it the better part of wisdom that you not come to Pacific Grove.

As things are working out, I shall not be here much longer myself. This area does not appear to need a typewriting service. (You may trust my judgment on this—I will not bore you with the details.) Therefore, when I have completed my six months as temporary keeper of the Point Pinos Light, I shall pack up and return to San Francisco. I will stop in along the way and visit you in Palo Alto, if I may.

I am sure your studies are going well, and eagerly look forward to our being together so that you can tell me all about geology, the science of the earth.

Your most devoted friend,
Fremont

There! I read it over, signed it, and experienced a flood of relief. It is quite amazing how much better one feels after reaching a difficult decision.

As I addressed and stamped the envelopes, I thought it would be wise to delay telling Michael my plans for as long as possible. You may imagine my surprise, therefore, when that very person opened my office door and stuck his head in.

"Speak of the devil!" I said. "Or think of him, as the case may be."

"I beg your pardon? May I come in?"

"Of course you may. I have just written a letter to Meiling, so perhaps it will come as less of a surprise that I was thinking of you. By the by, does Meiling know about the Misha transformation?"

Michael scowled at me, then turned his back and made a show of examining some truly awful paintings by Tom, Dick, and Harry—the Twangy Boys—that Artemisia had, as promised, assembled on my wall.

"Well," I needled, "does she?"

"No!" He turned again to me, positively glowering. "The members of her family to whom I was close are all dead, all except Meiling, and I do not wish to intrude upon her studies with trivial matters that cannot possibly be of any interest to her. I trust that answers your question?"

I covered the typewriter and slipped my letters inside my leather bag. "Rather more vigorously than I would have thought necessary, but thank you all the same. Is this a social call, or did you have something that wants typing?"

"Let's say my purpose is personal but not precisely social. Since we are finally having fair weather, I was hoping you might close your office an hour early and come out on the bay with me. I haven't taken the *Katya* out in quite some time, and as I recall you enjoy sailing."

I was vastly tempted. But even as I thought about how pleasant it would be to skim across the water with the wind in my hair, the sea spray on my face, I was swamped with a gut-level remembrance of the sea's ability to isolate. The nape of my neck began to prick.

"I suppose you will think it peculiar of me," I said cautiously, "to wonder why all of a sudden you want me to go out in a boat with you, when so many days went by without your troubling to inquire if I were recovering from that blow to the head. And then there is the matter of Phoebe Broom: I sent you a note about her very suspicious departure, to which I have had no reply whatever. These things rankle, Michael."

"You are being oversensitive. Taking the last first, I see nothing at all suspicious in Phoebe's deciding to go away for a while. She is a free agent and a mature woman, not required to discuss her plans with any of us. As for the rest: I knew you were recovering satisfactorily because I paid your man Quincy to bring word to me if you took a turn for the worse. As I've heard nothing, I assumed you were doing well—and I am happy to see that you are." He favored me with his most charming smile. "The bruise on your cheek is almost gone, as I was sure it would be. You're young and healthy, Fremont, there is no reason you should not heal rapidly and well."

"Oh, fine!" I crossed my arms and tossed my head. "You're not content with being a spy yourself and making a mess of your own life, you have to go and pay Quincy to *spy on me!* And I've told you before, don't call him my man! Quincy is as much his own man as anyone, so you can just leave him alone. Thank you very much." I fussed with the things on the desk. "And no thank you to the sail. I do not care to be isolated out on the bay with you just now."

"Fremont, please—"

"No. You have been acting entirely too peculiar of late. I am trying to get my life back in order, and I have the distinct feeling that if I let you influence me again it will only become more hopelessly messed up."

Some people, myself among them, blush in response to an excess of emotion; others do the opposite—they blanch. Michael's face drained of all color, which made his shapely nose appear yet more sharply honed.

He pleaded, "Fremont, trust me! I have something to tell you, and I dare not do it anywhere except the one place where I am certain we cannot be overheard."

I gave him a quick up-and-down glance. He was dressed head to toe in black, most of it leather. "Do you really expect me to trust a man who dresses like that? Who practically attacks an injured woman in her own kitchen? Whose entire personality—never mind his name—has changed almost beyond belief?"

"Your points are well taken," he said grimly, and he left.

After the midnight watch I could not sleep. I tossed and turned for a while, then got up, lit the lamp, and looked for something to read. In vain. I kept forgetting to obtain a library card, which was perfectly ridiculous considering the public library is free.

A whole host of things were keeping me awake, the principal one being Michael Misha Archer Kossoff; I feared I had shot myself in the foot, so to speak, where he was concerned. Probably I should have gone on the boat with him; on the other hand, he should be able to understand that after being hit on the head out of the blue (or green) it is not especially easy to trust *anyone*. And it is perfectly true that he has been acting strangely. So why should I have this feeling that Michael needs me?

"It is probably only wishful thinking," I said crossly, getting back into bed and punching my pillow into shape. I blew out the lamp . . . and fifteen minutes later I was up, lighting it again. I put on my bathrobe, an inexpensive tartan thing resembling a Black Watch plaid, belted it tightly over my white nightgown, and stepped into black felt slippers. With a ridiculously sharp pang of longing I missed my disreputable old once-viridian bathrobe. All my present clothes (which in sum total far fewer than I was once accustomed to own) are new and cheaply bought. I lost my former clothing, and virtually all my possessions, in an incident that occurred some months after the earthquake. Only my leather bag—which I begin to think has nine lives like a cat—and three pairs of shoes survived. And as for that incident, even now I still have nightmares about it.

I climbed the stairs to the watch room and stood for a moment looking out at the velvety-black night, split every few seconds by a sweeping white beam of light. I listened intently, and heard only the soft, swishing sound of peaceful seas. Then I closed the shutters so that I could work without the ever-moving beacon distracting me.

Though I had decided to close down my office, I still had Arthur's and Artemisia's manuscripts to finish. I'd brought the typewriter to the lighthouse so that I could do the work here in the watch room, a pleasant if somewhat cramped place to type. Since I could not sleep, and had nothing to read, I thought I might as well be doing something useful. It was better than lying awake and thinking myself into a mad tizzy.

I had spent more time thus far on Arthur's ghost stories, so in all fairness to Artemisia (and to be honest, I had a hard time being fair to her) I decided to type for a while on her novella.

I began on the second chapter of *The Merchant of Dreams:*

The very first night after I entered into the contract, I slept under the spell of Jonah Morpheus. I know this now, though at the time, upon waking I was only excited and a shade mortified by a dream of such vivid imagery and content.

Though by terms of the agreement I could have moved into the Morpheus Foundation, I preferred to remain in my own apartment even though it is little more than a hovel. So upon arising I dressed and broke my fast quickly, then went immediately by streetcar to the foundation, being careful not to speak to anyone along the way. The agreement was that the first words I spoke each morning after waking would be to Jonah Morpheus, an accounting of the previous night's dreams.

Morpheus himself answered my knock. He looked as if he too were not long out of bed, with his black hair somewhat disarranged and a white shirt, soft and curiously ruffled, flopping open at the neck. His trousers were gray, quite tight; he looked as if he belonged to another age.

"Come in," he said, "I have been waiting for you."

I tried to smile but my lips trembled, and I did not return the greeting because such words would have had nothing to do with my dream.

Morpheus led the way up the stairs into the upper regions of the house, where I had never been before. Gaslights burned in sconces on the walls, giving off only meager light and casting our own huge, wavering shadows before us as we ascended. Up and up we went and with every step I felt more curiously removed from day-to-day reality. I began to wonder: What if this, too, is a dream? I lost count of the landings, the turnings, the floors that we passed, but at last Morpheus stepped off the stairs. The cat, Shadow, was sitting between the balusters at my eye level; it blinked its great black-rimmed eyes at me as I passed, then lifted its handsome tail and with a subdued meow greeted its master. I debarked from the stairs and the three of us—man, cat, woman—proceeded entrain down a dim, high hall-way.

Jonah Morpheus opened a door and stood back for me to enter, which I did, preceded by his cat. His shadow goes before me, I thought, but I was not as amused as I might have liked. In truth I was more than a little apprehensive. The door through which I had passed led into a suite of rooms, sumptuously but oddly furnished. I blurted out "How extraordinary!" before I'd had time to think.

"Sshh!" whispered Dr. Morpheus, cautionary finger to lips. He touched a switch somewhere out of sight—or perhaps he was as much the magician as he looked and only snapped his fingers. But however he effected it, a chandelier glowed to life in the ceiling. It shimmered like diamonds hanging in rain. And like diamonds it refracted the light into a rainbow palette that played over the sheer draperies covering not only the windows but also the walls and doors. A room of veils.

"Sit, Heloise," said Dr. Morpheus, by a sweep of his hand indicating an empire-style chaise lounge, "Put your feet up, lean back, close your eyes. It will help you to remember."

The rainbow lights played over the chaise lounge, too, so that try as I might I could not tell what color the upholstery was. Nevertheless I did as he bade, for my dream had become heavy within me, a great burden I longed to be rid of—though how I would bear to tell its intimate content to a complete stranger, I could not imagine.

I arranged my skirts, turned my head, and looked at Morpheus and at his cat, which sat on the floor beside him. Those identical eyes . . .

"Heloise, tell me your dream!" he commanded. And I obeyed.

"I was walking upon a beach. At the cape, I suppose it was. The tide was low, the sea calm, the breakers merely lacy ruffles upon the sand, and the sand itself a shiny, silken, virginal stretch unmarred by footprints of human or bird. It was cool and quiet. I saw this scene all in shades of silver.

"But then it changed. The sun came out all gold, its rays shedding down heat from a deep blue sky. So hot! I took off my shoes and stockings and left them on the sand; bunched up my skirt and petticoats and waded in the surf. The salt water was warm; like a soothing bath it licked about my ankles, and the sea bottom softly oozed up between my toes. I swayed with the rhythm of the waves and I longed to go deeper . . . deeper . . ."

Realizing what I should have to say next, I felt my throat tighten and go dry. I glanced over at Morpheus and his pet, neither of whom appeared to have moved a muscle, although the doctor had a note-pad balanced upon his knee and a pen in his right hand. "Go on, Heloise," he said, as if he knew there was more to the dream.

I cleared my throat, closed my eyes, and raised the back of my hand to my forehead so that my bent arm partially obscured my face. "Then—" I paused to clear my throat again "—then as is the way of dreams, the scene changed yet again. I was still on the same beach but it was night. The sun had gone down and there was no moon, only stars twinkling in an inky sky. I had apparently disrobed, for I was emerging naked from the sea. Where I had been hot before, now I was cool, deliciously cool. A breeze sprang up and touched my wet skin, playfully, in places where—ah, where—"

"You must hold nothing back," said the voice of Morpheus, in a low tone so near my ear that my eyes flew open and my head snapped around. I thought I would find that he had moved his chair right up next to the chaise lounge, where he could touch me; that he was after all some sort of filthy if wealthy pervert with faked scientific credentials. But my ears had deceived me. Morpheus and Shadow sat exactly where they were before.

"Please, Heloise," he said reasonably, "you are not the only person involved in this project, you know. Time is precious."

I said, "I'm sorry," and composed myself. "The breeze touched me where, ah, only a husband may touch. It was actually quite . . . quite arousing. In fact I grew weak, limp with longing. I staggered up the beach and lay myself down upon the silky wet sand.

"I lay on my back with the breeze blowing over me, blowing stronger all the time, touching my, my nipples and the hair . . . down there. In the most intimate sort of way. And I was quite shameless. I opened my legs and let the wind be my lover. Stronger and stronger the wind blew, in great thrusts and gusts it swirled over me. Entered me. Took me to a height and depth of pleasure no mere man ever took me to before. . . ."

I opened my eyes and removed my hand from my forehead. My face was hot, as flushed as when I'd first awoken from that dream, and I was as wet in my secret place as I'd been then, too. The myriad of rainbow-colored lights on the ceiling whirled in a mad dance—but that was only my fevered imagination, for even as I blinked they slowed and winked as they should. "And that is all," I said, continuing to regard the ceiling.

I felt mortified.

"Was that the only dream you had last night?" Morpheus asked in a dry, clinical tone.

"The only one I remember."

"Very well. You may go."

I sat up and asked, shakily, for my pay. Dr. Morpheus said I would be paid once a week, on Fridays, and then he left the room. I thought that considerate of him, believing he must have understood I needed some time to get myself in hand, as it were. But the cat stayed. The cat stared. When I rose from the chaise lounge the cat darted under my skirts and twined itself about my ankles, purring.

I could not rid myself of the conviction that the damned cat knew—more, it wanted to be close to—my shameful secret: the sticky moisture of arousal was dripping down my inner thighs.

CHAPTER
ELEVEN

KEEPER'S LOG
February 1, 1907
Wind: W, mild to moderate
Weather: Foggy, cool, calm seas
Comments:

I felt hot, and damp myself in that most intimate place, when, on towards dawn, I left the typewriter. After opening the shutters of the watch room window, I went up the winding stairs and out onto the platform that surrounds the lantern. I did not know which galled me more: that Artemisia had the power to arouse me along with her Heloise, or that this same Artemisia who wrote so convincingly—not to mention erotically—was in love with my Michael.

"For shame, Fremont!" I said, astonished by my thoughts.

The wind took the words from my mouth and blew them away, even as it cooled my fog-damp face. The wind . . .

The story of Heloise's dream was stuck in my head, and somehow the wind-lover brought to mind a vivid visceral memory of Michael's kissing me in the lighthouse kitchen. As an antidote to such pointless passion, I said with conviction: "He is not my Michael, and never will be, not even if he should ask me to do the unthinkable and marry him!"

That did it: I cooled right down. I have strong convictions about marriage, one of them being that it fosters an unhealthy way for men and women to relate to each other. Marriage endorses possessiveness, especially in the man, who is literally likely to look upon "his" woman as merely one more possession. But women do it too. *My* husband, they say, emphasis on the *my*. That I, who feel so strongly about the independent worth of each and every human being, should have even thought the words "my Michael" filled me with consternation.

Yet you do love him, said the Voice.

"What does that have to do with it?" I responded crossly.

Deep within my memory, from some forgotten spot where the schoolgirl had stored her lessons, Shakespeare's words came bubbling up into consciousness:

Let me not to the marriage of true mindes admit impediments,
Love is not love which alters when it alteration findes . . .
O no, it is an ever fixed marke

and so on; I could not remember the rest.

"Hmm," I said. I was not so obtuse as to be unable to see the point some part of me wanted to make. But should I heed it?

I gripped the railing and looked out to sea, where through dense white fog I could just discern the humped outlines of the Point Pinos rocks. Looking like ghost-birds veiled in their own emanations, a flock of cormorants slid silently by. Drops of fog fell fresh on my skin. I breathed deep, and deep again; the air tasted both clean, like springwater, and salty like the sea. Above my head the beam of the Point Pinos Light threw itself against an opaque wall, but the deep voice of the foghorn regularly moaned a warning, so all was well.

But not for Jane Doe, who was perhaps Sabrina Howard; and probably not for Phoebe Broom, either. If anything had happened to Phoebe, I was certainly responsible. I had involved her; the sketch for which I had been hit in the head and (I very much feared) she had been kidnapped, or worse, had been my idea. I could not let self-protectiveness or pride get in the way; I had to do something, and I had to start in Carmel.

As I went back inside to make the day's entry in the log, I realized that this was a new month. Always with a new month there is the possibility of a new beginning. Unfortunately February is my least favorite month of the year, so it did not seem particularly auspicious.

I had the answer to one question, anyway: Yes, I should pay attention to the part of me that remembered Shakespeare's counsel—*Love is not love which alters when it alteration findes*. . . .

At midmorning it was still foggy. The wind had shifted slightly to blow out of the northwest rather than the West, and with the shift had taken on a wintry nip. I noted this in the log and wrote in the "Comments," which I'd left blank earlier: *logging schooner and freight steamer in from S.* Then I closed the logbook and went looking for Quincy.

He was nowhere to be found. I wrote him a note, using simple words that I hoped he would be able to read: *Gone to Carmel. Please take watch. Thank you, Fremont.* Then I wrestled with harness and traces until I got the rig put together, said a few encouraging words to Bessie, and took off for Xanadu. Michael's cottage, that is.

It was a good thing I had learned to trust Hettie's little mare, for the fog was thicker going over Carmel Hill than I had yet encountered during daylight hours. There were times when I could not see past the horse's ears. And a time near the summit when Arthur Heyer's ghost story about the demon-child grabbed me and I was sure I heard someone crying. But I found no demon-children; instead, an idiot in a motorcar found me. He was driving much too fast for the poor visibility and almost ran over the rig. Bessie was magnificent; she expressed her displeasure by putting back her ears, but she stood stock-still and waited for the idiot to whiz on by.

"If he goes over the edge it will serve him right," I remarked, and the mare whickered her agreement.

Eventually I found the opening among the trees that marked the Ocean Avenue turnoff. In the little village of Carmel there was less fog, but everything was gray and drippy. The car that had almost run me down sat dripping in front of the Pine Inn, so I surmised the culprit was a tourist who didn't know any better than to go tearing around blind. I went on past, started to lay the reins on Bessie's neck for the turn onto Casanova, then thought better of it. Instead I pulled her into a wide U-turn and went back up to Lincoln and along to Phoebe's cottage.

I did not even get down out of the shay. I didn't have to; Phoebe's cottage looked so forlorn it was perfectly obvious that no one was home. No lights shone through the windows, no smoke curled from the chimney. An emaciated black-and-gray-striped cat lay listlessly sprawled on the front steps, raising its head for a moment to stare at me with glazed eyes. A stray, probably. But maybe not. I had thought to continue on my way, but now I did get down from the carriage.

"Here, kitty, kitty," I called softly, feeling a bit like a fool. My parents had not believed in keeping animals as pets so I never had one as a child. Father, particularly, thinks it is evil to bend nature's creatures to one's will. I have heard him on occasion expound upon his conviction that the Fall of Man occurred not when Eve ate the apple but when Adam named the animals—presumably the first step toward domesticating them. Therefore I know almost nothing about dogs and cats, not to mention horses, cows, canary birds, etc. My personal opinion, though, is that once a species has been domesticated the damage is done and we must take care of them.

"Poor little thing, poor kitty," I said in what I hoped the cat would interpret as a sympathetic tone. She—or he, I had no idea which—did not run or so much as cringe from the touch of my hand. She was limp and light when I picked her up. In the carriage she dug her claws into my lap and made a pathetic, halting attempt to purr.

I took the cat to Xanadu. With her limp, furry body hanging over my arm like a black-and-gray-striped muff, I banged on the door, shortly thereafter interpreted a grunt from inside as an invitation to come in, and did so.

Due to the grayness of the day, the inside of the cottage was quite gloomy. A single lamp burned on the dining table. Involuntarily I tightened my grip on the cat, and she wriggled. Michael sat slumped over his elbows at the table like a dark shadow, and he was not alone. Either or both of them may have greeted me; it was difficult to hear anything over the roaring in my ears.

Nevertheless I advanced; not for all the tea in China would I have revealed the tiniest part of my true feelings. "Good morning," I said. My voice was steady and clear. "I wonder if either of you has anything we might feed this cat. It belongs, I think, to Phoebe and is quite starved."

"Oh dear!" Artemisia exclaimed. *Deshabille,* one of those rare words that looks like it sounds, could not even begin to describe her appearance. Her hair looked as if it had blown loose during a windstorm and frozen that way. The kohl she used to darken her eyelids had smudged in a raccoonish manner. She was more or less wearing one of those intentionally ragged layered things of hers, but without its underdress. In other words, when she moved and the layers shifted, one could see right through it. Like a naughty show in a stereopticon: *Flash, flash.* Now you see it, now you don't.

I put the cat down on the table. Kitty blinked and looked up at me, made a sort of peep, and began a wobbly exploration. Artemisia leapt up with a flash of nipples and dark triangle; *I* blinked. From the direction she went and the sounds she subsequently made, I presumed that she was getting the cat something to eat. I did not follow her with my gaze, because Michael had captured my eyes.

There is a Russian fellow who for the past two years has been taking the tsar's imperial court by storm—he is called Rasputin. In magazines I have seen photographs of this Rasputin, who did not look all that different from Michael at the moment. Michael's eyes burned in his head, burned into me; his dark brows were drawn together in the scowl of all scowls. He wore a nightshirt open at the neck. Black hair, sometimes shot with silver, curled everywhere: his chest, his arms, over his forehead, down into his collar, on the bare legs that stuck out beneath the nightshirt. Rasputin is said to be both a miraculous healer by powers of mesmerism and a terrible debaucher. At the moment I could believe Michael also capable of either or both those things.

Love is not love which alters when it alteration findes . . .

The cat wobbled over to him, delicately sniffing, and curled her tail under Michael's chin. His burning eyes never leaving mine, he began to stroke her, which oddly gave me hope.

He had not asked me to sit down at the table. I did so anyway, directly opposite him. "Are you growing your beard back," I asked, "or have you just forgotten to shave for the past several days?"

The corners of his mouth twitched, that sensual mouth, but he did not reply. Artemisia was chopping something, in sharp counterpoint to a low, continuous rumbling from the cat. A strong odor hung about Michael, both acrid and ripe, a combination of alcohol and something I could not exactly define, but I suspected it was sex. I have not had enough experience along those lines to know for certain.

"Fremont—" his voice cracked and his tongue showed pink for a moment as he moistened his lips "—this is not a convenient time."

"I do apologize. If you had a telephone I would have called first."

Artemisia returned with a bowl of something, which she put on the table. The cat came running over. "Chicken," she said.

Michael picked up both cat and bowl and set them on the floor, saying as he did so, "The cat should have water too. I didn't know Phoebe had a cat, did you, Art?"

"No, I didn't, but then I hardly pay attention to such things. Oh, bother! There's no water in the pitcher. I shall have to go out to the pump, Misha."

He was very involved with the cat, hunched over, supervising the eating process with repeated murmurings of "not too fast, puss," and so did not reply. I suppose I might have offered to go, as "Art" was barefoot and hardly dressed for the outside, but I did not. Instead I offered her my shawl, which she accepted. This shawl is black, knitted rather than crocheted, I have no idea by whom—another find from the donation bin when I was homeless after the earthquake, living in Golden Gate Park. Not a very grand garment, yet when Artemisia covered herself with it and flung one end back over her shoulder, the shawl took on an allure that it had never had on me.

"I should not have done that," I muttered after she went out the door, "now I'll never be able to bear wearing it again."

"Your generous, helpful nature gets you in trouble every time," said Michael with a touch of sarcasm, straightening up. "Now what exactly did you want? Aside from something to feed the cat."

"First, I want you to send your friend away. Or should I say your lover? At any rate, I need to speak to you alone, *Watson.*"

He shook his head. Hair fell in his eyes and he didn't bother to flick it away. "No. I can't do that. Not even for Sherlock Holmes."

I sat up as straight and tall as I was capable of. "Surely you mean that you *won't* do it. You can if you want to."

His eyes were burning again. "You could have gone out aboard the *Katya* with me too—but you didn't want to. I needed to speak to you. Alone. And you did not want to be alone with me."

"Alone on dry land is not the same as alone in a boat in the middle of Monterey Bay, and you know it!"

"Do I?"

A volatile silence shimmered between us. Artemisia broke it by banging through the back door with a pitcher so full she kept slopping water and muttering, "Damn! Damn!"

"I won't ask Art to leave," Michael said quite clearly, and quite loudly enough for her to hear. "Anything you have to say, Fremont, you can say in front of her."

"I have snakes in my house, so I can't go home," she said, plunking a small bowl of water down beside the larger bowl of chicken, which was fast disappearing. Kitty was ecstatic.

"I had gathered that you spent the night," I said evenly. "But that is beside the point," I continued bravely. "I've come because I'm concerned about Phoebe. I think there is something sinister going on."

"Sinister? How delicious! Do tell!"

Michael merely raised those eyebrows.

"I know something you do not," I said, and then I told them about the sketches of Jane Doe, told them everything, including

Braxton Furnival's frustrated attempt to identify the woman in person. "Michael," I said, leaning forward, deciding the hell with Misha, "you remember Wish Stephenson."

"The young San Francisco policeman whose honesty almost got him into trouble with a corrupt superior officer? Yes, I remember him."

"Wish?" asked Artemisia. Her face was animated, her dark eyes sparkled with interest. She was most attractive, in a full-blown, mature way I could not hope to achieve, and my heart ached—but I must not think about that.

"His real name is Aloysius," I said, "and he is the only person of his profession I currently feel I can trust. I wrote to Wish and asked him to check on the actress Sabrina Howard. I haven't yet had a reply, which is rather discouraging, because if someone had reported her missing I expect he would have replied by return mail."

"I told you before," Michael growled, "to leave it alone! Let the Pacific Grove police handle everything. But could you keep your inquisitive nose out of it? No! Dammit, Fremont—"

"Hush," Artemisia said, "don't be such a grouch." Then she said enthusiastically to me, "Of course we must help! How? What can we do?"

This was assistance from an unexpected quarter. I said, "I don't like to involve you, Artemisia. Look what happened to Phoebe. I wanted *him* to help. He's the one with all the experience."

"Misha?" She jabbed him with her elbow. "Well?"

"I'm retired," he said, glaring at each of us in turn. "I am a man of leisure. I will look after Phoebe's cat until she returns. That is the extent to which I am prepared to help. And don't badger me, either of you!"

I rolled my eyes. Artemisia stuck out her tongue at Michael and said, "Sometimes you are such an old fuddy-duddy!" Then she leaned eagerly across the table. "He's no use. Tell me what to do, Fremont."

I tried not to look at her breasts and to keep an open mind. A part of me wanted to tear a good deal of her hair out, but another part of me recognized that Artemisia was a person of exceptional talent and courage, and moreover she was offering what I so much needed: help. So I said, "You could come with me to Phoebe's and help me look through her things for any clue as to where she may have gone. An address book, perhaps, listing family and close friends. Letters with return addresses. That kind of thing. We must send telegrams. Then we wait a day for the replies. If there are none defining her whereabouts, as I am almost certain will be the case, then you could go to whatever law enforcement agency oversees Carmel—"

"Monterey County Sheriff," said Michael gruffly.

"Thank you," I resumed, "and report Phoebe as a missing person. No mention of the sketches, or Jane Doe, or any of that. Just that Phoebe is missing. Such a report would come better from one of her Carmel neighbors, as I'm sure you'll understand. Will you do it, Artemisia?"

"Of course I will!" She smiled radiantly. "Anything for dear old Phoebe. And for you, Fremont!"

Artemisia really did have snakes in her house. Getting them out became something of a production, a weird, impromptu ritual, Carmel-style. Khalid, the Burnoose Boy, beat upon a drum while Artemisia shook a gypsy tambourine; the Twangy Boys stood around looking dubious and every now and then saying together "Oooh!" like a Greek chorus; Arthur Heyer was full of suggestions that the principal snake-chasers, Oscar and Mimi, mostly ignored; and Michael, newly shaven, brought Phoebe's cat. Others, Irma and the man I'd called Diogenes at the picnic, and some I'd never met, hung around across the street simply watching. As did I.

The general idea seemed to be that noise of sufficient intensity or of a certain pitch would drive the snakes—two, supposedly—out of the house, whereupon Oscar would chase them toward Mimi, who had a long, forked stick and a net. It looked like a butterfly net to me, but I had never heard of a snake net, so what did I know?

These snakes, alas, proved impervious to noise. While various people were discussing what to try next, Michael walked calmly up to the front door of the cottage, opened it, and let the cat loose. Because I was listening, and because I know so well the timbre of his voice, I heard him say, "Go get 'em, kitty!" But the others did not hear him, nor did they seem to know that he had let the cat go inside the house. A few minutes later the two snakes slithered out, with the cat scampering behind, which is how the cat got its name: Patrick. The name was bestowed by Michael, with the explanation that Saint Patrick had chased all the snakes out of Ireland.

I believe that story about Saint Patrick and the snakes to be a metaphor—what Patrick really drove out was the old religion of the Druids—but I did not say so. Along with everyone else I smiled and congratulated the cat, but what I was actually most happy about was that now Artemisia could return to her own home. Of course that did not necessarily preclude her spending more nights in Michael's bed, but I preferred not to think about that.

I said good-bye to the motley group and went home myself, to the lighthouse. There was nothing more to be done today. When Artemisia got going she was like some force of nature: It was she who had found Phoebe's address book and she who composed the telegrams to people whose names I selected from it; she who paid when we sent them from the telegraph office next to the Carmel post office. "Don't be silly!" she'd said when I protested that as it was my idea to send the telegrams, I should pay. "I know you haven't any money. Misha told me." My humiliation would have been complete, except for some unfathomable reason I didn't feel humiliated.

Indeed, if we were not rivals for Michael's affections, Artemisia and I might well have become friends while we worked together on Phoebe's plight. She was lively, she was funny, and she was efficient. On parting she proposed to meet me at my office on Grand Avenue in Pacific Grove at two o'clock on Friday, the next day, to report on any replies to our telegrams, and to go over with me what she should say to the sheriff. I agreed without bothering to tell her that the office was now closed. After all, I'd paid through the end of the month and I still had a key. Anyway, I should have to tell them all sometime—Arthur especially, as I was still working on his manuscript—but not yet. It felt too much like admitting defeat.

Well, I thought as I clucked and cajoled Bessie into her fastest trot on our last leg home through the Point Pinos woods, after tomorrow they will all find out, because I will tell Artemisia and she will surely tell the others. I smiled. It felt like a good resolution for a task I'd dreaded. And besides, Artemisia had a car; she could take Tom, Dick, and Harry's paintings back to Carmel with her.

The truth was that I was beginning to rather like Artemisia, breasts and all. Life is so perverse!

Quincy was waiting along the track as Bessie and I came bucketing up to the lighthouse. His expression was particularly lugubrious, so as I pulled on the reins, bringing us to a halt, I asked him what was the matter.

"It's them cows, Fremont," he said, shaking his head slowly back and forth.

"Our cows? I mean, Hettie's? The Holsteins?"

"Yup." He took Bessie by the halter and walked her to the barn. I followed along.

When he didn't say any more I asked, "What about the cows?"

"We lost one."

"Well, for heaven's sake, Quincy, a cow shouldn't be too hard to find out here on the point. There's only just so many places it could go. In fact, I should think we could spot a lost cow from the lighthouse platform."

"Not this'un you can't. She's not lost that way. She's dead." Quincy looked at me with mournful eyes. "And two of 'em are sick. I reckon as it might be something in the water what's causing it. I reckon maybe you and me, we best be darn careful till I get this figgered out."

CHAPTER

TWELVE

KEEPER'S LOG
February 5, 1907
Wind: NW moderate, increasing in p.m.
Weather: a.m. fog, clear by noon; cool; increasing swells
Comments: Lumber schooner down from Vancouver reports Alaskan
storm headed S—this is the cause of increasing wind and swells

Our water had been poisoned. Not at the source, thank God, which is a well that also serves the dairy in the Point Pinos woods, but at a large tank where the water is held after flowing (downhill) through a pipe from the source. The lighthouse must have such a tank as a safety measure, in case of fire.

Of course I had to report the poisoning to the Lighthouse Service, as it caused expense. The water had been analyzed, and now the tank must either be thoroughly cleaned or outright replaced. I was for replacement, but of course the decision was not mine to make—that duty fell to some bureaucrat overseeing the Lighthouse Service.

On Monday morning I received, by messenger, a toxicology report: The water tank had been poisoned by the addition of kerosene. The concentration should not have proved fatal; therefore the cow that died must have had some constitutional weakness, probably of its complex digestive system, as that would be where the poison was absorbed. The sick cows had showed signs consistent with what the report suggested: a staggering gait, an attitude of stupor, decreased appetite, and poor milk production. Over the weekend, while we waited for the report, they had begun to improve; nevertheless I was so guilt-ridden that I wanted to have the veterinarian back now that the cause of the poor cows' problem was known.

The animals were Quincy's responsibility, so he was taking this even harder than I. He kept puzzling over how such a thing could happen, and I did not think I would be doing any favors by suggesting the various possibilities that leapt into my mind. Quincy is a complete stranger to malice—therefore the idea that someone might have poisoned the water tank intentionally simply did not occur to him. Of course to me it did, and so when Quincy had fetched the veterinarian, I set off on foot with the explanation that I had business downtown.

Once in downtown Pacific Grove, I hopped a horse-drawn trolley car for Monterey. With the toxicology report in my leather bag, I was on my way to the hospital to see Dr. Frederick Bright.

I confess I am no great fan of hospitals, which seem to me to have more to do with sickness and suffering than with making people well. I was glad to know where I was going this time, so that I could stride breezily along looking neither left nor right. Illness is so depressing, not to mention ill-smelling, and it seems that the available cures do not smell much better.

The dead smell worst of all. Even though I had no previous expe-

133

rience of such things, it was not difficult for me to conclude when I entered the pathology suite that an autopsy was in progress. My nose led the way, and I peeked through the double doors. Dr. Bright, easily identifiable by his unusually full head of white hair, was bent over a body; further details of the procedure were mercifully unavailable to me, due to his assistant's stance, which blocked much of my view.

The smell was really not so horrible once one got used to it. Soon my insatiable curiosity compelled me through the doors, first one step and then another. Being absorbed in their ghoulish task, neither doctor nor assistant noticed my presence. I moved a few more steps to one side, and then I could see what they were doing. What they were doing was eviscerating a corpse. They were wrist-deep in gore.

Without looking up, Dr. Bright barked, "Whoever you are, you'll have to wait. Outside, please!"

I didn't argue; I'd seen enough. My mother, rest her soul, used to belabor me with that old saw about curiosity killing the cat. From as far back as I can remember I'd refused to believe this, and had been delighted when at about age ten or so I'd learned the rejoinder "Satisfaction brought it back!" With indecent glee I'd hurled those words in her face, and with her great patience she had regarded me, saying, "Someday, Caroline, you will learn."

If Mother were still alive, I reflected as I walked back up the corridor to Dr. Bright's office, I would write her a letter tonight— she would be glad to know that my curiosity had at last found its limit. I shall in future be content to take people upon the merits of their outsides, accepting the fact that their insides are better left alone . . . at least by me.

Dr. Bright's office was unlocked. Leaving the door open, I went in and spent a few moments prowling around in search of something to read. I did not know how long I'd have to wait, and these days I do not do well with my thoughts unoccupied. At last I found something I thought I might understand—a tract about the use of mesmerism in surgical procedures. Then I selected the least-cluttered chair, moved its stack of papers to the floor, and sat down to read. The article was interesting, but I could not help noticing that the patients on which these mesmeric experiments had been tried were all women, while the surgeon and the mesmerizer were both men. This made me suspicious, although I would have been loath to put my suspicions in words.

Dr. Bright still smelled faintly of autopsy when he came into his office, but at least his hands were clean. "Aha," he said, "Miss Sherman, is it?"

I stood up to greet him but found I was reluctant to offer my hand, due, no doubt, to knowledge of where his had so recently been. "Fremont Jones, Dr. Bright," I said.

"Fremont, yes, I knew it was some sort of Army man's name. You're the one from the lighthouse; I remember you now. Wanted to know about the Jane Doe a while back." He plunked himself down in the chair behind his desk, which received him with a squeaky groan. "So what's it this time?"

"I am in need of advice, and a confidant," I said, feeling my stomach sink at the risk I was taking. I had reached the place where I did not feel I could trust anyone at all.

"And you chose me?" He chuckled and rubbed at the tip of his nose. "I'm flattered, to tell you the truth, really flattered."

"I hope you *will* tell me the truth," I said, and reached into my bag. I brought out the toxicology report and handed it to him. As he read it I watched his face intently. I expect that in time I will be a better judge of whether or not someone is lying to me than I have been in the past. At least I have learned, from experience, to be cautious.

"So?" After a quick read-through he looked up with beady black eyes.

"So I should like to know if this contaminated water, which sickened two cows and contributed to the death of another, would be lethal to humans? Or would it merely make us sick?"

He frowned, and rubbed at his nose again. "If you drank it, sure, it'd make you sick, but I doubt you'd die of it. For one thing, the water would smell and taste funny. You wouldn't be likely to drink much before deciding there was something wrong with it. You'd be sick at home for a few days, maybe even in the hospital, but that's all."

I said, "Hmm," and fell to thinking.

"Somebody tried to poison you, Miss Jones?" he asked jauntily, bending forward to fish in a cigar box on his desk. "Smoke? Some ladies do you know."

"No, thank you." I smiled. "That is not one of my vices."

"You don't mind if I do?"

I shook my head.

"What are your vices, Miss Jones?"

A good question—which I would have refused to answer had he been a younger man. As it was, I gave the matter some thought before replying, "I suppose my most glaring fault is a lack of good judgment. Also I have very little patience. Even the thought of injustice makes me wild, and there is so much of it—" I stopped short, biting my lip before I could say too much.

Dr. Bright grinned, his beady eyes jumped, and the moist inner membranes of his mouth gleamed as he pursed his lips and let out a few smoke rings. "That's what I thought. It's Jane Doe, isn't it? You still all in a twist about her?"

Maybe it was the smoke. I really hate cigars. Or maybe it was the lack of depth in those black eyes. Whatever; I decided to, as it were, take the information he had already given me and run. "Not a twist, exactly. It's just this terrible curiosity of mine. Her body was taken from the funeral home, but Mr. Mapson said the papers were lost so he didn't have the names of those who had taken it. I admit I was rather persistent; I may even have implied some criticism. And, I don't know, when there was a problem with our water, I—uh—" I broke off, shrugging helplessly and making my eyes as big as they would go.

"You seem none the worse for it," Dr. Bright commented.

Quincy and I were none the worse for it because our drinking and cooking water does not come from the tank, but rather from a pump at the kitchen sink that is connected directly to the waterline. But the person who put the kerosene in the tank would not have known that, and I wasn't going to tell the coroner. If someone was trying to scare me, I wanted that person to consider me scared. In fact I *was* scared—but I do not relate to being scared in the same way that some, one might even say most, women do. So I shrugged again and said, "At least I'm all right now. I just want to be sure to stay that way!" I stood up and slung my leather bag over my shoulder. "Thank you for the information, Dr. Bright. You've been most helpful. I won't bother you again."

"No bother, no bother!" He came around his desk and patted me on the shoulder in an unfatherly fashion. "You come back anytime!"

"Thank you so much." I forced one last smile at considerable strain to my facial muscles, then set off at a brisk pace.

I was so distracted that I lost my way in the medicinal wilderness and had to ask directions of a nurse in order to get out. I had hoped Dr. Frederick Bright might become an ally, one who had access to information from the police. I needed to know if Jane Doe was Sabrina Howard, and if so, what she had known that was so important it had to be buried with her. If I could not find out quickly, and quietly, it began to look as if some of us would be buried as well.

And what, I thought as I swung onto the streetcar, about Phoebe?

At last! I found a letter of reply from my singular policeman friend, Wish Stephenson, in the afternoon post. I was so eager to read it that I tore the envelope open and began my perusal as I walked back from the mailbox to the lighthouse, wind flapping the letter's two pages.

Dear Fremont:

As you may have gathered from the delay in my reply, Miss Sabrina Howard had not been reported as a missing person to any precinct of the San Francisco Police Department at the time I received your letter. I am happy to say—that is, as happy as one can be in the circumstances—that she is now on the books. Her case has been assigned to someone else, but I may be able to work a swap and get on it. I'll let you know.

Sabrina Howard was, as you suggested, an actress who had appeared at several of the theaters around town, most recently the Rialto. Her real name was Sara Mae Horvath, age nineteen, from up around Placerville. Her father's dead, and her mother runs a boardinghouse up there. Sara Mae, or Sabrina, apparently wrote home regularly and sent money when she could. It was the mother who finally reported her daughter missing—said she hadn't heard from her since right after Christmas and that was very unusual. The two women who shared lodgings with Sabrina are just barely cooperating with the police. They claim she had friends out of town and often visited them for extended periods of time, so they didn't think there was anything wrong with her being gone for so long. Except their noses were all out of joint when she didn't send her share of the rent at the first of the month.

I wish you could come up here, Fremont. I think another woman would get more out of these women Sabrina lived with, and as you know we have no females on the police force. I know you can't come—that's just Wish with some Wishful thinking. (Yuk, yuk!) Never mind. Maybe if I can get the case assigned to me I might be able to get more out of them myself.

I told the investigator assigned to the case that I had an anonymous tip about an unidentified body matching Sabrina Howard's description found in Monterey Bay. So he contacted the coroner's office down there, and they told him they didn't have any unidentified bodies. Anybody ever tell you, Fremont Jones, you get yourself in the darndest messes?

I'll write again when I have something more.

Your friend, Wish Stephenson
P.S. Here's a photograph of Sabrina Howard. She was really pretty!

Photograph? What photograph?

I looked in the envelope—no photograph. I had walked to the lighthouse as I was reading, gone through the door, and now was sitting at the kitchen table. I sorted quickly through the other mail, to no avail, and then realized that in my haste to get at Wish's letter, the photograph might have dropped out when I'd ripped open the envelope.

"Hell's bells!" I said, jumping up and running back outside. The mailbox was beside the road about a hundred yards away, beyond the cypress hedge that Hettie had planted to make a sort of visual boundary. The wind, stiff and cold, did not seem to bother the young cypress trees—already in the few years since their planting they had shaped themselves to it, grown flattened tops and back-swept branches. But it did bother me: It whipped the tails of my tied-back hair in my face with such a sudden gust that the black ribbon came loose and went flying, and so did my skirts about my knees. The cold wind cut through my clothes, through my skin, to lodge in my bones. Had this same cold wind snatched away the photograph, or had Wish forgotten to enclose it with his letter?

I trotted up the track to the mailbox, looking quickly from one side to the other and back again and continually fighting the hair out of my eyes. Yet the loss of my hair ribbon proved salutary after all, for the ribbon caught my eye as it descended sinuously in a lull to drape itself in some tall dune grass. In this same clump of dune grass was caught a square of something whitish. I loped over, seized the square object, and crowed with delight. Yes!

You are insane," I said to Artemisia about half an hour later, "but I suppose you know that."

"I haven't the slightest idea what you're talking about, Fremont Jones," she said, blinking with exaggerated innocence as she untied an orange scarf from beneath her chin. This scarf was confining the brim of an enormous straw hat, all wrong for the season but of course that did not stop Artemisia. Otherwise she was dressed more appropriately for the weather, in a long brown wool coat, smartly double-breasted with brass-rimmed buttons. As it was rather chilly in the lighthouse, she made no move to undo them.

"You've driven over here practically in the very teeth of a storm," I said. "I'm surprised the wind didn't blow you off the road."

She shrugged and said negligently, "Cars are heavy. I wasn't worried." Then nothing would do but that I must give her a tour of the lighthouse, which she had never been in before; I tried to be patient with all her *ooh*-ing and *ah*-ing because I'm well aware that Hettie's version of lighthouse living is unusual enough to merit a few *oohs* and *ahs*. Finally I was able to suggest that we sit in the kitchen at the table, where I could build up a fire in the stove that would warm us and boil water for tea at the same time.

"Although," she said, draping herself across one of the kitchen chairs, "I would far rather have a drink. You know, Fremont, a *drink*. It is, after all, that time of day."

"What time of day?" I asked, looking up from chucking wood into the stove. I knew perfectly well what she meant, so my question was not very nice, but it seems there are times I just cannot help myself where Artemisia is concerned.

"Teatime in some houses is the sherry hour in others. Not that sherry was what I had in mind, either."

"Well, I'm sorry," I closed the stove door with a resounding metallic snap, "but Hettie apparently doesn't drink because there were no strong liquors, or even sherry, in the house when I moved in. And I never thought to buy any. I can only offer you tea."

"Then Misha can't have spent much time here," she said rather maliciously.

Tit for tat; I could not complain. Since it was tea or nothing, I filled the kettle and put it on. Refusing to be baited on the subject of Misha, I stayed with my former line of thought. "Actually, Pacific Grove is a dry town. I have heard that there was a time, not so long ago, when people were not allowed to indulge even in the privacy of their own homes. There was a law that you couldn't draw your shades before a certain hour in the evening, to discourage immoral conduct."

"How boring," Artemisia said; "I can't imagine why you'd want to live in such a place, but never mind. I was serious in what I said about Misha. He's drinking too much, Fremont. Something is tormenting him, and he will not tell me what it is."

"I'm sorry," I said. I truly was, but not surprised. Not after what I'd seen, when she herself had been a more-than-willing participant. I joined her at the table. "Is that what brought you here this afternoon?"

"Oh, no." She began to unbutton her coat, as the room was heating up nicely. "He's a big boy. If he wants to be all moody and morbid that's his business, not mine."

"But if you truly care about him—"

"Sweets," Artemisia pushed her coat back and leaned toward me, "do you know what your problem is?"

"I suppose you are going to tell me."

140

"You're just *too* young and *way* too idealistic. How old are you anyway?"

"I'll be twenty-four on my next birthday."

She rolled her eyes. She wore a pumpkin-colored knitted garment—a very long sweater, I suppose it was—that kept slipping off her shoulder. The garment itself was shapeless, but sometimes when she moved one could see her large nipples poking against it. I began, God help me, to see more of a reason for corsets.

Since Artemisia made no response except for rolling her eyes, I asked, "And how old are you?"

"Thirty-five," she admitted readily, then laughed and winked, "a regular old hag!" Then she sobered. "He's too old for you, you know. He's forty-five."

"I do know." I got up and made tea. Perhaps it was the pending storm that made the atmosphere tense, or perhaps it was the direction our conversation had taken; no matter which, my hands trembled and I spilled more tea leaves than I got into the net tea ball. "But I'm not sure that age has that much to do with anything—whether it's my age, or yours, or his. If Michael is drinking so much that he's injuring his health, couldn't you at least try to, to—"

"To what? Just what do you think a person can do to stop another person from destroying himself?"

I brought tea, sugar, milk, and lemon to the table. I am sure my brow was furrowed, for I was out of my depth. "Surely it is not that bad? I must admit, I've never known anyone who is overtly self-destructive."

"Lucky you." She sighed, stirring milk and a very large amount of sugar into her tea.

I sipped and continued to ponder. "With Michael, you know, you never can tell," I said after a while. "It could be an act. He may not be as badly off as you think."

"Oh, he is. Believe me. Even I can't keep up with him anymore."

I winced involuntarily. "Then maybe you could distract him. Get his mind off whatever is bothering—"

"*Tormenting,*" Artemisia corrected me. "Don't belittle."

"All right, *tormenting* him. I just don't understand why he won't get involved in looking for Phoebe! It makes me so angry! Really

141

Artemisia, he's being terribly selfish. I just want to . . . to shake some sense into him!"

She smiled and raised her cup. "Yes, sister! That's the spirit! And that reminds me: I have news about Phoebe. That's really why I came."

CHAPTER

THIRTEEN

I waited with bated breath for Artemisia to tell me her news about Phoebe.

"You know I went to the sheriff," she said, tugging at her recalcitrant sweater, "and reported her missing when none of those telegrams we sent paid off. So I just thought you'd want to be kept up-to-date."

"That is thoughtful of you. I do appreciate it." I gritted my teeth, wanting to shout, *Get on with it!*

"We had two deputies in Carmel all day Saturday talking to people, asking all sorts of questions about Phoebe and her habits. By implication, about all our habits. It was rather annoying, actually, so I had to go around later and tell everyone it was for a good cause. The Petersons in particular were upset, but then Oscar is so overly sensitive."

"Mimi doesn't strike me as a particularly sensitive type."

"No, she isn't, but when Oscar gets upset, then Mimi gets upset that he's upset—if you see what I mean."

"Of course. I'm sorry for the inconvenience; I know how unpleasant it is to have the police prying into one's life. But Phoebe *is* missing."

"Yes, well, there's more."

She waited for me to ask. It was clear that Artemisia was intent on wringing every last drop of appreciation out of me; what she did not seem to realize was that I am far more likely to give it freely, and resent being wrung. So I merely raised my eyebrows in an interrogatory manner.

While we had this little war of wills the rain began. Flung against the lighthouse walls by the wind, it made enough noise to startle Artemisia. She jumped and her eyes darted around the room.

"The storm has begun," I commented.

"I suppose I really had better be going. It sounds a little worse than I thought we were in for." She reached back for her coat and, still seated, proceeded to shove her arms into its sleeves.

Curiosity won out over stubborn pride and I asked, "Before you leave, will you tell me the rest?"

"Oh, there's not much more. Just that one of the deputies came back this morning to tell me they'd searched the coast as far up as Half Moon Bay and as far down as Point Sur, and there's no sign of Phoebe. I told them she wasn't fond of camping, so there's no point going into any wilderness areas. At least they're working on it, which is more than you seemed to think they would do." Now she stood up to work on the coat's buttons.

"Thank you." I relented. "I do really appreciate your coming over in this bad weather just to tell me. I also received some news today." I reached into my skirt pocket and took out the photograph. "This is Sabrina Howard, who has disappeared from San Francisco.

She is also the Jane Doe that Phoebe sketched, but since the body and the sketches have all disappeared, there is only my word for it that Sabrina and Jane are one and the same."

Artemisia plunked her hat on her head and tied it down with the scarf. "I think you should tell the sheriff, Fremont."

"No, thank you. Having been disbelieved in the past by officers of the law, I am hardly eager to subject myself to that sort of treatment again. Besides, the one policeman in San Francisco whom I do trust has taken on Sabrina's cause. Believe me, he will make a far more valuable contribution than I ever could."

"You're probably right."

I walked with Artemisia to the door and opened it—no simple task against the thrust of gale-force winds. I had to raise my voice to be heard over the howling. "Perhaps you'd better stay here. This is bad!"

"Don't be silly!" To my great surprise, she stretched up and kissed my cheek (I am half a head taller than Artemisia), then continued, "I'll get wet, of course, but the car will take me home quickly. It hasn't been raining long enough to turn the roads to mud yet." She started down the path, but then turned back. Rainwater streamed off the sides of her hat onto her shoulders. "Fremont, I meant what I said about Misha. I'm worried about him. Go to see him, please. And make it soon."

KEEPER'S LOG
February 9, 1907
Wind: S, slight
Weather: Sunny and mild
Comments: Storm debris still washing up along bay; one shipwreck to be salvaged off Aptos

The storm stayed for four nights and three days. Quincy kept shaking his head and saying how unusual it was for a storm to be so severe and to last so long. Like the voice of doom he lamented how much worse this winter had been thus far than any in recent memory. I reflected, but of course did not say, that if Quincy ever had to make it through a New England winter he would be hard-pressed.

This was the third winter season I had experienced in California, and it did not seem so bad to me. Anything short of a blizzard would have seemed a relative lark, I suppose.

Our young cypress trees did not go down in the wind and rain, but many trees did fall in the woods of Point Pinos, and all over the Monterey Peninsula. It is an awesome, terrifying thing to wake in the night hearing the crack of one of nature's giants, and the great, tremulous groan of its fall to earth. More than once I thought we were having another earthquake, and my heart tried to jump out of my chest before my mind could take control.

Therefore it was with joy that I opened my eyes to sunlight early that morning. Barely taking time to don robe and slippers, I ran up the winding stairs and out onto the circular platform around the lantern. The sky was a tender new blue, with that scoured clarity that comes especially after storms. The familiar shapes of the Three Sisters, which had been obscured for days by rushing waves and pounding surf, were still there unchanged. Deer daintily picked their way, heads down, through the dunes, eating tender roots exposed by wind-shifted sands. Pelicans, cormorants, gulls of every stripe and color were wheeling, diving and feeding now that they could do so again with impunity. Far across the bay, the mountains scrolled their dark blue silhouette against the lighter blue sky. And I turned eastward, stretched my hands to the pale, winter-gold sun, and said a silent good morning. These quiet moments, this closeness to nature, I would miss when I went home.

Home: San Francisco. Four months and nineteen days until Hettie was due. I wondered if I could last that long. But then I thought: Of course I can! It is easy to be optimistic on the morning after the storm is over.

After breakfast Quincy set off to survey the damage in the woods. He was particularly concerned, he said, about the butterflies. It seems there are monarch butterflies that winter in the forests of Pacific Grove by the thousands, and falling branches and tree trunks would damage their cocoons. As we had already ascertained that our cows were all right, I told him that I hoped he would find the sleeping butterflies the same.

While washing the breakfast dishes, I felt an unexpected and unwelcome frisson of anxiety, the first in several days. Happy as I was

146

to see the sun again, I had to admit I'd felt safer during the storm. No one was going to venture out in Nature's fury to do mere human mischief. I had even finished typing Arthur Heyer's ghost stories, by lamplight with eerie wind accompaniment, and had not been scared for a minute. Not much, anyway. Yet now . . . I glanced quickly over my shoulder toward the kitchen door. There was no one there, of course.

Of course? Wiping my soapy hands on my apron, I walked quickly through the downstairs rooms. Someone *could* be there. I did not normally lock the outside door during daylight hours, nor had Hettie. Crime in Pacific Grove, she had told me, was practically nonexistent.

"Well, not anymore," I muttered. The poison in the water tank had changed all that for us here at the lighthouse, even if Quincy still thought it had been an accident. I went to lock the door, but with key in hand I paused. If I locked it, Quincy would want an explanation. "Miss Hettie never locks it," he would say.

Yet if I did not lock it, how many more times, for how many more days and weeks would I be looking over my shoulder with that cold, sick fear in the pit of my stomach? I shuddered and locked the door. I would tell Quincy that being attacked in the woods by the "robber" had spooked me, and that he must simply carry his key on his person from now on.

I went about my routine duties in a distracted state. Just as the storm had kept the mischief-makers away from the lighthouse, it had kept me inside . . . and I could not stay in here forever. Not that I would want to . . .

Yet as I went about my duties, slowly working my way up to the top of the lantern, I realized that I was feeling a bit like a princess locked in a tower—but with one difference: Those princesses were always wanting to get out, and I wanted to stay in. If some prince came and called for me to let down my hair so he could climb up, I would simply tell him I'd cut it all off!

From the highest point in the lighthouse where one could stand, I looked out through the glass. "The mirror cracked from side to side," I muttered, then finished the quotation: " 'The curse has come upon me!' cried the Lady of Shalott." The curse came upon her when she looked out at the real world, instead of watching its reflection in her mirror. The curse then compelled the Lady of Shalott to go out into that real world, where she died. Very prettily of course, as the poem had been written by Alfred, Lord Tennyson.

I rather doubted I would die so prettily when my time came; certainly I was not ready yet. I most definitely did not want to go outside, where the danger was, through the woods, and over the steep, taxing hill to Carmel—yet that was what I had to do. If my time came, then at least I would not take it docilely, lying down with my hands folded, like the lady of the poem.

"Hah!" I declared, and my breath clouded the glass. I rubbed the moisture away with the tail of the apron I still wore, then went down to the watch room to do some planning that had nothing whatever to do with the lighthouse. Unless, that is, one considers the health and safety of the temporary keeper as having something to do with it.

Noon is about the earliest one can go to Carmel and expect the majority of the Carmelites to be up and functioning. I dropped in first on Arthur Heyer, to deliver his completed manuscript. I had never been to his house before. It was called Heyer and Heyer. I understood the pun, of course, but to me it sounded an awful lot like a law firm. Still, I preferred it to Xanadu. "Pleasure domes," I muttered, thinking of Artemisia's breasts. I wondered if the same comparison had ever occurred to Michael.

Heyer and Heyer was palatial by Carmel standards. The structure actually looked as if a good deal of planning had gone into it, as well as professional construction; perhaps an architect had even been employed. Certainly some landscaping had been done—the plants and bushes and flowers and trees showed hints of discipline amid their profusion. The gray-shingled house had a porch with a railing all the way around it, broad windows with diamond-shaped panes, and a front door painted blue. I tethered Bessie to a tree branch and went up and rang the bell. This was a real bell tied to a leather thong, not the kind of bellpull one finds in most houses nowadays.

Arthur appeared not from inside, but from around the back of the house. From the condition of his hands and knees, I surmised he had been gardening.

"Hello, Arthur," I said, coming down off the porch. "Are you the gardener, then? I was just remarking to myself that your house is a cut above most of the cottages around here, especially the landscaping. Did you do all this yourself?"

"Oh, no. Not exactly. Welcome, Fremont. Excuse me if I don't offer my hand, but as you see—" He held his dirty hands out in a rueful gesture.

"Looks like good, honest dirt to me." I smiled. Here on his own turf, or the turf on him, as the case might be, Arthur no longer looked like a Medium Brown Man. He looked like a farmer, and a happy one at that. I held up a rectangular package, wrapped in brown paper and tied around with string. I hadn't had a box. "Your manuscript. I finished it last night."

"Oh, my. My, yes!" He pinked up, then glanced at his hands and said, "Oh, dear." Forget the farmer; he was reminding me of Alice in Wonderland's White Rabbit. He went on, "You just wait right there! Stay on the flagstones, the ground's all mushy, it'll ruin your shoes. Or go back up on the porch. Yes, do go up! I'll just dash in the back way and clean myself up in a jiffy. Then I'll let you in and we can have a look. Shall we?"

"Absolutely," I said, trying not to seem too amused.

The porch was neat as a pin, unlittered by so much as a single pine needle. Obviously Arthur had been working hard this morning to clean up storm debris. The front yard had already received his attention too. Although the daisy bushes seemed a bit beaten down, and the wild fuchsias had lost a lot of their red and purple buds, dead leaves and downed branches and other unsightly clutter had already vanished from the scene. I was impressed. My own gardening skills, which I learned from Mother, are rudimentary in the extreme; I am good enough at the planning of a garden but not so good at the part that requires digging in the ground.

"You were going to tell me how much of this you've done yourself," I prompted as soon as he opened the door, although he had not precisely said that.

"Oh," he shrugged, then motioned me to come in, "I had someone put it all together for me. More than one someone, to be exact. Architect, contractor, you know, those kinds of people. Poor little rich boy," he made a face, "that's me. After I got moved in, I discovered I like to muck about in the dirt and mud. Put the plants in with my own hands, pat them down, water them, and help them grow. Sometimes—" he pinked again "—I talk to them. I think plants like that, it makes them thrive. They like music too— Oh! I'm sorry. I do get carried away."

I laughed. "That's quite all right. I shall have to try talking and music on Hettie's aspidistras. They are looking rather puny. But shall we be seated somewhere and take a look at your manuscript?"

"Oh, by all means. Not very hospitable of me to keep you standing in the hall."

I had become so accustomed to small houses that it quite amazed me to walk down an actual hallway with rooms on either side. I guessed there were ten rooms in Arthur's house, all on a single floor. The room toward which he led the way was directly across the hall from the kitchen at the back of the house. "A library," I exclaimed from its doorway, "a real library!"

"Had to have it," Arthur said, beaming. He rocked back on his heels and stuck his hands in his pockets, in a prosperous banker's sort of pose—except that his denim trousers were all muddy at the knees and his plaid flannel shirt had one elbow out. Hardly a banker's sort of dress. He added, "Can't live without my books."

Suddenly I thought of Michael's books, how they had filled a whole wall of shelves at Mrs. O'Leary's house, how many trips it had taken to move them all before the fire following the earthquake rushed to claim Vallejo Street . . . and I wondered what had happened to those books. They were not in his cottage. Subliminally I suppose I had noticed, but I hadn't consciously marked it before. "Michael, I mean Misha, would love this room," I said, unable to stop myself from talking about him. "Has he ever seen it?"

"No. That is, not that I recall. You see I, uh, I . . . I'm not as gregarious as the rest of them. Professor Storch comes over now and then, and Phoebe used to, but the rest get too, uh, boisterous for me. May we unwrap the manuscript now? I'm so eager to see it!"

"Yes, of course." I handed the package to Arthur and could not help smiling as I watched him unwrap it. No child had ever been more thrilled with a birthday present. Here in his own home he blossomed; naturally he would be more comfortable with the quieter Carmelites.

"Oh my, it does look handsome!" said Arthur, carefully setting the stacked pages down on a handsome, oversized partners desk.

I moved over next to him. "I did two title pages," I pointed out, "so that you can decide which you prefer. I am only a typewriter, not an editor, but it did occur to me that the addition of the word 'California' to your 'Central Coast' designation might be desirable. That way, people in other parts of the country will not wonder, central coast of what?"

"That is very thoughtful of you." Arthur gave me a meltingly warm smile. "However, there isn't a chance in the world that this little book, once it's published, will be distributed anywhere but right around here. I do it all myself, you see."

"You publish your own books?"

"Yes and no." He hunched his shoulders and ducked his head as if, for a moment, he were trying to make himself disappear. Then he lifted his face and a beatific grin spread across his face. "It's like with the house and all. The experts do the part I can't do because I don't know how, and then I do the rest. They do the actual typesetting and the printing and binding, but I do the distribution. You know, I take my books around to various little towns that have bookstores, and sometimes I leave a few copies in a grocery market or a general store—anyplace they'll sell them. I like doing it. Sometimes I make enough from one book to pay for the printing of the next. I consider that a great success."

"Yes, indeed! But perhaps you are too modest? There is such an interest at the present time in spritualism and the occult; mediums communicating with the dead and such are all the rage, so surely ghosts are an equally fashionable topic. Have you ever tried to get a publisher in New York interested in your ghost tales? Or even one in San Francisco, if you want to stay closer to home?"

This time Arthur didn't pink, he turned scarlet. "Oh, I couldn't. I wouldn't—I'd just—"

"You're shy," I said gently, laying my hand on his arm in what I hoped was a comforting and friendly manner. "I quite understand. I certainly didn't mean to embarrass you. I enjoyed typing your ghost stories, and that is a great deal more than I can say for many things I've typed in the two years I have been doing this kind of work."

"L-let me pay you," he said, slipping out from under my hand and going around to sit at his desk. "Ten cents a page? How many pages did it turn out to be?" He turned the stack over to see for himself so I did not interrupt his calculations, although I remembered how many pages and so could have told him the price. By focusing on this activity he was recovering his equilibrium.

I reflected that I never would have guessed what a sweet, gentle person lay beneath Arthur Heyer's medium-everything exterior. Not only that, but a multifaceted and modest individual. It is rare in my experience to meet a man (or woman) of considerable wealth who is not interested, first and foremost, in either increasing or parading it. Arthur had turned out to be most refreshing.

He presented his cheque with a flourish and invited me to stay for lunch, which I declined, but I did take a glass of iced tea. We sat at a lovely casement window looking out over the back garden, where he had been working when I arrived. I said, "I shall have to ask you to teach me the names of the plants. Having come from the East, I am unfamiliar with so much of the flora here. For example, what do you call those trees with blossoms that look like red bottlebrushes?"

"Bottlebrush trees," said Arthur, and we both laughed.

When I judged the mood was right I reached into my leather bag, took out an envelope, and removed from it the picture of Sabrina Howard. "You mentioned that you are fond of Phoebe Broom," I said by way of introducing the topic in a manner I hoped would be palatable to him.

"I am," Arthur nodded. "Deputy sheriffs were here. They think something may have happened to her."

"I know. I think so, too." I put the photograph face up on the table and slid it across to him. "This woman may have something to do with Phoebe's disappearance, in an indirect way. Have you ever seen the woman in this picture, Arthur? Do you know who she is?"

"Oh, my." He picked it up and brought it closer to his face. Apparently he was a bit shortsighted. "Lovely girl, just lovely. No, I don't know anybody who looks like that. I wish I did."

"Take your time. She has been seen in this area. Perhaps, if you don't know her personally, you may have been at some gathering or social occasion where she was present."

His smooth brow wrinkled with concentration. I presumed that Arthur had a sharp memory; the collection and accurate recording of his tales would require such a trait, and practice would have kept it honed. At last his expression cleared and he said triumphantly, "Yes! I remember her in a white dress, and her hair was different. It was kind of—you must excuse me, Fremont, I don't know much about women's hair—anyway she had kind of a long curl or two hanging down in the back, and one of them she'd pull over her shoulder like this." He stroked the side of his neck, then pulled a long face. "But I can't remember where it was. I seem to see her with a lot of people around. So either she was somebody's guest at one of our parties, or else . . . I know! I could have seen her when my parents were visiting back in the fall. They stayed at the Del Monte Hotel, and there's always a crowd around there."

"It certainly sounds likely. Anything else? A name, perhaps?"

After a couple of frowning minutes, Arthur shook his head. "No, sorry."

"Not at all. You've been very helpful." I restored the photograph to its protective envelope and gathered up my things. "And I've truly enjoyed talking with you."

"You have?" He sounded amazed.

"I have." I smiled.

Arthur escorted me to the front door. As we reached it he said in a dubious tone, "I keep thinking I also saw the lovely lady in the picture somewhere else, not just the big party, but another time. But the exact place just won't come to me. It's as if I can almost see her in a different place, but then the picture gets all dim."

"Don't try too hard," I advised. "Your memory will surely sharpen in time, and when it does, I hope you'll let me know."

• • •

Oscar and Mimi Peterson were working in their yard in a rather desultory fashion; there was a kind of thick, sludgy quality to the atmosphere around them that made me think they might recently have quarreled. Not an ideal time for a visit, but since they'd already seen me it could scarcely be helped.

There was once a king—of England, I think it was—called Longshanks; King Longshanks had had nothing on Oscar. If anything, Oscar had grown leaner in the couple of months since I'd first met him, which only made him seem taller still. The habitual pallor of his skin had acquired an unhealthy grayish tinge. Even Mimi lacked her usual ruddy glow today.

"Hello," I called out as I approached. "Isn't it wonderful that the storm's finally over!"

Oscar sneered. "Hello, Fremont. It'd be a lot more wonderful if it had never happened at all. Gawd, what a mess! We'll be forever getting all this farking shite cleaned up."

"Excuse the crude language, Fremont," Mimi said with a strained smile. "Thanks for dropping by. You've given us the perfect opportunity to stop work for a while. Let's go inside. Oscar, are you coming?"

"No!" he said viciously. "There's too much to do."

"I can come back another time," I said in an undertone to Miami, "but before I leave—"

"Don't be silly!" Mimi swiped her hand on her skirt before firmly taking my arm. "I hope you'll stay. I can use a change of company."

Although I did not want to stay, after that I could hardly refuse.

I had never been inside the Petersons' cottage before, as they seemed to spend a good deal of time—and much of Carmel with them—in the woodsy clearing that was more or less their yard. The layout of the cottage was much like Michael's, with a kitchen and dining area at one end of the largest room. There were differences, though: The entire cottage was on a bigger scale, and Oscar had built a magnificent fieldstone fireplace at the opposite end of the main room.

"The fireplace is spectacular," I said.

"Oscar's masterpiece. Unfortunately we can't eat stones, and for every one in that fireplace there's a poem that didn't get written, and so won't be published, and Oscar won't be paid." She sighed. "If we didn't have my income— But you don't want to hear all that. Coffee or tea, Fremont? I haven't made any lemonade today."

"Coffee, please. Mimi, I know it's none of my business, but I thought Oscar was the one with the family money."

She laughed, bitterly. "His family knows him too well. Oscar's money is in a trust fund. It leaks out to us one lean trickle at a time, and he has exotic tastes."

"Exotic?" I inquired, but she would not be further drawn. She set about warming over the breakfast coffee without saying more.

I reached into my leather bag and removed a small round tin box printed all over with a pattern of red plaid, which I took over to Mimi. "This is for you. To thank you for spending the night at my bedside when I was hurt."

Her face lit up as she opened the tin. "Shortbread! How thoughtful you are, Fremont, but you don't have to give me anything. I was glad to sit with you. That's what neighbors are for."

"Nevertheless I am grateful. You must accept it."

"We'll open up the tin and have some with our coffee, shall we?"

Mimi and I gossiped and chatted in female fashion, and munched on the shortbread, which proved to be quite good. I ascertained that she did not see anything to be alarmed about where Misha was concerned, which meant either that Mimi was not very observant, or simply that the use of drugs, such as alcohol, did not much concern her. Probably the latter.

When at last I judged the moment was right, I took out the photograph and held it up before Mimi. I did not let go of it, for fear I should not get it back. The few anxious moments I'd felt with Arthur had taught me a lesson: From now on, the photograph would not leave my hands. "Mimi," I asked without preamble, "do you know this woman?"

Instead of drawing closer, she actually pulled back. Her face, which had become animated and pink-cheeked while we talked, went white. Slowly she shook her head. "No."

"Take your time." I leaned over and held the picture closer. "If you don't actually know her, perhaps you've seen her somewhere?"

"No, I've never seen her in my life." Mimi was recovering. Belligerance hardened her square jaw and flashed in her blue eyes. "What are you doing, carrying around a picture of somebody you don't even know? Who do you think you are, Fremont Jones?"

CHAPTER

FOURTEEN

Withstanding anger is not so difficult if one realizes that the angry person is not likely to be careful of what she says, and therefore one might learn something that otherwise one would never know.

Presuming that Mimi didn't really want to know who I thought I was, just for the sake of response I mumbled, "I'm terribly sorry—"

And she interrupted: "We don't need busybodies in Carmel, poking their noses into people's privacy. It's despicable!"

"I didn't mean to upset you."

Oscar came through the door, asking, "What's the matter?"

I spoke up. "Mimi seems to think I'm meddling, I'm not sure into what, but I was just trying to get to the bottom of something that may have to do with Phoebe's disappearance."

"Phoebe!" Mimi exclaimed.

Oscar shook his head and trudged over to the sink. "Don't understand what all the fuss is about. People in this country have a right to go where they want to go, when they want to go. Farking bang-bang shoot-'em-up deputy sheriffs . . ." His voice trailed off.

"What does the woman in the picture have to do with Phoebe?" Mimi asked. Her eyes looked round and scared, and her anger was gone.

"Perhaps nothing. Perhaps it's only a coincidence, but Phoebe was trying to help me identify her and then all of a sudden she—I mean Phoebe—was gone."

"Somebody else gone besides Phoebe?" Sitting next to his wife, Oscar removed his glasses and began to polish them on his shirt. Without the glasses his face looked worn and defenseless.

"This woman." Dead and gone, I thought. I held the photograph toward Oscar. "Do you know her?"

He craned his neck and squinted while continuing to polish the lenses of his glasses. "Never saw her in my life. But then, I don't pay much attention to people."

"That's true," said Mimi, leaning affectionately into her husband, "he doesn't. Oscar only just barely lives in the real world. I'm the one who has to keep up with things, and I can tell you for sure the woman in that picture isn't one of our circle. I'm sorry I jumped all over you, Fremont. It's just that Oscar and I have a mania for privacy."

I slipped the photograph back into my bag, saying offhandedly, "Really? You always have so many people around here I'd never have guessed you to have such a mania."

They looked at each other. "Not personally," Mimi qualified, "for Carmel. For the whole community. Having the police here—"

"Sheriffs," Oscar inserted.

"—was difficult for all of us. We just want to be left alone."

"Amen!" Oscar said emphatically. Then he put his glasses back on, carefully adjusting the earpieces.

I stood up and slung my bag over my shoulder. "I quite understand, and so if you'll excuse me, I'll be on my way."

Both Petersons mumbled separate versions of thanks-for-stopping-by. In the doorway I turned back. "Oh, one last thing I'd like to ask you. Was Phoebe in the habit of taking off abruptly, with no warning? Did she have someone in particular in whom she might have confided?"

"That's two things," Oscar observed mildly, without offering to answer either one.

"We didn't know her well enough to say." Mimi, of course, filled the gap. As a helpmeet sort of wife, she went more than halfway. "Phoebe kept to herself a good deal. She was very absorbed in her work."

"I see. Well thanks, and good-bye for now."

I left with my mind abuzz from the Petersons' odd dynamics. Even so, I could not fail to notice that the out-of-doors smelled wonderfully fresh after all that rain. I fancied I could almost hear trees and bushes and flowers responding, growing.

Bessie raised her head and whuffled as I came up. "One more stop, old girl," I said, giving her neck a pat, "and then we'll go back home." With a curious mixture of reluctance and anticipation, I turned her head toward Casanova Street, and Xanadu.

Michael had obviously done absolutely nothing in the way of afterstorm cleanup. His yard looked much worse than the Petersons'. I picked up my skirt so as not to drag the hem in the dirt as I went up the walk.

The front door was already open; as I approached, Artemisia's shapely form materialized on the threshold. "Oh, Fremont!" she wailed. "He's gone!"

"Gone? What exactly do you mean?"

She sniffled. Her eyes were swollen, so I assumed she had been crying. "I mean he left this morning, at a beastly early hour. I tried to stop him, but I couldn't, and he wouldn't take me with him either. He said he needed to be alone, and he went as soon as the storm was over. On that wretched yacht of his!"

"You mean the *Katya?*"

She nodded, so obviously miserable that I impulsively reached out and put one arm around her. I walked with her to a grouping of chairs near the cold fireplace and sat us both down. "The *Katya* is a sloop," I said.

"Sloop, yacht, who cares? I *hate* boats! I get *so* seasick!"

"Then it's a good thing he didn't take you with him."

"You needn't be so reasonable about it."

"I don't see why not. If he's gone, he's gone. Michael has a habit of doing this, you know."

"Doing what?" Artemisia wiped her eyes on the tail of the red scarf holding back her wild hair. Her dress, for once, was an ordinary blue cotton flannel with buttons all the way down the front.

"Going off by himself," I said. "Did you see him before he left?"

She nodded glumly.

"Was he, er, inebriated?"

"Hungover, maybe, but he drank gallons of coffee and ate twice as much breakfast as I've ever seen him eat. You may as well know, we had an awful row."

"Really?" I tried not to sound too happy about it.

Artemisia bit her lip and a single tear dripped down her right cheek. "I just don't understand him, Fremont. First I thought he was in love with a woman in San Francisco, who turned out to be you, but then he didn't bring her—I mean you—back with him; and when you finally did come on your own you didn't even take the cottage he found for you, so I thought you didn't want him anyhow. Which meant I had a chance. Lately I really believed I'd wormed my way into his affections, but—but—" She choked up.

"I do want him," I said quietly. It was the first time I had acknowledged this to another human being, including my very dear friend Meiling, and I went all dizzy with the risk of it.

Artemisia's brown eyes widened. "You do? But you're always pushing him away."

"I know. And he is always doing the same to me." I regarded the tips of my shoes peeking out from under my skirt. "That seems to be, at least in part, the nature of our relationship. Anyway, lately I'm not sure about anything." And I had begun to scare myself with this kind of talk.

"I know just what you mean! *Gawd!*" She threw the back of her hand against her forehead in a dramatic gesture and slid down in her chair with her feet sticking out pigeon-toed in front of her—a posture that even a four-year-old child would have been chided for.

From this position she addressed the ceiling, as if I were not there. "It isn't as if I wanted to *marry* the man, for heaven's sake. I only wanted to have some fun, for us to enjoy each other, maybe even live together; but not *all* the time because of course I have to have my own space to create my art. Which reminds me," she tilted her wrist away from her eyes and looked at me without otherwise moving a muscle, "you *are* typing my *Merchant of Dreams,* aren't you?"

"Yes, but there have been some unavoidable interruptions. It's a fascinating story. I'm awed by your talent, Artemisia. Truly."

"Thank you." She heaved a great sigh and addressed the ceiling again. "My publisher will hate it. He will say it is too sensational, and I will argue with him, and then he will make qualifications—he'll say it's too sensational to have been written by a *woman.* He will encourage me to apply a male pseudonym, like poor Charlotte Brontë did with *Jane Eyre*— That reminds me." Suddenly, in one fluid motion Artemisia righted her posture. "Phoebe is rather a Jane Eyreish sort of person, isn't she? I find I miss her a good deal. Surely she will come back on her own, don't you think? Someone like Phoebe couldn't *really* have any connection to this . . . this," she made a dismissive motion with her hand, "*Sabrina* person, could she?"

In the face of this flurry of questions I reflected that one finds prejudice in the most unexpected places. "You surprise me," I said. "I thought you would be sympathetic to Sabrina's plight, as well as Phoebe's. What I think is that they have both met with foul play, probably at the hands of the same person. I think further that this person is someone powerful enough in this locale to suppress whatever he or she wants suppressed. And further still, I think this powerful person wants me to cease and desist from investigating, and has laid down certain threats in order that I should take the point." I stood and hoisted my leather bag. "I had thought to tell Michael this, but as he is not here I suppose I will just tell you: I *have* taken the point. I have, if you like, been frightened off. Warned away. However one chooses to express it. Like Pilate's wife, I wash my hands!"

"You're getting that mixed up with Caesar's wife. It was Pilate who washed his hands. His wife, I think, had dreams. So did Caesar's."

"I stand corrected. And speaking of women who have dreams, I shall finish the typing of your manuscript in another week, provided nothing untoward befalls. I hope that is satisfactory?" I began to move to the door.

"Oh, yes. That will be fine. Fremont, what exactly did you mean about Misha having a habit of going away by himself?"

"Just that he has always done it, for as long as I've known him, which is slightly more than two years. Don't worry about him. He'll come back eventually, and when he does he won't tell you where he's been, and you will want to strangle him but it won't do the least bit of good."

She tipped her head to one side and smiled at me—a rather calculating smile—and she said, "You know him very well."

I smiled back. "I used to think I did, but I am not so sure anymore. He seems to have changed, Artemisia. You will probably be happy to know that you have had more effect on him than you seem to believe. And as for what I said earlier, about wanting him: Forget it, please. I am going back to San Francisco as soon as Hettie Houck returns to the lighthouse, which she has promised will be no later than the first of July. San Francisco is where I belong, not here; the only thing I want is to go home!"

With that I made a rather grand exit, or so I intended, but the effect was spoiled when Artemisia came running after me.

"Wait, Fremont!" she cried. "I forgot to tell you something."

One hand on Bessie's bridle, I forced myself to turn around. "Yes?"

"Misha—Michael, as you call him—wants you to take care of the Maxwell in his absence. He said to tell you he's left it in Monterey by the wharf, where the boat is kept. The keys will be with this man." The piece of paper she thrust at me was still warm—she had drawn it from her bosom.

I stuck it quickly in my pocket, then climbed into the shay. "Thank you."

She shrugged and smiled again, more genuinely this time. "I guess that should tell me where I stand. He leaves you the car, and I get stuck with the damn cat."

"Well, you do already have a car," said I, the paragon of reason, waving as I drove off.

KEEPER'S LOG
February 11, 1907
Wind: SW, moderate
Weather: Sunny after trace of morning fog
Comments: No commercial activity on the bay, due to this being a Sunday.

I waited impatiently for Quincy to come back from church. Yesterday I'd brought the Maxwell back from where Michael had left it near Fisherman's Wharf, and now I was dying to go out for a spin. Poor Bessie—my affections had quite completely deserted the horse as soon as Max was mine again. And just to think: I was the person who had said to Michael some ten months ago that automobiles would never catch on because they do not have the personality of a horse!

So I was fallible—the way things had been going lately, that was not exactly news to me.

I smiled, thinking of how pleased Quincy had been when I suggested that, as I now had the Maxwell, he might as well drive Hettie's rig to church. He'd driven off looking mighty sharp in his best suit, grinning from ear to ear, his usual laconic manner quite gone. "They will not know you," I'd teased, "they will think a handsome stranger has come in your stead."

When Quincy still had not returned by one o'clock, I was worried, but not greatly. He was probably doing what I wanted to do: driving around in the beautiful weather. Perhaps he had a lady friend to impress—if so, he would surely do it today, he would sweep her off her feet. I certainly didn't begrudge him a little time off. God knew he had taken the watches often enough for me.

On watch today there was little to observe, aside from the grandeur of the scenery. People do not seem to do much recreational sailing on Monterey Bay. On Sundays when the fishing boats do not go out, the bay waters belong to the seals and fishes. It occurred to me as I went back down the spiral stairs from the watch room that I had not seen a whale for many days. Apparently the migration was over. If the whalers did not stop chasing every whale that came into sight, one of these days the migrations of whales would be over permanently. Already along the East Coast some types of whales pass by no more.

I fastened the black shawl with a brooch at the throat so that it would not blow open, then taped a note on the lighthouse door: I WILL BE BACK SOON. F.J. The note was primarily for Quincy, which was why I kept it simple. I checked my pockets—yes, I had money in case anything happened, and a handkerchief if I needed it.

"Well, Max," I said as I climbed behind the wheel, "here we go again!" And we were off. I must say it was a great pleasure to drive again, and the requisite skill returned as if it had been only yesterday instead of months since Max was my companion and helper in the harrowing confusion of post-earthquake San Francisco.

Some automobiles cannot make it up Carmel Hill, but I knew that this was not the case with Max, as Michael had done the trip frequently, a few times with me along. Nevertheless I did not intend to pose that steep challenge to the Maxwell today, and drove steadily if bumpily toward the Pacific Grove gate to the Seventeen Mile Drive. I drove through Del Monte Forest all the way to the Carmel gate just for fun, then turned around and went back again. On the way back I made the turns that took me to Braxton Furnival's house—which had been my goal all along.

I passed through the gates with their bogus coat of arms, and as I approached the looming lodge I was glad to see there were not a lot of cars about. I had not been quite sure what I would do if he were entertaining guests, whether I should have the nerve to crash the party or not. Probably not. I am not particularly fond of large social gatherings, though I stood in for my mother at enough of them with Father after she died. I doubt anyone would ever know how impatient I'd been with all that socializing—I am sure Father never did.

Those occasions were my first exercise at dissembling, I thought as I stopped the Maxwell along one side of the driveway and unpinned the brooch so that I could leave the shabby shawl in the car. Standing on the running board I shook out my skirts. I am not overfond of clothes, and have not greatly minded the reduced state—not to mention quality—of my wardrobe, but for just a moment I thought with envy of Irma Fox and the fashionable traveling costume she'd worn when I first met her. Someday I should like to own a sporty duster—though I could do without those hats with the veils. I loathe hats almost as much as I do corsets.

I was wearing my second-best dress, which was also second-hand, and therefore of a better fabric and cut than I could have afforded otherwise. Bright blue in color, the dress has a jabot of lace at the neck and more lace at the hem of the sleeves, and a full skirt that should have had beneath it more ruffled petticoats than the single one I was wearing. It was hardly as exciting a garment as Sabrina would have worn, but Braxton was bound to find it more interesting than the skirts and blouses he had heretofore always seen me wear.

The role of seductress was a new one for me, so I was nervous as I lifted the heavy knocker and let it fall. I repeated the process, and tried not to fidget. Though I strained my ears, I could not hear footsteps or anything at all through that heavy door.

At last it opened, and I looked into the face of a man I'd never seen before. A devilishly handsome face that made me wonder if the *Californios* had reclaimed their state overnight. He was young, not far from my own age, I would guess, with obsidian eyes and a riot of glistening black curls, ecru skin, and the long thin nose of an *hidalgo*'s Spanish heritage. He looked down that nose at me without a word of greeting.

"Good afternoon," I said, smiling sweetly. "Is Mr. Furnival at home?"

The molten black eyes blinked once and he said, "Yeah."

"My name is Fremont Jones. I was just out driving in my automobile and decided on the spur of the moment to pay Braxton a visit. May I come in?"

"Yeah." He stepped back, turned around, and yelled into the gloom, "Brax!" Then he turned back, scanned me up and down, and said, "I think he's out on the terrace. You know where that is?"

"Yes," I said, gambling that I could find it from inside the house. But I did not have to go looking, because Braxton had heard the fellow shout and came on the run.

"Ramon," he said, "what— Oh, Fremont. Well hey, great to see you!"

"I know it is very rude of me, Braxton, but I have the use of a friend's car for a few weeks and so of course the first thing I did was to give myself a tour of the Seventeen Mile Drive, and I just couldn't resist dropping in on you. I'm so glad to find you at home."

"That's just fine, really fine." He took my hand and gazed warmly at me, the smile lines around his eyes crinkling. He had the ability to make you think, when he focused on you like that, that the rest of the world was no longer of any importance to him.

Oh my, I thought, I came to seduce and here I am being seduced. Well, at least this should be interesting.

While still gazing into my eyes Braxton stretched out his other arm and made a come-hither motion with his hand. The handsome young *hidalgo* obeyed the motion, and Braxton said, "Fremont, allow me to introduce Ramon Reyes. Ramon works with me from time to time."

"How do you do." I nodded to Ramon, as I could not very well shake hands—Braxton was still holding my right hand quite firmly.

"Fremont," Ramon acknowledged, sliding his eyes sideways and regarding me slyly. Half of his upper lip lifted, something between a smile and a sneer.

"Miss Jones to you, Ramon," said Braxton, cuffing him roughly but playfully on the shoulder. Why men have to hit each other as a form of communication I will never understand. At least he let go of me to do it, and I got my hand back.

"I never stand on formality," I said quickly, "I prefer Fremont. Truly."

"Miss Jones," said Braxton, ignoring my words, "is a woman of many talents, as well as obvious beauty."

"Oh, certainly!" I said, with my version of a flirtatious little laugh.

"Yeah, and I guess you wanna be alone with all those talents, not to mention the beauty. Right, Brax?" Ramon might look as if he had just sailed over from Castile, but he sounded like a cowboy straight out of Brooklyn, New York.

Braxton did not verbally reply to this, but aimed an exaggerated wink at Ramon and said in an undertone to me, "Clever fella, ain't he?"

My stomach sank somewhere down around my toes and I wondered what I had gotten myself into—but there was no other way. I

166

smiled and said, "I understand you were sitting on your terrace? I should very much like to see the view."

Braxton agreed that this was a fine idea, and offered his arm. We went through the baronial hall, which had crossbeams in the lofty ceiling and stairs, supported by more of those columns that resemble barely hewn tree trunks, winding around and around a square central core.

I paused in the middle of the hall, bringing us both to a halt, and looked up. "What an interesting house you have," I said. "It seems quite large for one person."

"I do a lot of entertaining." He tugged me forward. "For business purposes, of course."

"Ah yes. You are trying to attract buyers for large tracts of Del Monte Forest land, if I remember the letter I typed for you correctly."

"Estates, that's what we want to develop here."

"Like on Long Island, or in Newport?" I inquired.

"That type of clientele, yes." He pronounced it *klee-on-tell*.

"Only the wealthiest people will do, I suppose," I said as Braxton gestured for me to precede him through a doorway that led to a corridor with more doors on either side. While he gave me chapter and verse on selling land to the wealthy, I tried surreptitiously to get a glimpse through the open doors on either side with my peripheral vision. But alas, my eyes do not have the hyperacute capability of my ears. I can hear sounds that many people cannot, but my eyesight is only normal—I cannot see in the dark, and Grosse-Dark would indeed have been a fitting name for this house. My ears on this occasion were uninformative, but my nose performed well, picking up the scent of onions. I slewed a glance over that way and found a closed door that probably led to the kitchen.

A moment later I saw a bright blue and green rectangle that must have denoted an outside door. I turned rapidly, my skirts swirling, and put myself in Braxton's path while I grabbed his arm impulsively. "I have the most wonderful idea! Before we go out, why don't you give me a tour of your house? I'm sure it's fascinating, and I'd so much love to see all the rooms. I expect you modeled it after those European hunting lodges, did you not? The ones that are used by royalty when they go shooting in the woods?"

I had calculated that the word "royalty" would please Braxton and it did: He beamed and allowed as how he'd had something of the sort in mind. But then he said, "I'm afraid I can't give you the tour right now, Fremont. The housekeeper hasn't been here in three weeks—her mother took sick and she had to go look after the poor woman. So I haven't had anybody to clean up after the last house party. Things are a mess!"

"As if I'd mind something like that!" I leaned in toward him and allowed the side of my breast to rest for a moment against his arm. "Please?"

I could feel him respond to my nearness. He began to glow like a smoldering coal, giving off heat. Yet he said, "Another time, Fremont. Another time."

I broke away, chiding playfully, "Good heavens, what a fussy old housewife you've turned out to be, Braxton Furnival. Who would have believed such a thing?" Then I plunged toward the outside door, glancing gaily back over my shoulder as if to say, *You can't catch me!*

But he was bigger than I, stronger, heavier, with longer arms and legs. He could catch me, and he did.

CHAPTER
FIFTEEN

KEEPER'S LOG
February 14, 1907
Wind: NW, mild to moderate, with gusts
Weather: Fair and cold
Comments: Swells and surf high but not heavy. U.S. Coast Guard training ship in and out of bay. Tank of whale oil to be off-loaded from tender for light station.

*A*s I wrote the date, February 14, into the logbook, I realized today was St. Valentine's Day.

"Hah!" I said in a derisive tone—but then I sat gazing out the watch room window, lost in a reverie and trying to remember when exactly it was that I had first realized those tantalizingly frilly, heart-shaped missives could never be for me. Valentines were incompatible with the lifestyle I had chosen. Fremont Jones neither receives nor sends Valentines—I had known that before I even *was* Fremont Jones, back when I was still called by my first name, Caroline. "What a pity," I lamented, and for a while I did regret it.

But before I could pity myself for long, it occurred to me that this year my heartless duplicity might earn me one of those heart-shaped missives. A fine irony, indeed, if it came to pass: Braxton Furnival might very well send me a Valentine. He seemed smitten enough.

On Sunday, three days earlier, I had allowed him to kiss me on his terrace. I might have rather enjoyed it if I hadn't suspected him of having murdered both Sabrina Howard and Phoebe, and doing God-knows-what with their bodies. In fact, I did allow myself to enjoy the kiss for the briefest of moments, just long enough for Braxton to know it, before I broke away.

"Oh dear!" I'd cried, putting my hands to my cheeks in imitation of maidenly shock. "I'm afraid you misunderstand me, Mr. Furnival." Then I'd asked to use the necessary; ordinarily I just say "bathroom" but I was trying to be delicate. Fleeing from the terrace as I made my request, I had assured him, "Just tell me where it is, I'll find it!" And he, faced with a flustered female, did.

As I'd hoped he might, he directed me upstairs. There was probably a bathroom downstairs, somewhere in the proximity of the kitchen, but that would be for the help. As I ran up the stairs I strained my hearing, in an effort to determine if Ramon were anywhere in the vicinity, but I could not hear anything above the noise of my own feet and skirts and beating heart.

The stairs led to a gallery that ran around the square enclosure of the great hall; all the rooms appeared to open off this gallery. Counting doors I found the bathroom, opened and shut the door without going in, then continued stealthily on around the gallery. I felt horribly exposed, and edged along with my back skimming the wall, as far away from the railing as I could get.

A damp, slightly rotten smell hung about like a miasma. Perhaps

Braxton had told the truth about the rooms being in need of cleaning. If only one of the doors had been left open, or even ajar . . .

Footsteps! Holding skirt and petticoat up, clutched close to my body so that they wouldn't rustle, I ran back to the bathroom, slipped inside and pulled the chain to flush the toilet. For a crazy, disjointed moment I lost myself in admiration of the engineering skill that had brought a real bathroom to this forest when in Carmel they had only outhouses. Then I glanced in the mirror and decided I had best splash some cold water on my flushed face. I hate to admit it but this type of activity seemed to agree with me—my color was high, my eyes sparkled, and a couple of escaped tendrils of hair seemed to be trying to curl. I had seldom looked better.

While dousing my face, I heard the footsteps come to a stop outside the bathroom door. My heart thumped with uncomfortable force. I could feel the human presence on the other side of that door; how I wished for the clairvoyance to discern if it meant me harm or not! I had no weapon, nor any way to get one that I could see unless I broke the mirror and used one of its shards. Even as the thought occurred to me, I knew it would be an overreaction.

Though my fears were nearly running out of control, I managed to rein them in by telling myself that Braxton Furnival, no matter what else he may or may not have done, was for now only interested in one thing from me: sex. And until he had satisfied himself in that area, I should be safe from other threat. I took a deep breath and opened the bathroom door.

It was not Braxton who stood outside waiting, but Ramon. With a glassy-eyed stare he muttered, "It sure took you long enough," and pushed rudely past me into the bathroom. Braxton himself had waited at the bottom of the stairs, gazing upward with a lovelorn expression. "Tell me you will come again!" he said when I descended. And I had promised to think about it.

On Monday I received a note from Braxton, apologizing in flowery terms for his forwardness. On Tuesday he sent the actual flowers, via a sullen Ramon as messenger, with a note attached that said he would like to call on me if I would send a note of permission back. I sent one of the flowers, a yellow hothouse carnation, instead. Ramon smirked, so I told him not to eat it or lose it along the way or

Braxton would hear from me. And now I wondered what, if anything, today would bring.

It had better bring the tender with our supply of whale oil for the light, according to schedule. A "tender," I'd learned from Hettie, is a ship that tends to other ships by hauling supplies and communications back and forth; and as lighthouses (officially called light stations) are overseen by the Navy, tenders also tend to us.

I got up and went downstairs to look at the clock in the parlor. I no longer have a watch to consult—the one I was given when I worked for the Red Cross popped its mainspring, and watches are too dear for my circumstances. It was eight-thirty. The tender should come before noon, and there were certain things I had to do to get ready.

Speaking of things that needed tending: I had to count Quincy among that number, though he protested mightily. Quincy had a broken collarbone, not to mention a load of guilt that was almost as crippling. No matter how I tried, I could not convince him that the guilt was unnecessary. And of course I couldn't tell him that I believed the accident that happened to him was intended for me. If anyone should have felt guilty it was I—and as a matter of fact, I did—but if I let guilt cripple me and keep me from action then I should feel worse still.

Quincy drove Hettie's rig to church on Sunday, and as I had guessed might happen, he couldn't resist taking a lady friend for a ride in the country afterward. They'd gone up from Monterey toward Moss Landing. To make a long story (the version that came out of Quincy's mouth) short, the shay lost the wheel on the driver's side and Quincy went down, landing on his shoulder. His friend was unhurt.

They had kept him at the hospital overnight for observation, and it was nearly nightfall by the time he had convinced someone to come and tell me what happened. As one might imagine, I was by then more than a little alarmed. Poor Quincy blamed only himself: The upkeep of the shay was his responsibility, he must have overlooked a weakness in that wheel; he never should have driven out so far without permission; if he hadn't been "all puffed-up, showing off" for his lady friend he might have seen the rock that supposedly the shay had run over—etc., etc., etc. And now, just to make Quincy feel worse, he couldn't do his regular work properly because of having his shoulder all bandaged up and the use of only one hand.

I grinned ruefully. If the situation had been less fraught with uncertainty, and probable danger, I should quite have enjoyed pampering Quincy. I went outside and found him scattering feed for Hettie's white leghorn chickens with his one good hand.

"Good morning," I said as I approached. "Another beautiful day."

The chickens squawked and flapped their wings but they needn't have worried—I was not about to venture among them, much less threaten their food supply. If any of Mother Nature's creatures are less endearing to me than a chicken, I cannot think which. Possums might perhaps score a tie.

"Morning," said Quincy, bobbing his head in the battered black hat. He still wouldn't look me in the eye; hadn't since he came home on Monday.

"The tender is supposed to off-load some oil today," I said. "Hettie has put it on the schedule."

Quincy glanced up, surprised because he had forgotten, then quickly away. He put down the feed bucket and with his good hand clasped the hurt shoulder, unconsciously, I was sure.

I continued, "I want you to supervise. You'll have help—I've hired a man to work with you until your shoulder is healed, which as you know will be at least six weeks, and even then you will not be able to do any heavy lifting right away."

"But Miss Fremont—"

I ignored him, having expected all sorts of tiresome protests. "His name is Pete Carlson. I gather he is a sort of man-of-all-work about town. I've told him he is to report to you, and to do whatever you ask of him. I want you to really use him, have him do the work and don't strain yourself. Is that clear, Quincy?"

He regarded me with such a lugubrious expression that I longed to tickle him or make a funny face or *something*. But of course I simply waited for him to agree, and in a moment he began shaking his head slowly, rhythmically, from side to side in a way that made me think of dolefully swinging funeral bells.

"Quincy, whatever is the matter?"

"Wished you'da talked to me about it first, Miss—I mean, Fremont."

"If I'd done that you would only have insisted that you don't need help, or told me how terrible you feel that we have to spend money to pay someone to help you out when the accident was your own fault, or some such nonsense. You know you would have, so it would have been a complete waste of time to tell you beforehand."

"But Pete Carlson . . ." More doleful shaking of the head.

I have only just so much capacity to be amused by these things, and even that exceeds my small store of patience. I said curtly, "I took his name from a list that Hettie left for me. If he were not reliable, I'm sure she would not have put his name on the list. Nevertheless, Quincy, it is you and not I who will be supervising the man. If Pete Carlson's work is unsatisfactory in any way, all you have to do is say so and I will fire him and hire someone else. All right?"

Finally Quincy nodded, though he did not say anything and there was a dubious look in his eyes. The nod was enough for me.

"Good," I said. "Pete will be here at nine o'clock. Between the two of you, you can handle the oil delivery. If you need me, I shall be typing in the watch room."

I was about halfway through Artemisia's *The Merchant of Dreams*, eager to finish with the manuscript for reasons of my own that had nothing to do with typewriting, but also eager to find out what would happen next to the naive but intelligent Heloise.

> I began to live for the night. I no longer came fully alive until the sun went down. All day I waited for that delicious moment when I could lay my head upon my pillow, let out my breath in a long sigh and close my eyes. Dreams, I was finding, were like love—the more one gave them away, the more one had to give. That in my case the dreams were being paid for did not seem to matter; I still felt as if I were giving them away, and Jonah Morpheus received them with the most tender care and gratitude. He could not have been a more attentive listener. He hung on my every word.

There was just one problem, a minor problem surely, but still irritating because it would not go away. I became slightly, only very slightly ill. I had caught a chill that would not go away. I felt feverish from time to time, but not all the time; and my appetite was not quite right. So of course I grew a little frail. I told myself that this slight illness would pass, but a week went by and then another, and my condition did not change except, perhaps, to worsen.

My dreaming self was unconcerned; the dreams went on, more vivid, more exciting from night to night. There were nights—many nights—when I wanted the dreams to last forever; because it was with morning's light that the problems came.

My bones ached. My head felt as if it floated an inch above my neck without quite connecting, and if I moved in any direction too quickly, I became dizzy enough to fall. Getting out of bed was, therefore, a laborious task. Dressing myself was an effort that caused my pulse to race and beads of perspiration to break out upon my forehead. Walking to the streetcar was an unsteady affair that required the most minute attention to balance, and to the business of putting one foot in front of the other. And through all this, I carried each night's dreams within me like a woman nine and a half months gone, so desperately did I long each morning to deliver myself of them to Dr. Morpheus.

The angelic being, Thad, knew better now than to speak to me upon my arrival; rather he helped me up the stairs in the most solicitous fashion; the cat, Shadow, greeted me always by rushing beneath my skirts as soon as I crossed the threshold, and rubbing luxuriously against my ankles. In the room of veils, Jonah Morpheus would already be waiting; he would take my hand, dismissing Thad with a glance, lead me to the chaise lounge, and lay me tenderly—oh so tenderly—down. My heart would cease beating and my breath would stop until I heard him say the single word: "Begin."

The days passed in this fashion, and the nights; the weeks accumulated into months; I was paid over and over again. Money was no longer of primary importance to me—how could it be, when every morning I awoke feeling as if I might burst before giving Jonah my dream? But inevitably the morning came when something changed.

I had had a particularly hard time getting up and getting dressed that morning. I hadn't been able to put my hair up properly and strands of it kept tumbling down—I'd tuck them back but they would only fall down again, for I had scarcely enough strength to wield a hairpin. Exactly how I got to the Morpheus Foundation I could not say—presumably, as always, on the streetcar, yet upon my arrival and feeling the velvet softness of Shadow upon my legs, I realized that I could not remember a moment of the ride. And so when Thad took my arm to assist me up the stairs, I broke the rules. I said to him: "I think I may be too ill to continue."

"Shh!" he said, raising one finger in the manner that goes with that sound, and he frowned. Oh! The pain of that frown—it pierced me to the heart. Have you ever thought how you might feel if you'd made an angel cry? That is how I felt. And so when we reached the room of veils and Thad handed me over to Jonah Morpheus, all unwittingly I broke the rules again. I said to Morpheus: "Forgive me, I—"

And he pronounced: "Silence!" His voice reverberated like a great gong, sending ripples through all the veils. The chandelier flashed once, a great white light, then dimmed.

And I fainted.

"Oh, botheration!" I said, jumping about a foot when the doorbell rang. The bellpull was attached to one of those apparatuses that they have for the servants in large houses, so that it rang in the watch room—right over my head. Leaving poor Heloise was the last thing I wanted to do at the moment, but duty called.

"Coming!" I yelled as I wound my way down the circular stairs. I caught a toe in my hem and slipped; I would have fallen if I hadn't grabbed the railing and hung on. As it was, I felt a twinge in an old ankle injury and cursed myself for carelessness. With Quincy already incapacitated, we certainly did not need another injured person around here!

The bell rang again, but when I wrenched the front door open, there was no one there. "If you're in such a hurry that you can't wait for a person to get to the door . . ." I muttered—but then as I was closing the door, I looked down. The mailman had left a package on the step. A long, thin package. I leaned out, glanced to left and right, checked the stamps and the cancellation and the return address before taking the package in hand. It was from Gump's, a fashionable San Francisco store that specializes in imports. The sort of store that

Father—and one supposes his new wife, Augusta—might gravitate toward if they were in San Francisco rather than Boston, but as it is, no one of my acquaintance would be likely to frequent Gump's. No one except—

"Michael!" I pounced upon the box, which defeated my best attempts to open it until I took it into the kitchen and got a knife and performed dissection along the seam.

"Oh my," I said, drawing forth the item from within. Smooth as silk, hard as rock and as sturdy, crowned and tipped in— "Oh my!" I said again. Michael had sent me a walking stick of black walnut crowned and tipped not in brass, but in gold. The head of the stick was carved like the head of a dragon, and a secret button was hidden in the dragon's scales. I pressed and felt the click that released the blade, which I then drew forth with the most satisfactory sweep of arm and hand. The balance of the weapon was perfect, far superior to the similar secret weapon I'd lost many months before.

As I feinted and parried around the kitchen, a small envelope caught my eye—it must have fallen on the floor in my eagerness to unwrap the gift. I did not need to read the note in order to know who had sent me this excellent and most welcome of presents. My heart sang as I sheathed the weapon and turned it into an innocent-looking walking stick once more. He was in San Francisco, he was thinking of me, he cared!

The note was indeed from Michael. As I read it I could see in my mind his dear face:

My dearest Fremont,

If as I expect you would scorn a Valentine, you may consider this an early birthday gift. I have a feeling you may be in need of something along this line, not in April but now. Be assured that, in spite of all appearances, I have your best interests at heart.

Your devoted friend,
Michael Kossoff

I read Michael's words over three times and then I did a silly thing—I put the paper with the words his hand had written to my cheek and closed my eyes . . . and that is how I was standing when

Quincy came to tell me that the tender had been sighted coming up from the south.

Late in the afternoon I took my walking stick for a walk across the scrubby dunes. The deer, which feed at this time of day as well as in early morning, were so unafraid they did not move until I was nearly upon them. When I reached the rocks at the water's edge I turned to the right and followed the curve of the bay toward Lovers Point, about a mile distant as the crow flies—or gull, as the case may be. There was a particular rock formation that I thought might make a lofty seat, offering a different view from the one I saw so often out the watch room window.

I was walking both for pleasure and for the exercise. Typewriting is such a sedentary occupation, and due to my late reluctance to walk through the woods, I had been driving whenever I wanted to go anywhere. If not for the lighthouse stairs, I should have had muscles of mush—and that would never do. One of these days or nights I might literally have to run for my life.

The rock formation I'd had in mind did indeed have a high, flat place that made a fine seat. It was worth the fight I'd had with the wind to get there. I watched a few fishing boats headed in for Monterey; most, I knew, would have been out before dawn and back in the early afternoon. I wondered if these few were, like myself, unable to accomplish much that is worthwhile before midmorning. If my livelihood required landing a catch prior to that time, I'd starve to death.

A myriad of equally silly thoughts were chasing themselves around in my head, when what I wanted was peace. Peace and renewal. But the rhythmically breaking waves, which often have a calming effect on me, today seemed noisy and restless. I raised my eyes to the irregular scallop of hills far across the bay, and above them to long blue savannahs of clouds in the sky. Sweeping, trailing sheer clouds so high in the atmosphere that they seemed unmoved by the burgeoning winds. I caressed the walking stick and allowed myself to miss the Michael I once knew . . . to miss him, and to hope.

I got into a complete funk, tears and all; between that and the wind blowing constantly in my ears, and the waves not being any too quiet, I failed to hear someone approach. Without warning I suddenly felt a presence behind me. My thumb rubbed the dragon's scales and found the concealed button, and then I realized I had no space to maneuver, not even enough room to easily turn. One false step, a single ill-considered movement, and I could meet the same fate as Sabrina Howard.

"I thought that was you sitting up here all by your lonesome, Fremont," said the bluff baritone of Braxton Furnival.

CHAPTER

SIXTEEN

Somewhere around nine o'clock that night I began to think I'd been wrong about Braxton Furnival. He had walked alongside me back to the lighthouse, then presented me with a beautiful little heart-shaped box of chocolates, all tied up in red ribbons and lace. He had invited me to be his guest for dinner at the Hotel Del Monte, with the most abject apology for asking at the last minute. He'd waited downstairs without complaint while I changed into my one good suit, the olive silk gabardine. Now over dinner he was being an excellent conversationalist, all the more charming for his roughness around the edges. I looked across the table into those silvery eyes in their attractive nest of laughter-wrinkles, and could not find any real malice in him to save myself.

To save myself indeed! I must not forget that such an exercise might well become necessary at any time.

"So you see," he went on expansively, and I was sure his voice carried to the farthest corners of the elegant dining room, "we have room in the forest for a golf course to rival the one at Old Del Monte. Rival, hell—when folks see what Cypress Coast Company puts together out by Pebble Beach, they'll want to play our new course first. You mark my words, Fremont. 'Course, it won't hurt Old Del Monte none. The more the merrier where golf's concerned. People like it when there's several courses to play. They'll just stay longer, play more, spend more money . . ." His eyes glinted silver in anticipation of these things even while his voice trailed away.

"You are quite the entrepreneur," I said, smiling. The béarnaise sauce for the filet mignon had put me in a mellow mood. I had not had such a meal in quite a long time, and I reflected that I could easily get used to this sort of thing again.

Braxton leaned toward me and lowered his voice. "You bet! I'm selling advance memberships in the golf club. When the course is built, everybody who's bought in ahead of time will get their first year free. You interested, Fremont?"

"No, thank you. I am not overfond of golf. I prefer to do my walking without having to propel a little white ball ahead of me as an excuse."

He pulled a severe face but couldn't hold it for long. He knew I was joshing. "Too bad. Have some more champagne anyhow—I won't hold it against you."

Dessert was a red velvet cake with white frosting. To cut the sweetness, I asked for coffee even though I knew it would likely keep me awake past my usual bedtime. Then I ate slowly, working up my courage to approach the topic I'd avoided all evening.

"Braxton, do you remember that woman you tried to help me identify?"

"The one who drowned? Sure. I thought somebody came and took her away. Buried her, I reckon." He directed this remark at the cake, as if forking it up required minute attention.

"According to the coroner, she did not drown—but at any rate you were right about her identity. She was Sabrina Howard, an actress from San Francisco."

"Oh hey. I'm real sorry about that." He did look genuinely sorry. "No wonder I haven't been able to get hold of her for so long. It's too bad. Sabrina was real decorative. Useful, too."

"Decorative and useful?"

He completely missed my sarcasm. "You know, pretty. Hell, Sabrina was outright beautiful. She was a big help to me lots of times. Kept the men happy, put 'em in a buying mood. But you couldn't say Sabrina was smart," he shook his head and looked directly at me, "not like you. Brains and beauty, that's what you got, beauty and brains. Add some luck to that, Fremont Jones, and you'll have it made in the shade!"

"Thank you, Braxton—I appreciate your opinion. Thanks also for the fine meal. It has been a while since I had such excellently prepared food."

"Think nothing of it," he said negligently, then raised his hand to signal for the check. "There's just one thing I wonder, though. How'd you find out that was Sabrina Howard? Did I miss something?"

I tucked my napkin under the edge of the dessert plate, properly, without folding it. "I heard recently from a good friend who happens to be a policeman in San Francisco. He has been working with Sabrina's mother, who reported her missing at about the same time you and I went to that funeral home—so it could not have been the mother who took the body away. My friend has since been able to trace Sabrina's movements down to the Monterey Peninsula. I presume the police, or someone, recovered her body—but I have no idea how. The information he imparted did not extend to that."

My statement was deliberately laced with falsehoods; I wanted to see how he would react.

Braxton smiled. That was all—no twitches, no nervous tics, no wavering in the eyes—he just smiled and said, "Well, that's good then. Her mama can give her that Christian burial you were so het up about. Now to a more pleasant topic: How'd you like to take a turn in the garden outside before I drive you home?"

Since the Del Monte Hotel gardens are spectacular, and do not offer the opportunity of anything more dangerous to one's body or reputation than kissing in the shadows, I agreed. I do like kissing, and Braxton does it well.

KEEPER'S LOG
February 17, 1907
Wind: W, moderate and steady
Weather: Clear, cool, no fog a.m.
Comments: A body was found S of Point Sur early this morning and is being brought to Monterey for identification and coroner's examination.

I had stayed up all night typing *The Merchant of Dreams,* not only because I was eager to finish it so that I might have a reason to go over to Carmel, but also because I simply had to know how naive Heloise was going to get herself out of a situation that she really should have had more sense than to get into in the first place. Though I supposed to one in her circumstances, the money really could be a great temptation. At any rate, I am not averse to a certain suspension of disbelief when it comes to storytelling, and I was enjoying Artemisia's tale immensely.

When the sun came up I went down to the kitchen and put on a pot of coffee; while it perked, I went back up the circular stairs to make my morning observations and start the day's entry in the log. I was back in the kitchen grilling a piece of toast for my breakfast when the Coast Guard messenger came by with news of a drowning to be added to the logbook. This news neither surprised nor saddened me unduly, for a review of Hettie's previous two years of log-keeping had shown between three and five deaths in the water each year. Of course with two already and it only February, I thought, if the deaths didn't slack off we might break some kind of record in 1907.

By seven-thirty I was back at the typewriter, quite determined to finish *The Merchant of Dreams.* I had not much more to go. I rolled in a fresh sheet of white paper and flexed my fingers, meanwhile finding my place in the story. Heloise was living at the Morpheus Foundation now, in a bedroom adjoining the Room of Veils. (Actually, the Room of Veils might more properly have been called the Suite of Veils, but this seems not to have occurred to Artemisia.) She,

Heloise, was sleeping almost all the time and having dreams so erotic that it was a wonder the words describing them did not scorch the paper. I quite understood that most people would want to read this novella for the dreams themselves, but I was simply itching for Heloise to wake up and pull herself together! Surely Artemisia wasn't just going to leave her there with the evil Morpheus—and what was he doing with all those dreams he was buying, anyway?

I found my place and began to type again at page 110, vowing not to stop until the end. Once more I immersed myself in Heloise's voice:

Morning and night blended into one another until my mind, my very life, was as shadowy and insubstantial as the veils that swathed the room. My breath was shallow; I had little appetite. It seemed to me that they fed me less and less but I did not care. I did not care, that is, until I had a dream so monstrous that I woke myself out of it abruptly—and for once Morpheus was not beside me when I awoke.

In the dream I lived in a blue and green cave, a place that was glittering and cool, so magical that inside the cave it rained from time to time and the raindrops sounded like music. My body was covered all over with blue and green spangles like fish scales—these I wore in lieu of clothes. In the cave I led a languid life; I had no responsibilities whatever, except that I must not try to go outside, or even look through the cave mouth at the world beyond. But I was not lonely, for I had a lover who nightly came to be with me. He was called Oberon.

One night when Oberon entered me, waking me in that fashion as he always did, I dared to question him. I said, "My love, why do you only come at night, in the dark? The cave is so beautiful by day. I wish you could see it, and I might see your dear face."

"Be silent!" he whispered, his breath moving along my neck like a feather, softly, softly.

The spangles that shielded my skin by day dissolved in sparkles wherever he touched and left me naked, only for him. Vulnerable, but only to him; for as soon as he left me the shining scales would, in an instant, cover me again. It was magic, and our love was a magic that I had never thought to question—until that night.

When Oberon had spent himself in me and turned away to sleep, I could not be still. A flood of questions rose up and spilled from my tongue:

184

"Where do you come from, love? And where do you go when you leave me? Why can I not go with you? Why can I not see the world beyond this cave? What will happen if I go and stand in the mouth and look out, lifting my face to the yellow sun?"

He answered me in a low growl: "I come from darkness and darkness sustains me. You are my creature, made from the flesh of my groin for my own pleasure. Count your blessings, foolish creature, that you may stay in this cave and do not have to go out into the world by day to toil in the sweat of your brow. You cannot exist beyond these confines, so do not seek to go beyond your limitations. The light of the yellow sun will blind and burn you."

Certainly I did not want to be burned and blinded, yet the questions had awakened something in me and now I could not be still. When Oberon slept I left his side and slowly—very slowly—walked to the mouth of the cave. Surely I could not be burned and blinded at night, in the dark?

Not daring to breathe, I ventured to the lip of the cave, taking tiny glances like sips until at last I dared to look my fill, to drink it all in: a world vast and beautiful, of hills folded like black velvet and clear crystal stars winking in a never-ending sky of midnight blue. There was no moon. Yet I could remember the moon, a white orb that rides by night across the sky, an orb whose very constancy is ever-changing—it waxes and wanes and disappears, only to grow and bloom again. This, not the cave, was my world!

I stepped outside and stood poised on the brink of the world. The starlight touched me, and my scales fell in a flurry around my feet. "Oberon has lied to me," I said. "I am not his creature. He did not make me from his groin after all."

Behind me in the cave, a disturbance was growing. I sensed it as one may feel from afar a storm gathering. All the tiny hairs on my new-naked skin stood on end, and the hair of my head swirled and crackled. Sparks like tiny fireflies danced in the air, and in their midst a huge darkness coalesced, took shape, and ponderously unfurled its vast black wings—

That was when I woke myself out of the dream, instinctively reaching for Jonah Morpheus, who always slept beside me now, fully clothed, on top of the counterpane. This was—or so he said— so that he could be there to hear my dreams whenever I awoke during the night; and also so that he might keep watch over my delicate health. For a moment I was panicky when I found the bed empty . . . but then the meaning of the dream began to take hold.

I, Heloise, saw the nameless woman of the dream as myself, and Morpheus as Oberon. The dream was a warning.

Even as this realization came to me, Shadow the cat slunk sinuously from between the veils and leapt with cat-grace onto the bed. I knew that Morpheus would not be far behind. The cat looked at me, and I at the cat.

"Speak," I whispered, hissing on the sibilants, "I know you can. Say what you have to say!" But it only blinked its eerie eyes, then turned away as if I were not worth consideration. And perhaps I wasn't. . . .

Even as I had that appalling thought the full truth of my situation came home to me. Jonah came through the veils. I smiled and reached out for him with my poor thin arms. "I woke and you were not here. I was so frightened!" I said in a trembling voice.

He slid down beside me, stroking, soothing, seducing. "Tell me about your dream," he said.

I told him a dream, but I lied, and that lie was the beginning of my liberation.

"Fremont? You up there?" The voice that called up the stairs was Quincy's. I called down to say that I was, and he said, "Righty-o. I'm riding Bessie inta town. They 'sposed to have a new wheel on the shay this morning."

Botheration! I was torn, but my care for Quincy won out and I left the typewriter. "Wait, Quincy!" I took the twisting stairs so fast that I was a little dizzy when I reached the bottom. He was already at the door with his hand on the knob, his other arm still immobilized in a sling against his chest. I insisted, "You shouldn't try to ride or drive one-handed. The chance of your hurting yourself again is too great. Can't you send Pete?"

Quincy's eyes shifted away from mine and he said, "Nope. He didn't show up today."

"I can't imagine that he's sick. Yesterday he looked healthy as a horse." Pete Carlson was indeed a strong, muscular fellow in spite of his height, which probably was a sore point. Pete couldn't have been more than five and a half feet tall, which made him a couple of inches shorter than most men and a full three inches shorter than I.

Quincy reached up under his hat and scratched his ear. "Well, you see, the thing is, I told him not to come today. Thought we could do without him."

"Honestly, Quincy!" I planted my fists on my hips. "I don't see what you have against the man. He does the work well enough when you let him."

He mumbled something that I did not bother to ask him to repeat, because I suspected that Quincy was one of those people who, if he cannot do a thing himself, will never be satisfied with the way it is done by anyone else.

I love Quincy dearly, but at the moment I felt quite cross with him, and so I said, "This is really extremely inconvenient. I do not want you to reinjure yourself, but I do not have time myself to ride the horse in and drive the rig back."

"But Fremont—"

"Nor do I have time to stand around and debate with you about it, Quincy. You will not go, and that is that. I'll be driving the Maxwell over to Carmel in a little while, and I'll stop by the stables and ask them to bring the shay back using one of their own horses. Do you think, Quincy, if I can come up with a reason to tell Pete Carlson we no longer need him to work here, that you could get along with someone else better?"

"No siree bob! You better not let him go. Don't even think of doing that! It don't do to get Pete riled. Now we got him, I reckon we're stuck with him for a while. I'll do better, I promise, and I'm sorry for the inconvenience." Quincy trudged out the door, shaking his head.

I raced back upstairs. Soon I was typing Heloise's finest hour:

> By feigning sleep and keeping myself awake during the daylight hours—as best I could judge within the otherworldly atmosphere of the room of veils—I learned that there were long stretches when I was left alone. Except for Shadow. There were times I told myself I should not be so fanciful, this cat was just a cat; but there were other times when I was sure that Shadow was no more a mere cat than Jonah and Thad were mortal men. What sort of beings they were, precisely, I did not know—but the skills of Jonah Morpheus encompassed far more than mesmerism. I was beginning to claim my own mind again, to use it, to understand.

He had entered into my life through my dreams. The stuff of my dreams somehow sustained him, for when I gave him my dreams, he took from me some part of my life force as well. And when I slept he took me sweetly, racking my body with momentary pleasures; but that did not alter the fact that Morpheus was feeding on my soul.

With each day that passed now, I grew stronger. I withheld bits and pieces of every dream; I ate all the food given to me and asked Thad, not Jonah, for more. There was some small rivalry between the two of them, and I think it amused Thad to see me doing something—anything—without Jonah's approval. I explored the two rooms and found that they had only ordinary walls, the veils were only sheer curtains—but the chandelier I did not approach at all. There was something altogether too uncanny about it.

The day at last came when I was ready. I had not regained my normal strength by any means, but I did believe I could walk down the stairs and that was what mattered. I had a plan. After Thad took away my breakfast dishes, I went into the bedroom and climbed up on the bed. Day after day I had picked away at the top hem of one of the sheer panels until now it hung from the rod by only a few threads. I broke the last threads and brought it down in my arms, as gray and insubstantial as fog. Yet the fabric was incredibly strong and silky, like nothing I had ever held in my hands before, like something from another world. I bundled it up and shoved it beneath the pillows.

Not much later, Shadow paid his usual morning visit. The cat liked me—often it would stay all day. I petted and it purred. I crooned, in much the same tone of voice that Morpheus so often uses with me: "Shadow, sweet Shadow. You love me, I know you love me. You want to be with me, to stay with me, to go with me . . ." over and over I said these and similar words, until Shadow slept. Then I arose and put on the dress that I had not worn in so many weeks I'd lost count. The diaphanous nightgown I habitually wore, a gift from Morpheus, I draped over the foot of the bed. My old dress hung on me, for I was painfully thin.

Now I knew I must move swiftly. With deft motions I wrapped Shadow around and around with the curtain I'd taken down earlier. Wrapped the cat so thickly that it could not scratch me, picked it up, and ran. I ran through one door to another, suddenly panicked that I might find it locked. But it was not, and I had not really thought it would be. To all appearances, I had long been too weak to flee. I opened the door and listened. The cat stopped struggling, which somehow frightened me more than if it had continued to act like a trapped cat. There was a bond between Shadow and Morpheus—I had both seen and sensed it many times. I was counting on that bond to help me gain my freedom, but I had to get physically away first. It was time to fly, and I did!

Down, down, down the stairs, past dark and silent corridors: fly, fly! A door opened somewhere behind me but I did not turn. I was frail but fleet, my very lightness enabling me to move like the wind.

With a satisfied sigh, for Heloise was living up to my hopes for her, I continued typing all the way to the conclusion. I stacked the sheets neatly, all 148 pages of them. Then I sat for a few minutes thinking back on Artemesia's amazing story.

The Merchant of Dreams ended like a fairy tale, which I suppose in a way it was—though an exceedingly erotic one and certainly not for children! Heloise went back to her shabby apartment and placed Shadow in a golden birdcage she had inherited from her grandmother. When he came to retrieve the cat, Jonah Morpheus revealed his true nature—he was a shape-changer and an incubus. Shadow was the same but much younger, a sort of incubus-in-training, and Thad was a fallen angel. Heloise used the cat as a hostage in order to force Morpheus to release her from the contract, which he did do, and then both incubi dissolved into thin air. So all was well that ended well—or so one must believe or else have great difficulty sleeping.

I placed the typed manuscript in a box that had held a ream of paper, with Artemisia's handwritten original on top. I did wonder about one thing: the money. Did Heloise get to keep the money from selling her dreams? Would I have kept it, if I had been she? Would I reason that I had earned it, or would I be afraid that money obtained in such a manner would bring me bad luck?

"I trust you have had no further problems with snakes," I said to Artemisia as I entered her cottage for the first time. In keeping with her preference for things of the night, she had named the cottage Moonbow.

"What? Oh, that. No, I haven't—but Patrick may have something to do with that, even though he spends most of his time outdoors. Come in, Fremont. You must forgive me—I'm a little distracted this morning. What can I do for you?"

"I am delivering the typewritten copy of your novella." I extended the box and she regarded it for a moment as if she hadn't the slightest idea what I was talking about, then recovered herself and grasped the box.

"Thank you! Let's have a look." Artemisia went swiftly across the room to a cluttered worktable, put the box down on top of the clutter, and proceeded to open it.

Meanwhile I amused myself by gazing around the cottage. It resembled a small-scale anthropological museum, filled with things like masks and pottery and baskets and odd-looking figurines. Her furniture was covered with American Indian rugs. Nothing went together, yet everything had a kind of harmony that was extraordinary, like Artemisia herself.

"I must say, the typewriting gives it a very professional appearance," she said. "I almost feel as if it's been published already. What did you think of the story, Fremont?"

"I thought it was fascinating. I'm in awe of your fertile imagination, Artemisia. Yet as you yourself have said, the sensational nature of some of those dreams may give publishers a bit of a pause. Queen Victoria is dead, and they say her son is the veriest rake that ever lived, but—"

"Say no more!" Artemisia held up her hand, interrupting. "I can't bear to hear it. When I think of the hypocrisy of those men who sit in their offices like pompous prigs and then at night have their own sort of dark and degrading amusements, I just . . . just want to spit nails! I have decided that I'll be damned if I'll put a man's name on *The Merchant of Dreams* just in order to please them. So I expect Heloise and Morpheus will never see the inside of a bookstore—but who knows? Some publisher may surprise me. Now let me pay you. I have cash around here somewhere. . . ."

While she looked for her money, I asked, "Where do you do your painting?"

"There's a separate studio out back. It has one whole wall that is all windows. I suppose you may think it odd that a woman who paints nocturnes should want a lot of light for her studio, but I do.

I'd be glad to show you another day, but as I said before, just now I'm rather distracted. Something terrible has happened."

Having found some bills in an ancient jar, she came back across the room and pressed one into my hand. I looked, saw that it was a twenty, and dug into my leather bag to make change. While rummaging I asked, "What has happened? Can you tell me?"

"Keep the difference, Fremont. Consider it a bonus or whatever." She collapsed into a chair, and I noticed for the first time that her clothes were rumpled and dirty, as if she had not changed them for days. "It's Arthur. Or maybe it's Oscar. I guess it's both of them. You see, we don't know if Oscar's gone round the bend, or if he's telling the truth, or what."

I sat down near her, after putting five dollars and twenty cents on the table, where she would find it eventually. I had had that manuscript a long time, and did not in my own opinion deserve a bonus. "I don't understand," I said.

She released a long sigh and rubbed at her forehead. "I'm not sure I do, either. Mimi is no help. She's so damn overprotective!"

"I know what you mean. Why don't you tell me from the beginning?"

Artemisia looked at me with tragic dark eyes. "They went down to Big Sur to look for jade—you can find it on a particular beach there. Arthur and Oscar went together, but Oscar came back last night . . . alone."

CHAPTER
SEVENTEEN

I allowed the implications of what Artemisia had just said to settle, and then I said, "In other words, something happened to Arthur."

"Yes, and something has Oscar terribly frightened. Oscar has always been high-strung; many poets are, it seems to come with the territory. But he has never been so near to completely falling apart before, and I have known Oscar Peterson since my school days."

My throat went dry, and there was an odd tingling in the tips of my fingers and in my toes. I mustered enough saliva to swallow and then ventured, "Are you implying some sort of foul play, perhaps witnessed by Oscar? And if so, shouldn't we go to the sheriff?"

She shot me an ill-tempered look. "I'm surprised to hear you, of all people, suggest that. You have a remarkable talent for getting other people to do your dirty work, either with you or for you, Fremont Jones. I for one will have no further part in it."

My heart sank, though why I should care what Artemisia Vaughn thought of me I was not entirely sure. I said, "I'm sorry you feel that way, but to be perfectly fair I suppose I can understand it. It is not too great a leap, is it, to assume that whatever happened to Arthur may have some connection to both Sabrina Howard's death and Phoebe's disappearance?"

"Phoebe is most likely dead too, and I daresay so is Arthur." Her eyes blazed at me. "One must wonder if any of this would have happened if you had just left everyone alone."

I ignored that; I could not let myself believe it or else I would no longer be able to function. "What, exactly, does Oscar have to say?"

"He babbles. Sometimes he says Arthur fell from a cliff, which sounds like an accident, except for one thing: They went down the coastline by boat. What would they have been doing up on the cliffs? Have you ever been down as far as Big Sur, Fremont?"

I shook my head in the negative.

"It is absolutely breathtaking, especially at this time of year, when the mountains are a brilliant emerald green; but it is also formidable in terms of geographic features. The mountains are steep-sided and rise right up out of the sea, except that in one area there is a kind of shelf that was once an undersea plateau. Of course, there are these little coves tucked in all along the way, with sandy beaches. One would have to have a very good reason to leave the beach and climb up the cliffs, for it would be a perilous climb. Frankly, I can't imagine either Arthur or Oscar doing such a thing."

"Unless they were forced," I said grimly.

Artemisia wiggled uncomfortably in her chair, but I suspected her discomfort was internal rather than external and would not respond to a change of position. She continued, "The most peculiar thing is that Oscar keeps insisting there was no one else there. A couple of times he has just dissolved in fits of weeping, saying that Arthur is dead and he's to blame."

Something in my head went *click*. I allowed a few moments of silence and then said, "There is something you should know, and so should anyone who is concerned in this matter. At the lighthouse earlier this morning I had a report that a body found in the ocean was being brought up from south of Point Sur. For the coroner's attention."

Artemisia's hand flew up to her mouth. "Oh, no! Mimi will be . . . will be—I can't even think of the word!"

I stood up, my heart hardening. "Your reaction suggests that no matter how much he may have blamed himself, Oscar did not bring Arthur's body back with him in the boat."

"You can't expect a man like Oscar to deal with something so horrible as a . . . a dead person! He is far too sensitive. . . ." Her voice trailed off, one presumed as she realized the full implication of what she'd said.

"And highly strung. Yes, and as long as a man like that has a woman like Mimi to deal with things for him, I suppose one cannot expect much of him in the way of dealing with the dirty, messy little realities of everyday life. On the other hand, it takes a certain kind of person to go off and leave a friend's body in the water and make no attempt to return with help, wouldn't you say?" Without giving Artemisia a chance to reply, I continued talking as I walked to the door: "I am going to the Petersons'. If you want to come, I'd be glad of your company. If not, then I wish you as good a day as can be expected under the circumstances."

When Artemisia neither spoke nor moved from her chair, I took that as her reply. In the doorway I turned, experiencing an unexpected moment of self-illumination. "There is something you may as well know about me," I said. "I do not go out looking for trouble, but if trouble comes to me I won't run from it either. Particularly if an injustice is involved. Where injustice is concerned, I seem to be constitutionally incapable of looking the other way."

My little speech of self-justification made scant impression on Artemisia, but I felt better for having said it. I went on to the Petersons' alone, glad that I had my new walking stick with me. If Artemisia was hostile toward me, Mimi was bound to be even more so. In physical build Mimi is a strapping sort of woman, and while I did not really think she would physically attack me, it is always best to be prepared.

After parking Max in the bushes I took walking stick in hand, tested its balance, smoothed my skirts, took a deep breath, and began the longish walk through the trees to the Petersons' house. I walked slowly, trying to get my thoughts in order along the way. Mimi had reacted strongly to the picture of Sabrina Howard, but Oscar had not; Arthur had said he'd seen Sabrina, and I'd been counting on him to eventually dredge up from his memory exactly where. Ten to one, I'd bet wherever it was, Braxton Furnival had been there, too.

What connection could there be between Braxton Furnival and Sabrina Howard, and Mimi and Oscar Peterson, and Arthur Heyer? I knew where Phoebe fit—it was Phoebe who had made possible the identification of Sabrina Howard, that was why she had to be silenced. (One could only hope, not permanently!) What I simply could not get around in order to make the pieces fit together was the indisputable fact that the Carmelites are fanatically loyal to one another. No Carmelite would harm another; I was as certain of that as I am that breath equals life. So where, and how, did Braxton fit in?

Perhaps he didn't. For the life of me, I couldn't recall at that moment what had made me so suspicious of him in the first place. I was confusing myself.

I stopped on the far side of the clearing, with the house just beyond. Through the live oak trees, I could see the shingled roofline and the fieldstone chimney that Oscar had built with his own hands. A nearby plant, something between a bush and a tree, was filled with fluttering yellow finches. On another sort of day I would have smiled at these tiny little birds with their robust, sweet song—but as it was I went grimly on. Over the birdsong I could hear, from the house's open casement windows, a thin, pathetic keening. The sound was barely human. It was enough to break your heart.

I rapped on the door with the head of my walking stick. It was opened almost instantly by one of the Twangy Boys. "Dick?" I guessed. "May I come in?"

Either I had guessed correctly or he was accustomed to being mistaken for one of his fellows, for he nodded and stepped back to admit me. The keening was louder. I lowered my head and whispered, "Is that Oscar?"

He nodded again, an expression both grave and frightened on his young face. "They're in the kitchen. You heard what happened?"

It was my turn to nod.

Dick said, "Go on in, Fremont, but don't expect much. Oscar just about can't talk, and Mimi probably won't. I don't know what we're gonna do. This is awful, just awful!"

"I have some news that may speed things up," I said. "You should hear it, too. Come on in there with me."

Tom and Harry sat next to each other on a windowseat, holding hands; they both looked as grave and as frightened as Dick, who went immediately to join them. Irma Fox, in a severe gray dress, sat in a chair in a corner, as if she wished to be both present and absent at the same time. Khalid was nowhere about. Mimi and Oscar were both at the kitchen table, he slumped over the tabletop, crying as if his grief might dissolve him into the very wood; she, stroking and stroking his lank, longish hair. Her eyes were like the Medusa's— they could turn you to stone.

"I have some news," I said. My voice sounded too loud, or perhaps too rational, for this group, where everyone was to a degree in shock.

Mimi moved her head slightly and focused on me. "We don't need any news. We've had enough, thank you."

Oscar wailed again. His bony arms hid his face. The hair that Mimi so rhythmically stroked was filthy and appeared damp.

I went and sat on the other side of the table and spoke in a low tone. "This news I'm afraid you do need. I had word at the lighthouse this morning that the Coast Guard is bringing a body to Monterey for identification and examination by the coroner. They picked this body up south of Point Sur early this morning. I expect they will be in Monterey by now and if not, then shortly."

Oscar raised his head. His face was a skull with the skin stretched over it, no more—whatever flesh once covered those bones had wasted away. Only the eyes were alive, reddened and raw and streaming, as if his tears were supplied from an everlasting source. "Arthur!" he said. "Ar-thu-u-ur!" ending in a scream of anguish, his hands scrabbling and clawing at the tabletop.

"Hush," Mimi soothed, trapping his hands one at a time, stilling them and bringing them to her breast. Oscar slipped from his chair and slid to the floor, sobbing now and trying like some great dog to climb into his wife's lap. Meanwhile she studied me.

"He is right," I said gently, "it could well be Arthur."

The air of the kitchen reverberated with such tension that every word, no matter how softly spoken, rang hollow. My skin felt as if at any moment it might burst like an overripe plum.

Mimi blinked, and I saw a change in her eyes, a resolution. "I'll go," she said, standing.

I said, "You should both go."

From the corner, Irma Fox hissed.

Mimi's voice dropped to a low, deadly pitch. "Look at him!" When she stood, Oscar had collapsed on the floor beside her chair. He looked like a ragged heap of bones. "Do you really think he's capable of talking to anyone, much less of taking responsibility for his actions?"

"I think he might if you gave him the opportunity, and I expect he would feel better afterward for having tried."

This did not fit her agenda, so she ignored it.

Suddenly the heap of bones spoke in a loud voice: "I did it, I told you, I told you. I did it! I killed Arthur!"

"He has no idea what he's saying," Mimi said.

"Don't you think you need to let someone else—the police or the coroner—decide that?"

From the windowseat there came gasps and mumbles.

Mimi persisted: "Tell me, Fremont—if Michael were your husband and he might have killed someone, what then? Would you turn him in?"

I thought about it for a long time, and at last I said, "Yes. I would." It was the truth, but I felt as if I had stabbed myself in the heart. And when Mimi refused my offer of a ride in to Monterey and instead went off on her own, I neither protested nor followed her.

KEEPER'S LOG
February 18, 1907
Wind: W by NW, moderate
Weather: Fair, clear, cool; moderate waves and swells

Comments: Passenger steamer down from N, in and out; U.S. Navy brig Celestine *anchored in bay off China Point. Body brought in yesterday identified as Arthur Heyer, a resident of Carmel. Death presumed accidental, by drowning, pending further information from coroner.*

I did not really know if it was quite correct to put so much information into the log about Arthur's death, but as Hettie always seemed to record as much as she knew about deaths in and around this part of the coast, and as I had a great need to make note of it, I wrote all I knew myself.

Whatever Mimi had told the police, they apparently did not suspect Oscar of having a hand in Arthur's death. In spite of what Oscar had said, I tended to agree; but I did not think he was really out of his mind. I thought he knew what he was doing, and saying, although he was obviously distressed to an extreme. According to the morning newspaper, Arthur's body was to be sent to his family home in Sonoma for burial. Unless the coroner intervened, or some new information came from somewhere, the drowning would be labeled an accident: Treacherous Big Sur coastline claims another victim. Poor Arthur.

I sat in the watch room and forced myself to do the midmonth accounting. When I added up Pete Carlson's hours I felt a now-familiar flood of irritation and affection combined—Quincy had not used Pete for anywhere near as many hours as I'd authorized. If I were to go outside right now I'd probably find Quincy tugging away at feed sacks or raking pine straw or some such one-handed. I made a mental note to be sure none of the routine jobs around the light-house had fallen behind. I could easily do more myself, now that I was no longer trying to keep up my typewriting business.

Early in the afternoon, having satisfied myself that all was well with the lighthouse, I opened the wardrobe in the bedroom and surveyed my limited supply of clothes. I don't know what I was thinking, or hoping—that something suitable might suddenly materialize, I suppose. I knew perfectly well that I owned nothing suitable for what I had in mind.

"Aha!" I said, as an idea occurred to me.

The clothes Hettie had not taken on her trip were all on one side of the wardrobe, protected by dustcovers; mine, unprotected, were on the other. Hettie and I were quite nearly identical in size, except that I was somewhat taller and thinner than she. Surely she would not mind, and I would be extremely careful . . .

I selected the dreariest, most outmoded dress in the wardrobe. It was a dull satin, gunmetal gray, with tiny buttons all the way down the front and, in back, a swag skirt over a cascade of pleats that hung like a plethora of turkey wattles. On me it was a bit short, but I would wear my black high-button shoes so my ankles wouldn't show. Due to the fact that Hettie would have had a corset under the dress, it fit my own uncorseted waist just fine. If I didn't move too quickly, perhaps it would not be obvious that I wasn't wearing one of those strangulating inventions of the devil. Or of some man who could qualify for that position; surely it could not have been a woman who first thought up corsets?

Having gone this far, I looked into the hatboxes on the wardrobe shelf. Since moving to California, where I do not have proper Bostonians always breathing down my neck, I have seldom worn a hat—I think hats are a lot of foolishness and uncomfortable besides. Nowadays there are women who go around with dead birds and baskets of fruit and God-knows-what-all on top of their heads. It would be amusing except that the wearers themselves fail to see the humor.

If Hettie owned any outrageous hats, she had taken them with her. She did, however, have one that looked as if it might have been made for this very dress. Like the dress it was a bit out of style, a dark-gray satin chapeau shaped like a little flat cake with one thin black feather slanting skyward; it was meant to be worn forward on the head, held in place by thin satin straps that tied under the chin and looked for all the world like gray spaghetti. I put my hair up, and the hat on, and was astounded when I looked in the mirror. I looked quite respectable, and quite unlike myself.

Thus transformed I set off to beg an audience with the Matriarch of the Grove: Euphemia Wells.

"I hope you will forgive my presumption, as we have not been formally introduced," I said, using my most proper Beacon Hill manner, "but as it is a Sunday and therefore a day of leisure, I thought you might be at home to callers."

She frowned down at the calling card I had placed in her hand when she'd opened the door herself.

"The card," I hastened to explain, "still has my old San Francisco address. There have been so many things going on since the earthquake that getting new ones printed was the last thing on my mind."

"Understandable. Fremont Jones? You have no Christian name?"

"My first name, which I no longer use, is Caroline." The rebel in me longed to make some smart remark about what would I, a nonbeliever, do with a Christian name—but miracle of miracles, the heathen held her tongue.

This conversation was taking place on Euphemia's front porch. Behind me on Forest Avenue there was a good deal of traffic for a Sunday afternoon—the clip-clopping of horses' hoofs, the rattle and creak of wagons, the chug-and-wheeze of automobiles. The sky was blue, the air had a clean taste, and I was as nervous as any schoolgirl who has been sent to the principal's office.

"He was an upstart, you know. Relative of yours?" Euphemia performed the considerable feat of looking down her nose at me even though I am taller than she.

"You are referring to John Charles Frémont?" I asked.

She nodded; iron-gray curls like sausages bobbed against her chunky cheeks.

"He was a cousin on my mother's side of the family. That is how I got the name."

She narrowed her eyes, which had the effect of making her face appear bulldoggish. "What's wrong with Caroline?"

"Nothing. But as a woman in business, I thought I might do well not to advertise my gender."

Euphemia Wells snorted. Whether this snort denoted approval or disapproval was impossible to tell, but she stepped back and motioned for me to enter the hallowed sanctity of her home.

I swished across the threshold in my borrowed gray satin, and she creaked after me in her usual black bombazine.

A quick glance revealed that there was only one parlor, so that was where I went. A moment later I declined tea or coffee, and we both sat down.

"I know who you are, of course," said Euphemia. She sat very straight, her stiffly encased breasts jutting out like a shelf. "You're the temporary lighthouse keeper. From what I hear, it's no wonder Hettie Houck picked you. You're just like her, by all accounts. Except that I haven't seen you in church."

"I go to a different one," I lied, smiling. "Hettie is the reason I am here this afternoon. When she left, she said that if I ever needed advice about anything, I should come to you. She said, 'Euphemia knows everything that is worth knowing in Monterey and Pacific Grove.' I'm hoping she was right, and that your knowledge might extend a few miles into the Del Monte Forest as well."

When Euphemia Wells smiled, one worried that her face might crack, but it did not. She merely became a shade less formidable. "Do you find yourself in need of advice, Miss Jones?"

Anyone else I would have asked to call me Fremont, but on her lips Miss Jones sounded just fine to me. "Yes, but this is extremely confidential." I bent forward and lowered my voice to just above a whisper. "It concerns . . . money."

She too bent, from the hips, creaking like a mast in a gale. "Yes?"

"I am thinking of investing in some land. I am my father's sole heir, you see."

"I see," she nodded sagely, with a light in her eyes. The mention of family money does that to a lot of people.

"So I was wondering: What do you know, Mrs. Wells, about Braxton Furnival? Is he a trustworthy sort of individual?"

The light in her eyes went out. In fact, Euphemia glowered. "No, I wouldn't say so. I would not be able to say that at all."

CHAPTER EIGHTEEN

"Oh, dear!" I said. "That is bad news."

Euphemia leaned even farther forward, and said with an exaggerated air of confidentiality: "I have it on good authority that the development company has decided to replace him. They are only waiting for the new man to come down."

I pouted deliberately, even as it occurred to me that this information made sense of some things I'd seen—the sparse nature of his household furniture, for example. I said, "I am so disappointed. I had thought to buy into his golf club, but now I must question whether that would be a good investment."

"*His* golf club? It is true that there are some plans for a golf course in the forest some day, or so one hears, but Braxton Furnival has nothing to do with that. He is more or less a caretaker. That is why, I suppose, it doesn't much matter that he is—shall we say—such an uncultured sort of individual. Likes to give himself airs," she sniffed. "Don't let that sort of man pull the wool over your eyes, Miss Jones."

"Oh, my." I pouted again. "It's certainly lucky that I came to you. I rather liked Braxton, you see. I thought of him as a diamond in the rough. Do you mean he doesn't own that huge house he lives in?"

"I haven't the slightest idea where he lives!" She thrust her chin aloft in a manner that made it quite clear I had no business knowing, either. Which was perfectly true, if one were to adhere to the standards one had been brought up with. But then, one's life would be so terribly dull!

"His house," I said, "is an enormous place that looks as if it belongs in the Black Forest or some such place. Very rustic but very grand all the same."

"I do not venture into the forest much, either Black or Del Monte. I stay at home in Pacific Grove, where decent, God-fearing people live."

I have often wondered how it is that decent people must fear their God, and whether Jesus feared God in spite of God's being His Father, and if He didn't, did that make Jesus indecent? I should have liked to ask Euphemia Wells this question. Instead, I rose and extended my right hand; the left was on my walking stick. "I take your point. Thank you for your time, Mrs. Wells. I shall heed your advice and hold onto my money until the Cypress Coast Company sends the new man. I don't suppose you know when that will be?"

"Haven't got the slightest." She shook her head and got ponderously to her feet.

I started for the door. "I will be sure to tell Hettie how helpful you've been, when she returns. But that will be a while. She's not due until the first of July."

"I hope she is having a pleasant time. Where was it Hettie said she was going?"

"I don't know," I replied, with considerable satisfaction. How pleasant it is to be able to frustrate a person one senses to be a malicious gossip! "She didn't say. At least, not to me."

Euphemia was not one to give up easily. "Surely you must have a way to write to her. What if there were an emergency?"

"Then I would contact the Lighthouse Service, just as I do when I am in need of supplies. Good day, Mrs. Wells. Thank you for the advice and information."

"Good day, Miss Jones. Do come again."

With my foot on the first step down off the porch, I turned my head. "By the way . . . do you happen to know Braxton Furnival's friend Ramon Reyes?"

"I should say not! Mexican, is he?"

"Or Spanish." I walked down the remaining steps and turned my head again. "Mr. Reyes appears well bred."

"Miss Jones, it seems to me you'd be better off confining your activities to the lighthouse for a while. You are obviously in danger of falling in with the wrong crowd! Spanish or Mexican, doesn't matter—one has to avoid these foreign-speaking people."

From my safe distance, I simply could not resist a parting remark: "It is hard for me to think of someone who speaks Spanish as foreign, when California belonged to them first. But I will remember what you've said."

My next stop was the Hotel Del Monte. I enjoyed the drive, except for the part past China Point and the depressing ruins of the former Chinatown. The burned-out husks of former buildings there are fenced off, with guards posted; I had asked Quincy once why anyone would want to guard something that essentially was no longer there, and he'd said the owner of the land was doing it so that the Chinese would not attempt to move back and rebuild.

There is prejudice, I reflected, everywhere; even in so beautiful a place as this. Today Monterey Bay was a perfect azure mirror, the sun so pleasant on my satin-clad arms that I did not even need a wrap. Yet I allow I was in a somewhat grim frame of mind. I sensed that time was running out, things were working their way up to some sort of conclusion, which might well be my own disappearance. Or death.

I had reasoned that Arthur Heyer might have recalled where he'd seen Sabrina Howard, and mentioned it to someone in or around Carmel before he'd had an opportunity to tell me. Then this someone—probably Braxton or his friend Ramon—followed Oscar and Arthur down to Big Sur and whacked Arthur, scaring Oscar out of his wits in the process.

My theory, such as it was, was full of holes. For one thing, why whack Arthur but not Oscar? For another, where was the motive in any of this? Sabrina Howard must have known something she should not have known and threatened to tell. Perhaps she'd wanted to be paid to keep quiet—that would fit the picture of the ambitious actress with a taste for fine clothes.

Something else was bothering me: If Ramon was, so to speak, Braxton's henchman, then most likely it would have been Ramon who'd hit me on the head—but Ramon's eyes did not look to me like the eyes behind that mask. And another thing: For all that I could perfectly well imagine Braxton in some sort of shady business deal, he did not impress me as a man who would deliberately injure a woman. There are some men who genuinely like women; they like to look at them and touch their hair, admire their clothes, to treat them as exotic, expensive pets. Braxton seemed such a man to me.

"Yet I have so often been wrong before!" I muttered bitterly. The Maxwell chugged in agreement, its steering wheel vibrating under my hands and reminding me of the final thing—well, person—that bothered me deeply: Michael. Could he have had a role in any of this? "Of course not!" I declared . . . but I had to admit that if I had known him less well, I would have been obliged to seriously consider him as a suspect, if for no other reason than that (as usual) he had picked a crucial time to leave town. Add to that his recent uncharacteristic behavior, his refusal to help me investigate . . .

I saw that I had reached the sprawling building and grand grounds of the Hotel Del Monte. Giving the requisite hand signal, I turned into the drive and chugged on through to the parking area, at one side of the great Victorian structure. I could have had the parking valet take care of the car, but then I would have had to tip, and it is silly to waste money that way when I am perfectly capable of parking and walking a few steps myself.

Actually the walk was not a few steps but a considerable distance, along a covered walkway decorated with graceful arches and various architectural frew-fraws. Along the way I swung my walking stick and clenched my jaw, hardening my resolve. Chin up, I proceeded through the front door, using the walking stick to push it open in an imperious manner that I rather enjoyed.

The lobby was about the size of a football field, with palms and ferns and aspidistras and various articles of furniture dotted about. The walls were entirely paneled in golden wood, elaborately carved and polished to a high sheen. The hotel desk, long and sleek as some yachts out in the harbor, was made of this same wood. I strolled across the carpet and took a seat on one of those ridiculous round couches that one sees nowhere except in hotel lobbies, the sort that look like a giant sultan's hat with a rolled brim, the brim being the cushions. Acting as if I were waiting for one of the hotel guests, I glanced frequently in the direction of the stairs and elevators.

If I had been interested in a parade of fashion, I could have seen it here. But I was not. I was, actually, nervous. My palm on the dragon's head of the walking stick felt cold, slick, damp. I closed my eyes briefly and repeated to myself: *Phoebe, Phoebe. I am doing this for Phoebe.*

My intention was to find Phoebe, dead or alive. When I had found her I would go to the sheriff. The diligence of the deputies in questioning the Carmelites had made a favorable impression on me. Surely if I had enough facts at my command they would listen . . . and then perhaps the culprits would be caught and Quincy and I could rest in peace.

Rest in peace, *requiescat in pace*—an unfortunate choice of words. *RIP* is what they put on tombstones. Heaven forbid! It was too late for Sabrina but oh dear God, I hoped that Phoebe was not dead. I also hoped that I would not be joining either or both of them. An unexpected and most unwelcome chill spread through my body, and I suddenly found it difficult to breathe.

I have found that this sort of breathless panic may be relieved by taking action. So: Time to get moving! With one last glance in the direction of the elevators, I slipped over my shoulder the strap of the black reticule I was carrying instead of my favorite leather bag, took up the walking stick, and stepped briskly toward the desk.

Stopping a couple of steps short of my goal, I surveyed the three clerks on duty and picked one: an older man with a narrow face and serious mien. On him the ostentatious uniform that all Del Monte employees wore looked less ridiculous than it did on the other two raw-faced lads. I fixed my gaze on the older man and moved forward.

"Good afternoon," I said, placing my reticule on the desk's high counter, "I wonder if you could help me?"

Nodding gravely, the man came forward. "I'll certainly try, Miss."

"I'd be so grateful." I reached into the reticule and withdrew an envelope containing the photograph of Sabrina Howard. Placing it on the counter I slid the photo out and kept my hand on its edge. Then I leaned forward and said in a low voice, "This woman has, I believe, stayed here often. Do you recognize her?"

"That would be Miss Howard, a famous actress from San Francisco. She does come here a lot," he said, still nodding, still grave. "However, she hasn't been with us in recent weeks. I expect you might find her in, as one says, the city?"

When he said "the city," he smiled, and it was like the sun flashing briefly out from behind a thin gray cloud.

"You are from the city yourself!" I said with unfeigned joy. "So am I!"

For a few minutes we exchanged information and condolences on our losses from the earthquake, an exercise with which I was by now (alas!) all too familiar, and then I got back on track. "Sabrina—Miss Howard—has not been seen in any of her usual haunts for quite some time. I am trying to help her mother, and a member of the San Francisco Police Department, gather as much information as possible in order to locate her." Of course Wish Stephenson didn't know I was helping, but one cannot put too fine a point on these things.

The clerk gave me a look and I nodded significantly, even as I prayed he would not ask me for any sort of official identification. I leaned forward again. "If you could check the hotel register and see when she was last here, I would be so grateful."

He grinned, letting out not the whole sun but one warm ray. "I expect I could do that."

As in many large hotels, the register was not a single book but rather a series of bound books, like ledgers, one for each month.

Only the current one was kept on the desk. The others were arranged on a shelf behind. While the clerk located the ones he wanted, I put the photo back into my reticule. It had served its purpose.

He returned with a scrap of paper to which he referred, but he did not pass it over to me. "The party you're interested in was here twice early last month. The first time she arrived was actually in December, the thirty-first, New Year's Eve. She left on January second for five days and came back on the seventh."

I nodded; I had sighted Sabrina Howard's body on January ninth. "And when did she check out?"

The clerk scrutinized the paper he kept cupped in the palm of his hand. "The tenth."

That's impossible! I almost said, but managed to swallow the words instead. "Was she by any chance checked out by Mr. Furnival? I presume it was he who made the reservations on her behalf."

This got me another look. "Just a minute." He went back to the bank of little cubbyholes where the keys were kept and opened a drawer down below. In a moment he returned, chuckling and gazing over my left shoulder. "Speak o' the divil! I guess you wouldn't want to say hello?"

"I beg your pardon?" But even as I cautiously turned my head, I understood: The familiar large form of Braxton Furnival was striding across the lobby toward the elevators. "Good heavens!" I said, but so softly that it came out sounding rather like a hiss. I kept my face turned away and could only hope that the gray satin and all those pleats down my back would be enough of a disguise. To the amused clerk I whispered, "I would of course be most grateful if you were to keep my inquiry to yourself."

A prosperous-looking couple with two shrill children came up next to me and were pounced upon by one of the raw-faced lads. The other lad was helping a man in a homburg down at the far end of the counter. My clerk and I moved in that direction, away from the couple, who really ought to have thought about shushing their children.

"Anyway it was not he," said the clerk, the very model of proper diction.

"Not Furnival? Are you sure?" From the corner of my eye I could see Braxton standing with his head tipped back, watching the elevator's floor indicator.

"We don't record the actual checking out, but a Mr. Peterson paid the bill on that day, the tenth of January."

"Oscar Peterson?" I recalled Oscar's face looking down at the photograph, the total lack of recognition registered on that scrawny, somewhat ascetic visage. "How odd!"

"Not when you consider that about half the times when she was here over the last six months, it was Mr. Peterson rather than Mr. Furnival who paid for her to stay. Now mind you, this is confidential information, and I wouldn't be telling you if you weren't working with the police."

"Of course!" I agreed, with only a small qualm. I heard the elevator ding and its doors slide open. I felt—but surely it was my imagination—a pair of eyes bore into the back of my skull.

Sotto voce the clerk said, "And I don't think the two of them were exactly cooperating on taking turns, if you know what I mean."

"I expect I do, yes," I said, hastily gathering my things, "and I'm extremely grateful for the information. Extremely. So will Sabrina Howard's mother be, I'm sure."

I sat in the Maxwell with so many ideas whizzing around in my head that I was almost dizzy. What now?

A glance at the sky and the angle of the sunlight through the surrounding grove of shaggy eucalyptus trees told me the afternoon was drawing to a close. I should return to the lighthouse. I had not even left a note for Quincy, and I'd been away the whole afternoon.

I bit my lip, jiggled my legs impatiently, and pounded a couple of times on the steering wheel. Botheration! I didn't want to leave; I wanted to know what Braxton was doing in the hotel, whom he was seeing, and where he'd go next. Oscar Peterson and Sabrina Howard—surely an impossible combination?

"Jealousy?" I wondered aloud. Had one of the men found out about the other, subsequently quarreled with Sabrina, and in the heat of the quarrel killed her? And if so, which one?

"But then," I mused, "where does Arthur Heyer fit?"

Slowly the picture became clear to me, like a scene taking shape out of the fog: Oscar Peterson, a brilliant man, a sensitive poet—with all the emotional maturity of a two-year-old. Oscar came, I had been told, from a prominent family. His father, and possibly Oscar himself, were members of the Bohemian Club. A real member of the Bohemian Club would be irresistible to a beautiful actress from San Francisco: Sabrina Howard. They must have met at Braxton Furnival's party. Oscar, mothered but also smothered by Mimi, was smitten.

"Oh my God!" I said, as yet another idea came to me. "Mimi!"

Just at that moment the parking valet jumped into an auto a couple of rows up from mine, started it with a few loud, healthy revolutions of the motor, and backed out. I knew that sporty, distinctive car, I'd ridden in it—it belonged to Braxton Furnival. I prayed that Max would start for once without my having to crank, and by great good fortune it did.

While the valet drove right up to the hotel's main entrance, I lingered just around the corner of the building. Braxton bounded down the steps and into his car. He was alone, so I could not ascertain whom he had called upon. Out of pure curiosity, or perhaps just for the practice, I was determined to follow and see where else he might go.

I have not had much experience at following people. Most of what I know about real detection I have learned by reading the adventures of Sherlock Holmes, the rest by trial and error. Since Braxton had mentioned Pinkerton's female operatives to me, I'd had a few thoughts about how I might remedy my ignorance in the future, but for the moment I seemed to be doing all right. Braxton's car was distinctive and the traffic was not heavy, due to its being late on a Sunday afternoon. I could stay well back and not lose sight of him, although I did not think he would recognize me in Hettie's gray satin getup. Nor was he likely to take note of the Maxwell, which being black and boxy was so much like most other cars on the road.

Braxton did not take the Seventeen Mile Drive, which actually begins to count its seventeen miles at the Hotel Del Monte. This surprised me, as it was his logical way home, and my alertness increased. He drove instead straight to Pacific Grove.

I had begun to wonder if he had decided to visit me at the lighthouse, when he turned abruptly left off Lighthouse Avenue onto Ash Street, which goes rather steeply uphill. The street is narrow. I would not have dared follow except that, as in much of Pacific Grove, trees with huge trunks and low-hanging branches grew right out over, and in a couple of places into, the street itself. I coaxed Max up behind the cover of a giant cypress, and peered out cautiously while keeping my foot firmly on the brake.

The houses along here were tiny, not much more than shacks. I knew these small houses had not been intended for year-round living when they'd first been erected, back in Pacific Grove's days as a religious campground. But now for many working-class people they made inexpensive permanent homes. Braxton parked in front of one and tapped his horn, which instead of the usual beep emitted an *A-oo-gah!*

And out came the short, strong, compact figure of Pete Carlson. Pete, the man-of-all-work, detested by Quincy yet high on Hettie's list of odd-jobbers. Well, why shouldn't Pete be on Braxton's list too? I couldn't think of a single reason why not.

Disappointed by this unexciting development, I decided I would do well to leave before I was discovered. So I slipped the Maxwell into neutral and allowed the car to roll silently back downhill. In very little time I was backing onto Lighthouse Avenue, thence through the Point Pinos woods and to the lighthouse.

The sun hovered about a foot, or so it seemed, above the ocean. The horizon line was smudged with veils of long, trailing clouds in ever-modulating shades of peach and purple. I stood out on the lighthouse platform with the binoculars to my eyes. I had been counting an extraordinarily long string of brown pelicans, mostly as a way to divert myself from an internal argument. A part of me had argued that it was neither necessary nor wise to go to Carmel tonight and confront Oscar Peterson—especially since I would have to drive over at twilight, not a particularly safe time for driving, and back after dark. The very thought of taking Carmel Hill in pitch-black darkness with nothing but the carriage lamps for illumination was enough to give me the willies. But another part of me had simply been itching to get back into the Maxwell and go!

Strangely enough, the cautious side of me seemed to be winning this time. As I am not exactly Miss Prudence, I left off counting pelicans and puzzled over why this should be so. Well, for one thing, I would far rather be able to talk to Oscar without Mimi present. Given Oscar's condition the last time I'd seen them, the chances of that happening were remote—but still I would be more likely to catch him alone during daylight hours.

The more I thought about it, the more wary of Mimi I grew. How far would she go to protect her husband? As far as she had to? Probably. I would be well advised to have all my ducks in a row before she had an inkling of my suspicions. Speaking of birds in a row . . .

More pelicans—or was it the same ones going past again? Had they done a loop out over the bay and come around once more? Feeding pelicans will do that, I've observed, when particularly taken with some food supply.

As I watched the pelicans skimming along the surface of the water and reflected that once I start trying to figure something out I don't know where to stop, a human figure walked into the forefront, blurring the view. I refocused, and suddenly had a close-up of Joe, Junior, bent, scruffy, and none too clean. His pungent personal fragrance almost reached me through the lenses. I was curious, as before, about what he might have in his burlap sack.

Junior is a coastal scavenger. He walks the beaches, picking up everything that might even remotely have value. Suddenly I had an idea, and wondered that I had not thought of it before. Probably it was too late now—how often he sold his finds I did not know—but anyway I hurled myself around and down the circular stairs, out the door, and across the dunes. I was completely out of breath by the time I caught up with him.

"Good evening, Junior!" I called out when I was still some distance off. He raised his head and I waved, still coming on. My shoes were full of sand, my calf muscles protested all the slipping and sliding, and the tails of my long hair kept hitting me in the face. I had changed out of Hettie's dress into my usual blouse-and-skirt combination, and now my skirt was full of stickers from the sea grass that grows on the dunes.

"Miss Hettie, that be you?" Junior closed one eye and squinted at me with the other, presumably the better one.

"No, Hettie is still away. I'm Fremont, the temporary keeper. We have met before."

Junior nodded. "Yep, I recall it. Shame, ain't it, what happen to ole Quince."

I agreed it was a shame about Quincy's broken collarbone, and listened politely, if somewhat impatiently, to the tale of how Junior had once lost his footing over at Cypress Point and broken his ankle, and had to lie there with the tide coming in and aggressive sea lions barking at him for quite some time before help came. Finally it was my turn to speak.

"I suppose you must find many interesting things on your walks," I said.

"Yep. Never can tell what'll wash up out the sea or blow out from off'n the land. But valuable as opposed to interestin'—now that's another thing altogether. Why one day not too fer back—"

I simply had to interrupt him. "Please excuse me for breaking into your story, but soon it will be too dark to see and I wondered if you would very kindly let me look through the objects in your bag? If I find anything I want, I will of course pay you for it."

"Well . . ." He scratched the side of his face, where several days' growth of beard made a rasp like sandpaper. "I don't see why not. We'll just dump 'er out right here." So saying, he did.

Various odors assaulted my nostrils—the mustiness of burlap, the fetid, salty stench of a large seashell with its creature dying inside, several scents I could not readily identify, plus the unique odor of the man himself. Fortunately the wind, which blows constantly in from the water surrounding Point Pinos on three sides, quickly carried the smells away. Junior, who knew how to take advantage of an audience when he had it, went right on telling about his latest valuable find while I sorted through his stuff.

"Aha!" My exclamation caused Junior to stop midmonologue. I held up my prize: a shoe that, if I were not much mistaken, would be an exact match to that on Sabrina Howard's one shod foot when her body was recovered. "This shoe, Junior—do you remember where and when you found it?"

He took the shoe in his dirty, gnarled hands and brought it up to within an inch or two of his ruined eyes. Shaking his head he said, "Ain't worth nothin', this shoe. One shoe don't do a body no good. Thought I might find t'other, that's why I kep it. A pair of 'em would bring a pretty penny, that's fer sure. Good leather, that." He handed it back to me.

"How much will you take for this shoe? I'd like to buy it."

Junior named a price that was certainly high for a single shoe, but I didn't dicker because I wanted him to rack his brain for me. "Where, exactly, did you find it?" I asked again, since he seemed to have forgotten my question.

More sandpapery *scritch-scratch*. "Wasn't too fer from where I live. Found it stuck in the rocks above the tideline. Couldn't think how it woulda got there. Couldn't've washed up that high, weren't stuck so hard you couldn't pull it right out."

"So you found the shoe on Point Joe," I said with a sinking heart. For although I could easily imagine the scenario—the desperate struggle, the stuck foot, the twisted ankle, the shoe wedged in the rock as she fell to her doom—that location was not the place where Sabrina's shoe should have been found.

Junior straightened up as best he could, turned, and gestured down the coast to where Point Joe was visible as a finger of land extending into the sea far across the shallow curve of Spanish Bay. "Called after my pa, Point Joe, that's right."

Like a huge red India-rubber ball the sun slipped beneath the horizon, for one moment blazing with such splendor that both Junior and I were rapt. "Reckon I be blessed to live where I can see that every night, even if the old house Pa built be falling apart," Junior said when the last sliver of scarlet flashed and died.

"I reckon," I agreed, with an involuntary sigh. I stuck the shoe in my pocket and began to shove the other stuff back into the burlap sack. "But to get back to the shoe," I persisted, "when did you find it? How long ago?"

"Oh, it's been a while. More'n a month."

So not only the appearance of the shoe, but the timing was right for it to have been Sabrina's. I asked Junior to come back to the lighthouse with me so I could pay him, and as we were walking I recalled his keen sense of direction when he'd told me how to find Braxton Furnival's house. He had wandered this stretch of coast all his life; surely he could help with this dilemma?

It could do no harm to ask. "Junior, tell me something. The current flows southward along the coast, doesn't it?"

"Yep. Now that's mostly, but it depends. You got your wind, you got your waves and your swells relatin' to the direction of the wind, and o' course you got your tidal currents."

He was losing me but I didn't interrupt.

"Then you got these other deep currents come up from time to time, like we been having this winter." Junior wagged his head back and forth rhythmically, like a metronome. "Haven't seen such a winter since back before the turn of the century. Too many storms, bad weather."

"What about these currents we've been having this winter?"

"Odd, that's what they are. Odd. Back last month we had us a warm current up from the south with a northerly flow. Came along with them storms started south of the Sur. You remember."

"So last month if something went into the ocean, for example, and got caught in one of these currents with the northerly flow, it would travel up the coast, not down? North, not south?"

"Exackly," said Junior, "you got it. You live by the water long enough, you get to know these things."

"That's very useful. Thank you."

I paid him, said good night, and took my prize up to the watch room. The shoe was new, barely worn on the sole but deeply scarred along one side. I believed it was Sabrina's. I believed she had been hit over the head and thrown into the ocean at Point Joe, and from there she had drifted not down to Carmel but up to Point Pinos, because of that anomalous warm current with the northerly flow. Perhaps the shoe was not perfect evidence, but I thought it could be used to shake up the murderer, perhaps enough to get a confession. First thing tomorrow I would send a telegram to Wish Stephenson.

I thanked God or whatever had led me out onto the platform to find Joe, Junior through the binoculars, and then I silently thanked Junior for being such a pack rat, because I'd been close to accusing the wrong person of Sabrina Howard's murder.

. . .

I struggled in my bed, twisting and turning, caught in the bedclothes. I was having a nightmare from which I could not break free, a nightmare like the ones I'd had for so long after the earthquake. I dreamed of fire, of San Francisco, of my whole world burning. Burning and burning and burning!

Wake up, I told myself, wake up!

Finally I did. And there was smoke, and it wasn't a dream.

CHAPTER

NINETEEN

I coughed, fought my way out of the bedclothes, and leapt to my feet. Automatically I reached for my robe at the foot of the bed and with shaking hands put it on, even as I tried to gain control of the fear that raced through every nerve and vein and sinew. I threw back the blackout shutters, without which no one could sleep in a lighthouse; the revolving light immediately came round and revealed thick gray smoke seeping over the windowsill. I'd left the window cracked for ventilation. The small patch of my brain that remained unparalyzed by terror told me I might not be in immediate danger. This fire was outside.

"Quincy!" I had been sleeping with my walking stick beside the bed. I grabbed it and unsheathed the hidden blade with a swish, letting the base of the cane fall wherever it would. I hadn't the patience to wait for the light to revolve around again, and the floor was black as pitch so I couldn't find my slippers. Barefoot and blind, I tore out of my bedroom beneath the eaves. Up or down? No time to debate. I went down, based on a hasty conclusion that the barn and Quincy's lean-to were on fire, not the lighthouse itself.

Smoke rose through the stairwell, gray and wispy, winding its way up to the height of the lantern. Smoke that came through the open front door . . .

"Hey-a-a-ah!" I yelled at the top of my voice, and yelled again, as a year or more ago I had instinctively learned the reason for war cries; and I charged full tilt at the bulky figure silhouetted against the open door when once again the light came around. My robe and gown billowed with the speed of my flight, and my long, unbound hair streamed out behind me. I daresay I must have appeared a screaming banshee—but this banshee was no specter, she was armed, and knew how to use her blade.

The intruder was no match for me, especially as the light had gone as quickly as it came. I felt the tip of my blade pierce flesh, heard a grunt and the sound of something heavy, with a metallic clunk, dropping to the floor.

"Back!" I commanded. "Move back! As you've already learned, I know what I'm doing. I wouldn't hesitate to slash your throat."

He backed into the doorway, and when the light came around I saw it was Pete Carlson. For the space of a heartbeat this confused me, but then the fleeting light gleamed for a moment in his eyes before moving on, and they were the same eyes. The eyes of my attacker, the bandito in the woods.

"You bastard!" I said, jamming the tip of the blade into his throat.

"Hey!" He sounded scared. As he went on he began to whine. "Leave off, lady. None of this was my idea. I'm just the hired hand!"

"You can tell me later. And believe me, you will—you'll tell me everything!" I tossed hair out of my eyes. "But right now you're going to help me undo some of the damage you've done here."

"Hey, I didn't touch the lighthouse. Lighthouse is gov'ment property. I'm not that stupid."

I pulled the tip of my blade back an inch from his throat. "Bully for you. Now turn around. That's right." I put the rapier's point between his shoulder blades. "Move!"

As soon as I went through the doorway I saw fire-glow on Hettie's carefully cultivated rectangle of lawn. I heard the roar and crackle and lick of flame, tasted bitter ash on my tongue. I shot a glance over my shoulder and saw: The barn was burning.

San Francisco's post-earthquake conflagration had left me with a morbid fear of fire. For months afterward the simple stoking of a cookstove's belly had been too much; I would cringe before it, my hands would shake. Yet now, fueled by my own rage, I knew I could face this fire without the slightest hesitation. Relentlessly, step by step, I drove before me the man who had hurt me and my friends and invaded the sanctuary of my home.

"I ain't going in that!" Pete wailed. "You can't make me!"

"Is that so?" I jabbed, forcing him to keep moving. By the firelight I saw blood seeping through his shirt where I had already wounded his left shoulder. "I am armed and you are not. You dropped your weapon, didn't you? What was it? A gun?"

"Yeah," he sneered. Suddenly he ducked and turned on his heel to face me, making a grabbing motion with his right hand. In my super-alert state I did not even have to think, but stepped back and with a flick of my wrist slashed his palm. He looked tremendously surprised.

"Any more false moves and I swear I'll run you through! Now walk toward the barn. You are going to get Quincy out of the fire, and release the animals. If you burn up yourself in the process, it will serve you right!"

The terrified cows were mooing, bellowing, really, at the top of their lungs, while the bay mare's hooves pounded the walls with the force of John Henry's hammer. Over and over I yelled Quincy's name. Just as my captive and I got close enough for me to send Pete through the flames, the door of the lean-to flew outward with explosive force.

Quincy had kicked out his own door. His spare form hurtled out and he landed rolling in the grass, coughing, wheezing, spitting. The first words out of his raspy throat were "Bessie! Cows!" but I was already ahead of him. Without a shred of mercy I forced Pete Carlson to unlatch the burning barn door and let the horse and the Holsteins out. Sparks sizzled in his hair and burned holes in his clothes and so of course he commenced whining, but he was not badly hurt. I have observed that it is always the bullies who are most cowardly at heart.

Quincy recovered quickly. At what cost to his healing collarbone I do not know, but he tied Pete Carlson to a fence post, muttering all the while, "I told you he was no good, Fremont, I told you he was no good." Then Quincy and I, using the emergency water tank, put out the fire. The blaze had not been so huge as it had at first seemed in the black of night, and due to the isolation of the lighthouse, I doubted the Pacific Grove Fire Department had been alerted. That was fine with me.

Quincy wanted to go for the police.

"No," I said, "if you will trust me, Quincy, I have something else in mind."

"Fremont, I trust you almost as much as I do Miz Hettie, and that's a fact!" He looked both earnest and comical, with his smudged face and sparse gray hair sticking out from his head in odd directions.

I smiled and patted his arm in comradely fashion. "Thank you. Pete is going to provide me with the answers to some important questions. I'll tell you later all about it, but for now, would you kindly just keep an eye on him while I go and put on some clothes?"

It was five o'clock in the morning; the sun would not rise for some time yet. The fog had begun to roll in from the south, over the Santa Lucias, while Quincy and I were putting out the fire, and now a dense whitish mist covered everything. I had seen thicker fogs in San Francisco, so I was not at all concerned. There was about five feet of visibility around the Maxwell, which was plenty for me.

I turned and addressed Pete Carlson, whom Quincy and I had previously tied with sturdy ropes in the passenger seat: "Now you are going to tell me some things, because if you do I'll see to it that you get some special consideration when I take you to the police. And if you do not—well, who knows what I might do?" I paused to let him think about that, then resumed. "My first question is: Do you know the whereabouts of Phoebe Broom?" My heart pounded as I waited for the answer. The longer he delayed, the more I was afraid my hopes were soon to be dashed.

Finally Pete said sullenly, "Yeah, I know."

With my heart in my throat I asked, "Is she alive or dead?"

Pete laughed. It was an ugly, mirthless sound. "She's alive. That Mr. Braxton High-Falutin' Furnival ain't got the stomach for killin'. He near-bout turned me in himself just for hittin' you upside the head. Said I could've kilt you. As if I'd give a shit."

I winced, but nevertheless this was interesting stuff. "Then the first order of business now is: You are going to give me directions to wherever Phoebe is hidden." I started the motor, which Quincy had previously cranked for me.

"Well," Pete drawled, recovering his confidence, "I just don't know as I can do that. For all that Brax is a yellow-bellied ladie's man, he paid me pretty good."

In my lap I had Pete's gun, having found it on the floor when I went in to change; I picked it up now and pointed it at him. It was large and heavy, the type that is called a revolver. I am nowhere near as practiced at shooting as I am at slashing, but Pete did not know that—which was just as well. "I disagree," I said. "I think you will tell me exactly where she is, and you will not try to misdirect me, because if you do I will shoot you in the foot."

"You bitch."

"I am quite serious. May I point out to you that if shooting you in the foot does not suffice, you have another foot, and knees, and so on."

Pete shrugged the shoulder I'd pierced, then winced as the motion pulled at the cloth stuck with dried blood to the wound. The pain must have made a timely reminder, for he gave up the bravado. "I guess you do mean it. Okay, she's in this kind of mee-dee-val tower down to the end of Brax's property. Some old guy built the thing out of rocks like you find down by the water, back a long time ago when all that land was El Rancho Pescadero. I helped Brax fix it up, turn it into sort of a hideout. The ladies like a tower, he says, they think it's romantic. Har! I bet your friend Phoebe ain't been finding it any too romantic."

The Maxwell's carriage lamps gave our passage a ghostly glow in the fog. I had no difficulty staying on the road, but I did involuntarily shudder now, both at his words and because we were passing the place where Pete had knocked me out. Though it was low on my list of questions, thus reminded I could not resist asking, "Why did you hit me in the head?"

"To get them pictures for Brax."

"You were wearing a mask and bandana over your face—I couldn't have identified you. You could have just asked me to hand over the pictures, and I would have. You didn't have to hit me, especially not that hard!"

"So?" He looked away from me, out into the fog. "I like to hit people. I ain't no sissy. Brax shoulda let me take you too, along with that Broom bitch. But he said you bein' the lighthouse keeper, if you disappeared it would cause too much of a fuss, I should just get the pictures."

I let that pass. "Braxton paid you to kidnap Phoebe?"

"Paid me to help him do it. I told him you was a troublemaker, you'd never let it alone. From the minute Tom called Brax and said there was these women been messin' around and we better go get that body—"

"Tom, at Mapson's, told Braxton that Phoebe and I were there?"

"Yeah. Didn't you figure out none of this? I thought you was supposed to be so smart. Brax thinks you're really something, you know, that's mainly why he didn't want you hurt. He wanted me to do stuff that'd scare you but not really hurt you. I told him it wouldn't do no good."

"Like poisoning the water and loosening the carriage wheel. And tonight, setting fire to the barn."

"Yeah, except the fire tonight was my idea. That sanctimonious son of a bitch Quincy, I hate his guts. It was kinda amusing for a while, workin' out here, knowin' the damage I'd done, plannin' what else I could do—but after a while I just couldn't take no more of Quincy. So I thought I'd do him some mischief, burn up his barn.

Maybe he'd get out and maybe he wouldn't. If you hadn't woke up so fast, I'da got you too!"

I turned the Maxwell into the Del Monte Forest at the Pacific Grove gate. Ghostly, mist-shrouded trees closed in all around us, even overhead. I said, "I'd like to know exactly what you mean by that but before I ask, there is something I want to go back to. The woman whose body was at Mapson's, Sabrina Howard. I presume either Braxton killed her, or paid you to do it."

"Heh, heh, heh!" A low chuckle, wicked, tinged with twisted amusement. "Then you presume wrong."

I had to slow the car. Here in Del Monte Forest the fog was so thick I could barely see the edge of the pavement. "But her shoe was found near where Braxton lives. If he didn't kill her, then all the rest of it makes no sense. You can't expect me to believe that."

"Brax, he had his reasons."

I took my eyes from the foggy road for a moment. All this time I'd had one hand on the gun and one on the steering wheel. I raised the weapon and aimed it at Pete's nearest foot. "And what were his reasons?"

"Hey, he didn't tell me. Okay? All I know is, when we went to get the body from Mapson's, Brax said it would be bad for business if anybody found out who she was, on account of her havin' been known to work for him."

I mulled this over. It made a certain amount of sense—if Braxton were doing something shady or criminal, he wouldn't want the police coming around and asking him questions—but still it was hard to believe. I decided to move on to the next obvious question. "What did you do with Sabrina's body after you took it from the mortuary?"

Pete's eyes shifted from my face to the gun in my hand, and back, before he answered. "I buried her out here in the forest. Nobody'll ever find the grave. Brax didn't want to know where I buried her, and I don't even think I could find it again myself."

Damn! But I had to admit he was being cooperative. I lowered the gun and a few moments later asked casually, "By the way—if you had *gotten* me tonight, what did you intend to do with me?"

Pete Carlson didn't answer for a long time. I watched him from the corner of my eye, saw how he stared at me. He exuded an ugly feeling that I supposed must be hate, but what had I ever done to make Pete Carlson hate me? He didn't even know me! Finally he broke the silence with a snort of derision.

"Your friend Mr. Braxton Loves-the-Ladies Furnival is gone. He left early last night. He said I could have the bitch in the tower to do anything I want with. All by herself, she's not much fun—I know, 'cause I had her already. She just lies there, don't wiggle nor squeal nor nothin', and besides, she's ugly as a foot. So I was gonna take you over there . . ."

He half turned toward me. His eyes were glittering, and I could feel the hate. My right hand closed over the gun while my left kept the Maxwell on track through the fog in the murky half-light of approaching dawn. I let up on the gas a little more, slowing the car to a crawl.

Pete said with a sneer, "I was gonna take you over there to the tower and fuck the both of you."

Having never heard that word before, I had no idea what it meant, but from the context I could guess. I steeled myself not to show the reaction Pete was waiting for.

In a moment, when I didn't react, he continued: "I'da kept you alive for a while, played with you. Who knows, maybe you'd have figured out how to escape, seein' as how you're so smart. 'Course it's pretty hard to get out of a place with nothing but bare stone walls—"

In a flash, bonds and all, he rose up and flung himself sideways at me. There was no time to think, only to react. My hand was on the gun but I never felt the heft of it, or the recoil after. I shot Pete Carlson.

My ears rang. The car tilted off the road. Pete's weight fell across me; I could reach neither the gearshift nor the steering wheel. So I used my feet, jamming both of them quick and hard onto the brake, hoping that way to kill the motor before I crashed into a tree.

With a lurch and a cough the Maxwell came to a rolling stop right up against the broad trunk of a cypress. Even before the car stopped rolling I pushed open the door and scrambled out, frantic to get away. My blouse and skirt, where Pete had fallen on me, bore a wide band of blood. Panting and wild, I aimed the gun, my hand clamped to it like a vise. I blinked, shook my head, took in great gulps of air.

He wasn't moving. His head lolled upside down in the open car door, half off the seat. Still pointing the gun and holding it now with both hands, I took a step closer. Then another. Pete's eyes were open and so was his mouth. He looked a little surprised.

"Phoebe! Phoebe, it is I, Fremont Jones!" I called out loudly as one by one I tried the keys on the ring I'd taken from Pete Carlson's bloody pocket. I was not sure how long it had taken me to find this picturesque tower that held Phoebe prisoner. Since the fog was thinning, every now and then letting through a strong shaft of sunlight, I estimated the hour to be later than nine o'clock.

"Phoebe? Do you hear me?" I myself could hear nothing on the other side of the stout oaken door, which was banded in rusting iron and secured with an equally rusty padlock.

At last a key slipped all the way into the lock and turned easily; in spite of its ancient appearance the lock's inner mechanism had been oiled. I pushed the heavy door inward on creaking hinges and announced as I entered, "Phoebe, it's Fremont. I've come to take you home."

Phoebe stood near a fire pit centered in the floor of this round room. She had lost a great deal of weight. Her eyes were huge in her small, bony face, deeply shadowed and darkly ringed. Her hair and clothes were unmentionably filthy, and she looked at me without comprehension. Then she looked up over our heads, and back at me again. I wondered if perhaps the long imprisonment had played havoc with Phoebe's wits.

I too looked up, to see what drew her eye. The round tower walls leaned slightly inward, like a funnel, and were open to the sky. At the top, some twenty-five or thirty feet above our heads, perched a large, handsome bird with feathers of ruddy gold.

"A goshawk," said Phoebe. Her voice wavered a little. "He flew away when you opened the door. I've been taming him. He is my only friend."

Looking up again at the bird I said, "He's beautiful." I looked back at her. Her head tipped to one side, she studied me. "You do remember me, don't you?" I asked.

She nodded and began to walk around the fire pit toward me. She looked like a ragged child with an old face. "Fremont. You're not with them. Not one of them. Are you?"

"No, of course I'm not!" I wanted to run to her and take her in my arms, but I dared not. There was something feral in Phoebe now, and who could blame her for that?

Suddenly I knew how to gain her trust and ease her pain at the same time. I would tell her the very thing I myself had not yet come to terms with. "I killed him, Phoebe, I shot Pete Carlson. His blood is on my clothes—see? He can't hurt you or frighten you anymore."

She stood stock-still. "Pete. The short one, ugly and mean. What about the other one? He said he would get me out. Is that it, did the other one send you to let me go?"

"Braxton Furnival has gone away, or so I have been told. No one sent me—I came on my own. I took the keys to this tower out of Pete's pocket after I shot him. I've been looking a long time for you—not just this morning, but ever since you disappeared. I'm so glad you're all right!" Tentatively I took a couple of steps forward.

"Not Braxton," she shook her head, "I don't mean him. After they put me in here Braxton only came once. The other one is young, dark, handsome. He never told me his name but he said he would take me away, rescue me, he promised!" Her voice rose to a high hysterical pitch and her eyes burned. Then she slumped and the light went out of her face. "But that was days ago, I don't know how many; I keep count by making marks on the wall, but sometimes I can't remember when I last made a mark—"

"You must mean Ramon," I said hastily. "I haven't seen him for some time either." I held out my hands. "Please Phoebe, come with me now. I have a car outside. Let me take you home."

With fragile dignity Phoebe came, lifting her bony little chin. "Home. To Carmel?" I nodded and she said matter-of-factly, "Yes. That would be good. I believe I am badly in need of a bath."

Phoebe wandered through her house and out into her yard, touching things, and it seemed that with each one she touched, she came back more and more into reality. I had set up the old hip-bath she used for a tub in the kitchen, and while water heated on the stove I began to deal with some realities of my own.

I had killed a man. I had not meant to kill him, but I could not precisely say that I'd acted in self-defense either. As soon as I'd realized Pete Carlson was dead, I had pulled him out of the Maxwell and examined him. He'd worked one hand loose of the ropes that bound him, but I hadn't known that when I fired the shot. The bullet had entered his left side and gone right through him, to lodge itself deep in the car's leather upholstery. I had shot Pete Carlson through the heart. Then like a thief I had gone through his pockets, looking for the key to Phoebe's tower.

I did find the key, but I hadn't stopped there. Other things I did, almost without thought, on sheer instinct—the survival instinct, perhaps. Those other things could be undone, but not without difficulty, and I was not at all sure I wanted to undo them.

I decided to discuss the matter with Phoebe, who wandered in from her sculpture studio-cum-garden just as the water on the stove began to steam. She was smiling through her grime.

"It's really true," she said, "I'm really home. This is my cottage. Those are my sculptures, I made them—with these hands." She held up her hands and inspected them. "Gawd, are they filthy!"

Phoebe giggled. That giggle was like a ripple in a stream—it grew wider and wider until it encompassed me and I giggled, too, and then our giggles became laughter. We both laughed until we cried, only to laugh again until we were spent. In the midst of all this, somehow, Phoebe got her bath. It was the most hilarious bathing experience I have ever participated in, and I do believe it was good for both of us even if the whole thing was slightly hysterical.

So it was not until Phoebe had dressed and was brushing her hair dry that I told her exactly how I had shot Pete Carlson. "I'm afraid that isn't all," I said.

Brush upraised, from under a canopy of shining-clean hair she shot me one of her old savvy looks. Phoebe was recovering quickly. "Oh? You killed him. He was scum. What else could there be?"

"I covered my tracks. I can't say why exactly; I just did it out of some sort of instinct. I unwrapped the rope Quincy and I had tied him with and put it in the Maxwell, in the back under the traveling rug. I left Pete's body there on the side of the road. What is worst of all, I threw his gun—the one I killed him with—into the sea."

Phoebe moved the brush in languid, rhythmic strokes through her hair. In an unconcerned tone she inquired, "Are you positive no one saw you do any of this?"

Carefully I searched my memory of the grisly business, which was almost preternaturally clear in every detail. "Yes. I am positive."

"He raped me, you know, many times. He beat me. The other one was nice, after Pete. But he forced me, too."

"I am so sorry," I said, my voice sounding hollow with horror.

"If you hadn't shot Pete, he'd have gotten loose and killed us both—but not before he'd done other unspeakable things. It was self-defense, Fremont."

"Not technically, it wasn't. He was still tied up and had no weapon. I would have a hard time proving self-defense in a court of law."

"So?" Phoebe shrugged, put the brush down, turned and faced me. She was not her old self after all; she was profoundly different in more than appearance, and I wondered if forevermore she would have this feral edge. "So you continue to protect yourself, which is what you were doing when you shot him. You make sure you don't have to try to prove self-defense. That is why you removed the rope and threw away the gun. Believe me, Fremont, if I could have got hold of any sort of weapon, I'd have killed that bastard a hundred thousand times!"

Slowly I nodded, accepting a burden I knew I would carry for the rest of my life. "And that is why I must now go out and clean the Maxwell, and when I get back to the lighthouse I will tell Quincy I made Pete tell me your whereabouts and then I let him go."

"Good!" Phoebe said vehemently. She rose, came over to where I sat, and leaned down to place her cheek next to mine. So softly that I barely heard, she said, "Thank you, Fremont, for saving my life."

I walked to the Pine Inn on the corner of Lincoln and Ocean Avenue to buy some already-prepared soup for Phoebe. Like Mother Hubbard, all her cupboards were bare. I had covered my bloody blouse and skirt with a fringed Spanish shawl, one of Phoebe's artistic props. I would not have worn such a thing in Pacific Grove but it seemed just right for Carmel. In fact, I rather liked all its bright bands of color. I found myself smiling and humming, giddy, light-headed, the way one becomes when a crisis is past.

But when I emerged from the Pine Inn with the soup in a covered pail, I discovered that I had let down my guard too soon. There was another crisis, right here in Carmel, and it was just beginning.

CHAPTER

TWENTY

Somewhere in Carmel, someone was ringing a great, deep bell. I thought at first it might be the bell at the Mission; but since the Mission is in near-ruins, on second thought that was hardly likely.

When one lives near the sea, one soon learns to look in that direction for whatever out-of-the-ordinary thing may be happening. Thus in response to the ringing bell, people were coming out of their houses and places of business and walking—or in some cases running—down Ocean Avenue toward the beach. I continued on back to Phoebe's. Of course I was curious, but first things first: A woman who has been kept a prisoner on starvation rations should have her food!

Phoebe, however, had other ideas. When I was still half a block away she came out of her cottage, tottering a little in her haste. "That's the alarm!" she said breathlessly. "We must go down to the water. Someone must be drowning!"

I could not dissuade her, but I did convince her that she was in no condition to walk that far; so I drove us both down in the Maxwell.

"Park here." Phoebe pointed to a grove of trees still some distance from the white sand. "I can walk the rest of the way. But before we see any of the others, Fremont, I want you to promise me something."

"Anything!"

"I don't want anyone to know I was kidnapped, held prisoner and all that. You can think of something else to tell Quincy about why you let Pete Carlson go. Tell him . . . tell him Pete got loose and grabbed his gun from you and took off into the forest. Please, Fremont. The note they made me write when Braxton and Pete forced me to go with them, it only said I was going away for a while. I remember telling them it didn't need to say more than that, because in Carmel we don't question each other's comings and goings." She put her hand on my arm, her fingers gripping like claws. "I just don't want to have to talk about what happened, it was too humiliating, I don't want them to know!"

I hugged Phoebe and stroked her hair. "Of course I won't tell, if that's what you want. You can give whatever explanation you like for the time you've been away." Artemisia would have a field day telling me I-told-you-so, and somehow we would need to placate the sheriff, but that could all come later. I had been accused before of filing frivolous missing persons reports, and survived.

"Thank you," Phoebe said, "you're a good person, Fremont Jones."

I smiled. "Now shall we go see what all the commotion is about?"

They were all there on the beach: Artemisia in her layered purple dress; Irma Fox accompanied by Khalid, the Burnoose Boy (sans burnoose today); Tom, Dick, and Harry, alias the Twangy Boys; my Diogenes, Professor Storch; and the skinny La Señorita, who was so shy and reclusive I had never gotten to know her. But Arthur Heyer, the Medium-Everything Man, was absent—and if I did not miss my guess, the alarm bell was ringing for the person who missed him most.

Oscar Peterson, naked as the day he was born, had a long-barreled revolver in one hand and a bottle of either gin or vodka in the other. His skin was fish-belly white and loose on his long bones. His testicles swung when he moved like stones in a withered pouch. He looked part crane, part mad prophet. He was either chanting or singing—one of his own poems, perhaps—and he seemed intent on wading into the winter-cold waters of Carmel Bay.

"Oh, no!" Phoebe exclaimed. "What has been happening here?"

"Let Artemisia explain it to you, but if she mentions me, I hope you'll take whatever she says with a grain of salt," I said. "I'm going to see if Mimi will talk to me."

Mimi Peterson stood alone at the north end of the beach on a broad, flat rock that had been exposed by the low tide. Her cornsilk hair was loose, not braided as I had always seen it, and rippled in the onshore breeze. Tears rolled silently down a face as set as marble and she wore black, as if she already mourned. I expected that she did.

I hung back. At this moment, Mimi was unapproachable.

It went on for a long time, Oscar croaking nonsense at the top of his lungs, swigging from the bottle and waving the gun. A crowd gradually gathered, not only the sunset group of core Carmelites but others I had never seen. Whenever anyone ventured into the water, Oscar raised the gun and fired wildly. I counted five shots, one of them a near-miss on the Twangy Boys; after that, they left him alone. All the while the tide came in.

I still stood near Mimi, noting that her best friends were all giving her a wide berth. I wondered why—perhaps it was not so much a wide berth as a respectful distance. Still I had not spoken.

Finally the waiting was too much for me. I yelled, at Mimi or at anyone who would listen, "Why don't some of the men get together and rush him? He's not trying to shoot anybody, and anyway, he's almost out of bullets. Isn't it obvious that if we don't intervene, Oscar will drown himself?"

Slowly Mimi turned her head toward me; not another muscle moved, only her head and neck, and her expression did not alter. I felt chills from the coldness in her stony eyes. "Oscar confessed to all of us last night. I knew, of course, that he was having an affair with that actress Sabrina Howard. He paid her bills at the Del Monte, lavished money on her when we were practically starving. Then at New Year's Oscar found out she was still 'entertaining' Braxton Furnival and his friends, and he started to come apart with jealousy. Oscar killed Sabrina Howard. It was not an accident. If he couldn't have her exclusive attention, then no one else could have her at all—that's how crazy he'd become over that woman."

I did not say anything; there was nothing to say. Down below, now waist-deep in waves, Oscar ranted on.

Mimi had not finished. "It might have all blown over. I was the only one in Carmel who knew—who cared to know—that Sabrina was Oscar's *whore.*" She spat the ugly word from twisted lips, yet still no other part of her body moved; the effect was eerie, like a statue come to life. "But then you came around with that photograph. And Arthur—poor, pedantic, thorough Arthur—remembered how Oscar had spent a lot of time talking to Sabrina at one of Braxton's parties. So Oscar had to kill Arthur, so that Arthur couldn't tell. Oscar drowned him . . . but it broke my husband's heart, and what was left of his mind. Now Oscar intends to drown himself in reparation, and we are all agreed to allow him to do it. This is the best way."

Suddenly Mimi whirled on me, her black skirts swooping like a vulture's wings: "You will not interfere! Do you understand that, Fremont Jones? *Go away and leave us alone!*"

I opened my mouth to speak, but no sound would come out. The force of her anger buffeted me; I staggered backward, slipping on the smooth rock. I would have fallen but for an unseen pair of arms that closed around me and buoyed me up. Unseen, but not unknown. A soft, luxuriant beard filled the hollow behind my ear—so, he'd grown it back. I was glad.

"Your sense of timing was always impeccable," I whispered, turning in Michael's arms.

Michael kissed me right there on Carmel Beach, in front of God and Artemisia and everyone, but of course they didn't see. Their eyes were on Oscar Peterson, playing out the final act in his tragedy.

"Come away, Fremont," Michael said, "don't watch this."

"I can't leave. I have to take Phoebe home. You don't know—" I bit my tongue, remembering my promise. "She has been a little ill and I doubt she could walk back up the hill as far as her street."

"They will see that she gets home. Come with me now, Fremont. Phoebe will understand."

I looked across the beach, where Phoebe was surrounded by Carmelites, and saw that he was right. Then I looked back at Michael; I gave him all my attention and all my heart.

I went with him. Of course I did.

EPILOGUE

"*I* am not going to ask you to marry me," Michael said.

"I am relieved to hear it," I responded, in a stout voice I could only hope would give the lie to my ambivalence on this risky topic. Indeed if he were to do to me again the things he had just done, who knew what I might end up agreeing to? It had been a mere ten days since Michael's return and (at least privately, with me) the end of the Misha charade, and already I could scarcely remember that the two of us had ever been other than as close as we were now.

He went on: "I know how you feel about marriage. I've heard you expound on the subject often enough."

"Um-hmm." I traced my fingertip around and around one of his totally useless nipples until he shivered and trapped my hand. It is quite amazing that men's nipples get these tiny little erections. I looked down and saw that his magical member was also transforming itself again, and I smiled.

We were having a two-day holiday up the coast, in a little cabin on Half Moon Bay. Quincy was minding the lighthouse. I'd never been before to Half Moon Bay, which is some miles north of Santa Cruz. Michael had chosen the place for its seclusion; we'd sailed up on the *Katya* without letting anyone know our destination. There were things he needed to tell me, Michael had said, that required the most absolute privacy.

He had begun with the reason for his recent bizarre behavior. Michael Archer—or rather, Mikhail Arkady Kossoff—was more than just a spy. He had been, for most of his adult life, a reluctant double agent for both Russia and the United States. This was a role he had inherited, not chosen.

How this inheritance came about was, actually, quite fascinating: Michael's great-grandfather Kossoff had come to this country early in the last century as a fur trader, and he had prospered. Michael's grandfather had therefore inherited a thriving business, which he proceeded to increase to such a point that his wealth attracted the attention of the tsar. The tsar raised the grandfather to nobility, with the title of duke—but there was a price: Along with the furs Grandfather brought from California to Russia, he was also expected to bring information. The Kossoffs were thus bound in service to the tsar. And so they had remained, from that day to this.

Michael's father had not been the hard-driving risk-taker the grandfather was. When California became a state in 1850, all Michael's father wanted to do was settle down and be an American; but Michael's mother, a minor Russian princess, wouldn't hear of renouncing their place at the tsar's court. So Michael had grown up in two worlds. In temperament and appearance he was more like his grandfather than his father, and recognizing this, his father had thrust the information-carrying (that is, the spying) role on Michael when he was only nineteen.

At first, with the enthusiastic hotheadedness of youth, Michael had enjoyed the intriguing side of being a Kossoff. But then he'd met and fallen in love with his Katya—and Katya had been killed by the Russians, on the assumption that Michael had shared certain secret information with her. Tragically, he had not; but there was no convincing her murderers of that. Feeling vengeful and betrayed, he had then volunteered his services to the United States government as a double agent, and he had been leading a perilous life ever since. Yet, he said, he had been perfectly happy with it until I came along two years ago and turned him upside down.

Now Michael wrapped his hand in my hair and pulled my face close to his. "Aren't you going to try to change my mind?"

I licked the tip of his noble nose, because it was irresistibly close. "About what?"

"Marriage, of course." His hand strayed down the valley between my breasts, and below. "I've just robbed you of your virtue, after all."

"If you didn't realize that I was not a virgin, and therefore had lost my virtue a while back, then you are less experienced than I supposed." I drew back a bit and scrutinized him: sensually curving lips, rosy cheeks, and the bright eyes of an imp. "You don't seem displeased with my lack of virginity."

"If I were, you would probably have something to say about pots calling kettles black."

"No doubt." I laughed; into my open mouth he plunged his tongue, which got us involved in something else for quite a while. When we had disentangled ourselves again, Michael stroked the hair back from my forehead, raised himself up on one arm, and said seriously, "You do understand about Artemisia, don't you? She was just a part of the ruse."

I frowned a little, and did not reply immediately. The ruse to which he referred was that whole Misha persona. Michael had sought to appear as if he'd become dissolute and unreliable, because he wanted out of the spy game and neither government would agree to let him go.

"The problem is, Michael, that Artemisia didn't know it was an act. She thought Misha was the real you, and she could have been hurt. Deceiving people is so, so—" Thinking of the people I myself had deceived, albeit for (supposedly) good cause, I could not complete the sentence.

"I didn't deceive her," Michael said patiently. "I told her from the beginning that I was in love with someone else. Of course I meant you, Fremont."

"It might have been nice if you'd told *me.*"

"I'd intended to. Back at the end of the summer I thought all I had to do was announce my resignation to both sides, and I'd get some sort of letter of dismissal and that would be that. But that was not what happened. During the fall when you had to stay in San Francisco for Mickey Morelock's trial, I found out that neither the Russians nor the Americans would let me go. Their refusal panicked me. I became obsessed with the morbid idea that what had happened to Katya would also happen to you the minute I said the words 'I love you.' "

"So you became Misha."

"Yes. By the time you arrived in Carmel I'd perfected the act. Believe me, I didn't always enjoy it."

"But you did sometimes?" I teased. "Like the time Artemisia spent the night with you?"

"I told you," he grumbled, "I was drunk. I'm human. And I'm sorry."

"I forgive you," I said, reaching up perversely to tweak his ear; but somehow the tweak became a kiss of delicious tenderness.

Outside our little cabin the wind picked up and went moaning like a ghost at the cracks around the door and windows. But we were safe and warm. We had built a fire in a hideous potbelly stove, the room was gilded by the glow of many candles, and we had the comfort of each other lying side by side, full length, skin against skin.

"It has all been worth it," Michael murmured.

"What do you mean?"

"You demonstrated something to me that makes all the difference."

"I was not aware of giving demonstrations."

"No, you were just being yourself. Fremont Jones. That is what I learned: You are not Katya."

238

I turned my head on the pillow and tried to find my way through Michael's eyes into his soul. My throat felt dry. To speak of Katya was like treading on holy ground; one must go respectfully. I cleared my throat and admitted: "I still don't understand."

"For years I felt the guilt of her death. How could I love you, and want to have you with me, when for Katya loving me had been the same as dying? But you, Fremont, are different. In fact, you're completely impossible! You have a talent for getting into risky situations that equals, if not exceeds, my own. You may listen to advice, but then you inevitably draw your own judgments from it and go your own way. You're so strong, or maybe just so stubborn, that if an avenue doesn't open up in the way you want to go, you will just hack your way through the obstacles regardless. It has become perfectly clear to me that you are going to continue to get into these situations no matter what I or anyone else does."

A remarkably accurate assessment, but I was not entirely sure I liked it. I sat up, tossed my hair back, and put my fists on my hips. "So?"

Grinning, Michael pushed himself up against the head of the bed and folded his arms over his hairy chest. "So I may love you and I may be concerned about you, but I'm not enough of an idiot to think I can control you—which also means I don't have to feel responsible for you."

"All right." I sighed. "That's good. In fact, that's really fine." I let down my guard and leaned back against him, snuggling into the soft hollow beneath his arm.

For a while we were quiet, and then Michael said, "Oh, by the way. You might want to know that the Cypress Coast Company has charged Braxton Furnival with fraud and theft, and the district attorney has also charged him with murder. It seems that when the new man from Cypress went to his house in Del Monte Forest—which incidentally didn't belong to Furnival, it's a lodge for the developer's guests—he found a dead body, subsequently identified as Ramon Reyes, a speculator from Paso Robles. They're looking into the possibility that Reyes was shot with the same gun that killed the fellow they found in the woods—Pete Carlson. There's a warrant out for Furnival's arrest."

I had wondered what happened to Ramon; there were any number of questions I wanted to ask, but I dared not. All I said was "They'll have to find Braxton before they can arrest him."

"Do you know where he is?"

"No. Of course not!"

"Hmm. At any rate, he was selling memberships in a nonexistent golf club," Michael went on, "and taking cash for options on property to which he didn't have the title, and pocketing the money. Some of it, of course, went into bribes to cover up Sabrina Howard's death. Fremont, I have an idea you know a great deal more about all these things than you put in your letter to Wish Stephenson."

When I made no reply, Michael said softly, "Look at me, love."

I looked at him mutely. I suppose there may have been a plea in my eyes but if so, it was unformed, for in truth I wanted to tell him everything but felt bound to hold my tongue.

He said, "I do have a proposal for you, but not a proposal of marriage. I propose that we be partners, you and I. Fremont Jones and Michael Kossoff. Partners in life and in work, all burdens, all secrets, all joys to be shared. What do you say, Fremont; will you be my partner?"

A smile spread slowly over my face while in my head I repeated the words and let their meaning bloom full in my mind. Then I said, "That makes eminently good sense."

I sat up in the bed, folding my legs Indian-style, and Michael did the same. We faced each other. I held up both my hands, palms out, and Michael fitted his palms to mine—a spontaneous, solemn salute.

"Yes," I said, "Michael Kossoff; I, Fremont Jones, will be your partner in life and in work, all burdens, all secrets, all joys to be shared."